MW01137805

Love's Healing Path

LACY WILLIAMS

Chapter One

MADDIE FAIRFAX EXITED Mrs. Barrigan's tent without looking where she was going. Head bent, one hand rifled through the wicker basket she held.

She sensed someone hovering nearby, a little behind her and a few feet from the Barrigans' tent. That wasn't unusual. Since the first week she and her sisters had begun traveling with this Oregon-bound wagon train, folks had sought her out when they needed help.

She wasn't anything special. Not a nurse, not officially. But she'd learned about herbs and home remedies from a dear neighbor, Mrs. Murphy, when growing up in Dublin. When her father had been sleeping off the drink, when her older sister, Stella, had gone to work in the factory, Maddie and Lily had needed someone to watch over them. Maddie had needed someone to nurture her love of learning. Keep her from drowning in loneliness.

Mrs. Murphy had done that for her.

She was still rifling through the basket—where was that

yarrow?—but she heard the crunch of footsteps on the dry prairie grass behind her.

"Excuse me."

She stopped, surprised at the cultured male voice. Her fingers closed around the sprig of yarrow as he stepped closer to her elbow. "I've been hoping to meet you," he said. "I understand you've—"

Her bonnet slipped back slightly as she glanced up. And up. My, he was tall. Piercing brown eyes studied her. She recognized him immediately—the man who'd accompanied Owen Mason and his wife, Rachel, when they'd returned to the wagon train days ago.

A doctor, she'd overheard during a late meal one evening.

He was striking, with a patrician nose and strong jawline with only a hint of stubble. Dark hair peeked from beneath his hat.

His eyes took her in just as she was doing with him. His nostrils flared wide and his lips firmed in disdain.

She knew that look. Seán had worn the very same one on the night he'd told her he *'hadn't ever loved her. Not really'*. He'd broken her heart.

She couldn't help the minute narrowing of her eyes. What right did this man have to look at her so? To dismiss her before she'd even spoken to him?

He cleared his throat, expression shuttering. "I'm Dr. Jason Goodwin. Folks call me Doc. I thought it was time we met."

Jason.

For a moment, time grew sluggish. Or maybe that was the beat of her heart in her ears.

She smiled tightly. "Maddie Fairfax."

She stuck out her hand, offering a polite handshake even

though he still looked as if she were a bug that had landed in his supper.

It took a beat too long for him to reach out and take her hand, a flush high on his cheeks. He barely touched her before he dropped her hand like a burning coal.

She didn't understand this instant dislike. She had a very good bedside manner. It made her bristle.

He jerked his thumb toward the tent she'd vacated moments ago. "Perhaps I should examine the patient."

"Why?" she asked warily.

"I've heard good reports about how helpful you've been to the company thus far..."

She didn't smile. Simply waited.

"But I'm a doctor by profession."

Surely he didn't mean the words to offend.

Her eyes cut to the tent and back to his tight-lipped expression. She could give him the benefit of the doubt, couldn't she? She shuffled closer so that she could lower her voice. This wagon train was full of gossips. No need to give them any fodder.

"Mrs. Barrigan asked for me. As you said, I've formed a rapport with the travelers in this company. They know me."

She hadn't meant to deliver the last so that the words sounded like a challenge, but as his shoulders grew more tense under his dark suit coat, she allowed her chin to jut up.

His eyes flashed. "And where did you gain your medical degree?" Now his words threw a gauntlet. "A woman's college? Apprenticing with a professional doctor?"

Uncertainty slithered through her. A voice from the past, one that sounded like Seán's, whispering, *you're a child. You don't understand how the world works.*

"Ah. You don't have one." His superior tone irritated like a burr rubbing against bare skin. "I'm sure you mean well, Miss, but I've seen firsthand how home remedies and old wives tales can do more harm than good. The trail itself is dangerous enough."

So this was it.

The source of his disdain. He thought she was beneath him because he had a medical degree—and likely years of experience, based on the brushes of silver at his temples.

But wasn't there value in what both of them could provide? She opened her mouth to ask whether they couldn't work together, both helping the travelers, when he spoke over her.

"Mrs. Mason almost died from an infection," he informed her in a know-it-all tone. "She *would've* died had it not been for my medicine." He patted the black bag in his left hand as if it were a chest full of gold, not medical supplies.

Mrs. Mason's husband, Owen, was tangentially related to Maddie's brother-in-law, Stella's husband, Collin. Owen was Leo's half brother, Leo was Collin's half brother. The Spencer and Mason families were tight-knit because of Stella's connection. Maddie was often in close proximity to them as well. She'd seen how pale Rachel had been when she and Owen had returned to camp. Had witnessed how quickly her energy flagged even now. Part of that could be attributed to being the mother of a newborn, but Maddie had also heard from her friend Alice Spencer about how near a thing it'd been, Rachel almost dying from infection.

Before she could say anything else, a young voice rang out.

"Miss Maddie, Miss Maddie!"

Happy for the interruption, Maddie moved toward Alex Miller, who was running toward her. Alex was all of ten years old and related to one of her former patients—sort of. She would be happy to leave this conversation with the doctor behind.

Unfortunately, Jason was right on her heels as Alex reached them. The boy bent over, hands on his knees, as he tried to catch his breath.

Maddie knelt at his side, one hand going to his shoulder. "What's the matter?"

"Tommy's stitches came loose."

Tears streamed down the boy's cheeks as the words tumbled out. He wiped his face with one grubby hand, smearing dirt through the moisture.

Maddie had stitched up a small cut on the dog's leg just yesterday. She'd cautioned Alex and his brother Paul to keep the dog barricaded inside their wagon or tied up so his movement would be restricted—but the small brown dog was incredibly energetic, and she wasn't surprised he'd torn open the stitches already.

She started to comfort Alex when Jason interrupted her again.

"Where is this patient?" Doc demanded.

The boy sniffled and glanced from Maddie to Jason.

Jason kept his eyes averted from her. It had been on the tip of her tongue to tell him that this *patient* was a dog—except his disdain rolled over her again like a wave. He seemed to think the situation dire—did she really need to correct him? Perhaps she could let this play out...

No. Her concern for the boy and his emotions had her putting her hand on his shoulder. "It's all right, Alex."

"He's in our wagon." Alex pointed across the clearing. "Miss Maddie, ya gotta stitch him back up."

Of course she would.

5

Jason bent to speak to the boy. "I think it would be prudent if I went with you and put in the stitches."

Alex looked tearfully up at him, suspicion evident. "Who're you?"

"This is Doc," Maddie said gently. "He's got a fancy medical degree from back East."

He bristled. Had he heard the slight condescension that had leaked into her tone?

The doctor's smile turned into a grimace. "I've performed countless surgeries and assisted in many more. I'm certain I can put in stitches that will stay closed for your patient." Spoken as if Maddie's stitches had been inferior.

Her lips wanted to twitch. Perhaps he wouldn't argue quite so hard if he knew the patient was a canine. She straightened and motioned Doc across the clearing. "By all means."

The boy looked between them, though his eyes had taken on a new shine. "You're a real doctor?"

"I am," Jason confirmed.

"C'mon!"

Alex left at a jog. Jason followed. Maddie trailed behind both of them.

"I'm certain I won't need assistance," he called out over his shoulder, not even deigning to look her direction.

But she trailed the pair anyway. If Jason became angry at being deceived, she didn't want that to boil over onto Alex. And someone would need to stitch up the dog. If Jason refused, she'd happily do the task.

Alex climbed into the wagon. "You better wait there, Doc. Ma doesn't like anyone tracking mud in our wagon."

Jason started to protest, but Maddie stayed him with a hand on his forearm.

He jerked away from her. "If you please."

She felt the punch of hurt before she blanked her expression. She'd reached out without thinking. What possessed her to stop him in that way?

But surely he didn't have to react like *that*.

The doctor set his bag on the ground and opened it, ignoring her completely.

What she'd thought was simple contempt for her lack of education must be more. Perhaps there was something about *her* that had rubbed him the wrong way. It didn't matter. Shouldn't.

But that didn't stop the misty haze from slipping over her eyes. She blinked it away, firming her lips into a line.

She'd make sure Alex and Tommy were taken care of, and then stay out of the doctor's way. With such a big company, surely she wouldn't have to speak to him again.

Alex edged out of the wagon and dropped to the ground with a small brown dog in his arms and sidled up to the man.

"This is Tommy. He don't like strangers much."

The little dog growled at Doc, baring its teeth.

"This." Jason went stiff, his voice quiet. "Is Tommy?"

Maddie remained silent as Alex waited with a hopeful look on his face. He held the dog securely and presented one front paw. A gash stood out on the dog's forearm. Just yesterday, she'd shaved the fur away from the cut. Her neat row of stitches was visible, at least where they hadn't been torn out by doggy teeth.

Silent anger emanated from the man, and she was suddenly afraid he would lash out at Alex.

"Would you like me to take over for you?" Maddie asked. "I'm sure such a prestigious doctor such as yourself has more important tasks to look after."

There was a definite hesitation before Jason shook his head. "I'll be happy to stitch him up."

Fine.

She waited only a moment to ensure he would take good care of Alex and the pup before she slipped away.

If she never had to speak to Doctor Jason Goodwin again, that would be too soon.

* * *

"Miss Maddie says Tommy is the best dog she's ever met." The boy, Alex, spoke as Doc slipped the first stitch into the dog's leg.

Although Alex held the dog's head against his shoulders with one arm, Doc eyed those canine teeth warily. They were only a few inches away from his fingers.

Maddie Fairfax had done a decent job shaving the one-inch cut, and her sutures were neat and tidy.

Maddie Fairfax had been a complete surprise. He'd meant to meet the camp nurse that everyone praised so heartily, make a connection so they could perhaps work together. He hadn't been prepared to come face to face with her beauty, for the bolt of attraction that had caught him unawares and turned him inside out.

He hadn't so much as looked at another woman since Elizabeth had passed. Hadn't been tempted in the slightest.

When Maddie'd spoken with the gentle Irish lilt to her words, it hit him like a blow to the kidney. The spray of freckles across her pert nose, the intelligence in her blue eyes framed with sooty lashes that could tease or flirt. Beneath the bonnet, hair the color of fire. Strands had come loose somewhere along the way and framed a graceful jaw.

Her youth had come as another blow. Hearing folks talk, he'd expected to meet an experienced nurse, someone in her thirties or even older. Maddie looked to be eighteen or nineteen at most.

"D'you like dogs?" Alex asked, his curious voice breaking Doc from his distracted thoughts.

Doc shrugged.

Please can we have a puppy? Papa, please! The voice from the past—Hildy's voice when she'd been only six years old—echoed inside him, the split-second of memory threatening to overpower him with pain.

Men's voices from nearby offered a welcome distraction.

Doc cleared his throat. He put in another stitch even as he widened his awareness to a bigger circle than this untidy campsite.

Something was going on. He caught sight of Owen Mason on horseback outside of the circle of white-covered wagons. Owen seemed to be having a word with two other men on horseback, his expression a fierce frown.

Doc had only known Owen for a matter of weeks, but he was well aware of the other man's brand of stubbornness. They'd met when Owen and his wife Rachel had been seeking to join an Eastbound wagon train. The very company Doc had joined with earlier in the spring. When Owen had gotten into an altercation with one of the wagon masters, he and Rachel had been ejected from the company. Wary of the wagon master's temper, Doc had set out with the pair.

Thank heaven he had. For Rachel had grown sick from an infection after the birth of her infant daughter. Owen didn't sleep for three days, building a shelter, toting water, praying over her. Willing her to live.

"Miss Maddie says he's the best dog ever," Alex said. The

boy almost buzzed with energy, even as he stood holding the dog.

Miss Maddie. She'd only just gone, but Doc was still reeling with awareness of her presence. He burned with shame. Not only was he far too old to be noticing—he must be at least fifteen years her senior—but his heart still belonged to his wife. It didn't matter that she was gone—

Deceased.

His mouth turned down in a grim frown as his thoughts focused. He couldn't let himself twist the words.

Face the truth. Elizabeth was deceased.

But he was still her husband. And it wasn't right, the bolt of instant attraction he'd felt for Maddie.

As far as he was concerned, the less he saw of her, the better.

Another stitch finished. Only a few more to go.

Another boy—twelve or thirteen, he guessed—appeared from around the wagon. "Yeah, but Miss Maddie says yer supposed to take a bath every week and wash behind yer ears, and you don't do that."

He tossed the words over his shoulder with a smug brotherly grin and headed off somewhere else among the camp.

Alex's mouth twisted into a grimace. "Ya got any brothers, Doc?"

"No." Doc kept his focus on the animal's paw. The dog squirmed in Alex's hold now. "Can you hold him tighter?"

"I dunno." Alex readjusted the dog in his arms. "He's rumblin' an' growlin' at me. C'mon Tommy."

There.

The last stitch. Doc quickly tied off the catgut and grabbed some disinfectant from his medical bag.

"Good boy," he said stiffly as the dog wriggled in Alex's arms.

Alex started to put the dog on the ground, but the animal leapt away, landing on its feet.

"You'll want to keep him from being too active—don't let him run around so much," Doc cautioned.

That seemed a lost cause, as the dog was already bounding through the nearby field, chasing a butterfly.

Alex stood with hands in his pockets and a lift of his chin that reminded Doc of another little boy. Alex squinted slightly. "I ain't go no money to pay ya."

Doc shook his head. "It's all right."

Alex brightened. "I knew you was a kindred spirit. Ya like dogs, doncha?"

Hildy had loved dogs. Cats. Birds. Lizards. Animals of all kinds. He could vividly remember the way his daughter's eyes had pleaded when she'd asked for a puppy of her own.

And then the memory-image of his daughter changed to darkness and a thunderous noise. Her screams echoed in his ears.

"Doc," Alex prodded.

The boy's voice had shaken him out of the nightmarish memories, but there was no escaping them. Not when they lived inside him.

He stiffened. "Goodbye Alex."

The boy's face fell, but Doc snapped his medical bag closed and turned on his heel. He strode away, needing to run. His chest locked up, breaths sawing in and out of his lungs.

"Doc, you hungry for lunch?" Rachel's friendly call hailed him, but Doc barely spared her a wave.

He strode out of the circle of wagons, away from camp, as far as his feet would carry him.

Maybe he'd keep on walking. Forever. Just disappear into the land.

Like his family had.

But in only a quarter of a mile he slowed to a stop.

There were a lot of folks on this wagon train heading to Oregon. Close to two hundred souls. These folks needed someone with medical expertise to help them—not someone with patchwork knowledge and a handful of herbs, like the young Maddie Fairfax.

He still didn't know why he'd been spared on that fateful night. What did God want from him? But one thing he did know. He couldn't walk off into the sunset. Couldn't give up, couldn't stride out into the wilderness and die.

No matter how badly he wanted to.

Lily Fairfax heard the jaunty whistle as she dragged the large pile of canvas that made up the tent she shared with her sister Maddie from the wagon to a bare patch of ground nearby. The playful tune was familiar, and she couldn't help glancing over at the group of hired hands gathered around their campfire just outside the circle of wagons.

Harry Ransome was building the fire while holding an animated conversation with another man lounging against a saddle nearby. A third man was picketing his horse.

Lily quickly ducked her head, not wanting to draw attention to herself. Or maybe she did, because her fingers fumbled and lost their hold on the canvas and the unwieldy bundle fell to the ground with a loud thump.

Bootsteps hurried in her direction as she knelt to gather the tent back up, but it had unfolded too much.

"Need some help?"

She'd had a smile ready, but it slipped when she looked up to see the cowboy who'd been settling his horse. Not Harry.

"Oh. Um. Thank you."

He smiled broadly, a flash of white teeth against his tanned skin. Reached for one corner of the canvas, opposite her, and began to unfold it. "I'm Luther. Most ever'body calls me Lucky."

"Lily."

"That's a pretty name."

She fumbled the corner of canvas she'd been trying to straighten and had to bend to fix it. And was a little glad of the chance to hide her face.

That's a pretty name. They were the same words Harry had said a handful of weeks ago when he'd introduced himself on a lengthy walk back from the creek where Lily had been tasked with washing laundry.

He'd smiled at her, too, eyes sparkling beneath the brim of his hat as he'd offered to carry her laundry basket full of wet, heavy clothing.

That had been the first of numerous days they'd bumped into each other. She'd grown to count on his smiles to break through the drudgery of this never-ending journey. Harry made her laugh. He made her heart flip inside her when he looked at her in that way that only he could. They'd grown close.

She'd waited each day for the handful of minutes—sometimes more—they would be together. Until two weeks ago, when he hadn't come to her at all.

Lucky asked a few questions about placement of the support pole inside the tent as they worked together to set it up. But Lily was mostly aware of Harry at his campfire, so close he could probably hear every word she and Lucky said.

She'd prayed for this very thing for days. For the wagon that belonged to the three Fairfax sisters to be parked near Leo Spencer's when the wagons circled up for the night. There were two hundred travelers in their company. Leo was one of the captains. And he was the man who'd hired on several cowboys to help him bring his herd of cattle to Oregon. At night, the cowboys who weren't on watch bedded down near the Spencer wagon.

It should be Harry helping with her tent. She'd spent a frantic few moments with her head and shoulders ducked inside the wagon to tame the wisps of hair that always seemed to curl around her face. To pinch some color into her cheeks.

But Harry hadn't even left his campfire. And she didn't know whether she had the courage to walk across the expanse of grass—with the other cowboys watching—and speak to him.

Once the tent seemed sturdy enough, she thanked Lucky for his help. The young man walked back to join the cowboys, and she heard the cadence of voices ring out as if they were ribbing him.

And at that moment, Harry glanced up. Their gazes met and held. The flickering campfire gilded his skin gold and turned the tips of his hair a burnished copper.

He averted his face without smiling.

Her stomach tumbled. She turned away from the tent and walked to the wagon on wobbly legs while her stomach churned. It had been doing that a lot lately. Every time she remembered his tender words, whispered into her hair. Remembered his kisses.

And then his silence.

She dragged her bedroll out of the wagon and had no choice but to cross the campsite and put it in the tent. The sunset cast vivid colors across the sky. It was beautiful—or it should have been. She was too heartsick to enjoy it. She wanted nothing more than to curl up inside her tent and hide. But Stella and Collin and Maddie would be expecting to find supper cooking over the fire.

She took the few steps toward the tent. Suddenly Harry was there, his boots hesitating at the edge of her campsite.

Her heart flew into her throat as she pretended casualness. "Hullo, Lily."

"Hello." It wasn't the smile she'd meant for him earlier, but she gave it anyway.

He didn't smile back. She couldn't understand what had changed between them. Had she done something wrong?

"Why haven't you been around?" She wanted to call the words back as soon as they escaped. She hadn't meant for the first thing she said to sound so accusing.

His eyes flashed before he looked at the ground. "Been busy. The cattle. And all."

And all.

What did that mean?

The words were there, on the tip of her tongue, to ask him whether he'd meant any of the lovely sentiments he'd shared. If someone else had caught his fancy. If he regretted the kisses they'd shared. And everything else.

But as the silence grew longer and more awkward between them, everything bottled up inside her.

As she moved toward the tent, she loosened her hold on the bedroll. It shifted in her arms. The circlet of flowers she'd kept hidden away inside it tumbled to the ground.

For a fractured moment, she registered him staring at the daisy chain before she bent and scooped it up, face flaming.

Never seen such talent, he'd teased her as she'd woven the chain of blooms the last time they'd been together. It was a girlish trick, something to keep her hands busy as they'd talked long into the night, sitting on a picnic blanket under the stars well after the campfires in the company had winked out. She'd wanted something to keep her hands busy because she'd ached to reach for him. To feel his arms around her, to experience his kiss.

She'd gotten her wish that night.

Weeks of silence had followed.

And now he'd seen that she'd kept the flowers as a memento. He must realize she was still pining over him.

"Excuse me," she mumbled, making quickly for the tent so she could hide her humiliation.

"Lily—" His voice stopped her in her tracks, but another voice called out, too.

"Do you need help with supper?" Stella said from behind the canvas-covered wagon.

By the time Lily looked up, Harry was striding into the dusk to where the horses were tethered.

Chapter Two

TWO WEEKS LATER

COOP SPENCER HAD LIVED through his share of barrel fever.

He liked to imbibe when the occasion was right, and the occasion was right pretty often.

But he'd never been knocked on his hindquarters like he was right now. From the typhoid.

He'd heard the frightened whispers from other pioneers in their company. Dismissed them, the same as he had the whispers about bear attacks and raiding parties.

He'd been wrong.

Three days of heaving his guts out, with a fire inside his stomach and crawling through his skin. And far as he could tell, he seemed to be doing better than most everyone in his family, except for his sister Alice.

Right now camp was quiet. Lotta folks sleeping off the illness. He fed a bit of kindling into the fire from where he lounged against his saddle and watched as his older brother

Leo crawled out of the tent he shared with his wife and young adopted daughter. Leo made it to his feet but only took two steps forward before he had to lean on the nearest wagon for support.

"Why aren't you out with the cattle?" If Leo's voice had held concern or even curiosity instead of derision, Coop would've pointed to the pot of broth on the edge of the fire. He'd have told Leo that he'd spent hours on wobbly legs toting bowls of nourishment to Collin and Stella, August and Felicity, Owen, Rachel, and checking on little Molly.

Leo had been the recipient of one of those bowls when Coop had delivered food to him and Evangeline and Sarah just this morning.

But since Leo had asked his question with such an air of disdain, Coop drawled, "I checked on the cattle earlier."

"Where's Owen?" Leo leaned heavily on the back of the wagon. His face was pale, a feverish flush high on his cheeks. His eyes were sunken. He looked as if a stiff wind might blow him over.

"Been down for days."

Leo hadn't asked about Coop, only expected more. Like always.

Leo had known Owen for all of four months. Apparently, the man was the spitting image of Leo and Alice's father—the same one who'd abandoned them and divorced their mother before the two siblings could even walk or talk. Twins Coop and Collin had been born after Leo's mother remarried. It was Coop—and Collin—who had stepped up to help the family after losing first their father and then their mother.

It was Coop who'd held things together for the past few days while everyone else had been so sick they couldn't get out of their bedrolls. But Leo didn't seem to remember who'd spoon fed him broth early this morning when he was too weak to lift his head from the pillow.

Several of the cowboys Leo had hired on—Coop had come to consider them friends—had been hit hard with the typhoid, but two of the men had recovered enough to sit in the saddle, and they'd been watching over the herd.

"You should be out there," Leo chided.

Coop shifted from where his right shoulder leaned into a large fallen log. His stomach protested every movement, threatening to bring back up the broth that he had eaten an hour ago. He ignored the queasiness, movements slow while breathing steadily through his nose. He took the lid off the pot, giving it a stir with the long-handled ladle.

"I sorta thought humans were more important than bovines." He gave the pot a good stir, keeping his focus there. He didn't have to look at his older brother to know Leo's expression would be a mix of disappointment and suspicion.

Two weeks ago, Coop had made a promise to himself that he was going to clean up his behavior. Stop imbibing so much. Prove to his family that he could provide and protect just as well as Leo or Collin. With both his brothers married on the trail, and distracted by their pretty wives, Alice needed more help than ever.

But it'd meant long nights of fighting off his demons, trying to drift off to sleep without the whiskey relaxing his muscles and making him forget. And Leo was still riding him, watching Coop's every move. He hadn't seemed to notice any improvement in Coop's manner. His constant disappointment and frustration wore at Coop like a burr under his saddle.

"You want some broth?" Coop asked as he tapped the ladle against the side of the pot. Maybe Leo would go back to bed and leave Coop alone. But his question seemed to jolt Leo out of his thoughts.

"Where's Alice?" he growled.

Coop felt the grim expression slip over his features. "Gone. She rode off yesterday." *With Robert Braddock.* Coop kept that news to himself. Leo would have a fit if he knew. "Headed for the fort, I think."

Almost half of their company had gone off and left the rest under Owen's leadership. Hollis and the others had hoped to find help at the fort. Maybe Alice thought she could do the same.

"You let her ride off alone?" Leo's voice exploded out of him, but the man himself could barely take a staggering step before he had to cling to the wagon's side for balance. If he'd been hale, Coop might've found himself knocked to the ground at the vitriol in his brother's voice.

"No one *lets* Alice do anything."

Leo was overprotective and controlling. A quintessential older brother. But Alice was strong in her own way. She wasn't one to be pushed around. She was the backbone of their family.

"What if she rides into trouble?" Leo demanded.

"Been trying not to think about it too hard," Coop let the words drawl from his mouth again, knowing they would infuriate his brother.

Coop had fought off his own worries about Alice over the past days. At least she wasn't alone, even if Coop didn't trust Braddock one whit.

"You should've stopped her. Or gone with her."

Coop ignored his brother. When she'd left, Coop could barely stagger out of his bedroll long enough to fetch water to keep himself alive. He'd puked his guts out, fought off a fever that made every muscle weak and shaky.

And after he'd realized Alice was gone, what she'd done, he'd known there was no one else among their family that could keep the fire going long enough to boil water or make broth to sustain everyone.

A silent roar of anger lodged in Coop's throat. It wasn't fair that Leo couldn't see what he'd done for the family. Only his failings.

"You just don't think, do you?" Leo spat the words. "You're careless. Still. After everything this family's done for you."

Coop slammed the pot lid down, hand shaking.

"What this family's done for me?" He got to his feet, ignoring the wobbly feeling in his legs, the streak of heat down his spine. "You made us leave all our friends. The only home we've ever known."

Coop had visited his mother's grave in the scant few hours he'd been given to pack up before his siblings abandoned the tenement. He still ached thinking about leaving her there alone.

"You're the reason we had to leave," Leo said coldly. "The reason Collin and I lost our jobs."

The reason their friend had died. Leo didn't have to say the words for them to batter Coop. He'd heard the whispers when his siblings thought he wasn't listening. They'd believed the coppers were coming for Coop because of his negligence in the explosion at the powder mill where the three brothers had worked. The mill owned by Braddock's grandfather.

Neither of Coop's brothers had cared to ask him the truth.

Bitterness welled.

"I guess you can get your own broth." Coop stalked off into the night, slowly. For a moment, he thought his stomach would revolt, but its contents stayed put.

Why was he torturing himself? Why try to stay on the straight and narrow when Leo couldn't see past his own prejudices to recognize the contributions Coop had made?

Leo treated him like a toddler.

And Coop was finished settling for it.

If they'd been in a city or even a town, he'd walk away from his family. They didn't want him here. Didn't need his brand of trouble. Leo might as well have said as much.

But the company was in the middle of the wilderness. He couldn't just walk away with no money and no supplies.

Leo thought he didn't contribute. Let his older brother see what things were really like if Coop slacked off completely.

Because he was done.

* * *

"What do I do if his fever won't come down?" the young mother asked.

Doc lifted his ear from the small boy's chest, where he'd listened to a good, strong heartbeat and several breaths.

"It will come down, in time," he reassured her.

"Mama," a new voice with a note of whine that made Doc want to slip into a memory from his own past.

He held steady and kept his focus on this new patient, the small boy who crawled into the pallet this young mother had crafted underneath the stationary wagon. The tot couldn't be more than two. He was flushed with fever, eyes glassy as he settled beside his mother and brother.

"Beh-yee," the toddler whined. *Belly.*

The young mother looked as if she wanted to weep, but she held out her arms and the boy crawled over his older brother's feet to come to her. She took him in her arms, settling him on her lap.

His head rested against her shoulder and she reached for the bowl of cool water Doc had brought along with him when he'd come to check on this family. She dipped a rag in the water, squeezed out the extra with one fist, and pressed the damp rag to her boy's forehead and cheeks.

Doc reached to close his black medical bag on the ground next to him. There were many other families to check on, and it wouldn't be long before night fell.

Days ago, when the first few pioneers had fallen ill with typhoid, Owen had been in a fierce argument with Hollis, the wagon master. Hollis had insisted on pushing forward, trying to reach the fort for supplies and help.

At least half the company had gone with him, including Maddie Fairfax. Doc had been glad of it. Her presence was a distraction he didn't need. But over the past days, the worst had happened. Nearly the entire company had been afflicted with typhoid. Every family had been infected.

People were dying.

Owen was sick. His wife, Rachel, too.

Doc was fighting a losing battle.

He'd be lucky to catch a few hours of sleep.

Doc glanced up to give the young mother a few more words that might reassure her. When his glance cut to her, he caught sight of the boy's flushed face and small hand that came up to rest against her neck. An innocent embrace, a silent need for comfort. The young woman bent to press her cheek against the boy's forehead, eyes shining with love and worry.

The shared moment between mother and son pulled Doc into his own memories and he was helpless against them.

Elizabeth had been up late with JJ, their second child and oldest boy. Jason had awoken to find her sitting up in bed, the four-year-old curled in her lap.

"He sick?" Jason mumbled the words, pressing one hand against his right eye socket to try and wake himself. It'd been a late night delivering a baby; he felt as if he'd barely closed his eyes.

Now his son needed him.

"Go back to sleep," Elizabeth whispered. "It's only a bad dream."

A bad dream. Not sickness.

Jason relaxed back into the softness of the feather-tick, one elbow behind his head. His son's soft cries faded to an occasional snuffle and Jason reached out his other hand to press against JJ's back.

His hand tangled with Elizabeth's. She'd lit a candle at some point and the soft, flickering light filled the room, illuminating her profile and gilding the edges of her hair gold. Her humming was soft enough not to wake the other children.

Jason could barely keep his eyes at half-mast, but he saw the way JJ's body sagged in her embrace. Nearly asleep again. JJ's hand came up to rest against her neck. Completely secure in her love. Safe from whatever had haunted his nightmares.

A wave of love swept over Jason. Elizabeth would always be there, the perfect partner for him.

He snapped the medical bag closed, forced himself out of the torturous memories.

But it was too late.

The cloak of grief and sorrow slipped around him, heavy and choking.

"I'll come around to check on you in the morning." He steeled himself against the sight of the tears standing in the young mother's eyes, the fear deeper inside them.

He paced away, past the edges of the circled wagons, out into the twilight prairie. He couldn't help the young mother. There was no medicine to eradicate the sickness. Peppermint candy could soothe a stomachache, but it wasn't a fix. And even that was scarce now that the company had been on this journey for months. Willow bark tea could help with the pain, but it was only managing a symptom.

He was helpless.

If the two children could overcome the fever and stomach cramps, hold down some food over the next few days, they'd survive. Doc had nothing more to give her. No more comforting words.

He might as well have died in the rockslide.

His clenched back teeth caged a scream. If he opened his mouth, or breathed too deeply, he wouldn't be able to hold it in.

Keep working.

The single thought that penetrated the self-hatred and choking grief was enough to give him the fortitude to take a breath. That one thought was enough to cling to.

He made himself turn back to the company, stride through the circled wagons.

There. Someone was up and around in Owen's camp. Doc headed that direction.

Owen fed sticks and twigs to a fire, making it crackle and grow in the deepening light. Doc sidled next to Owen, who squatted next to the growing flames.

"Still feverish?"

Owen nodded, looking peaked. "I thought to make some more of that willow bark tea for Rachel. She needs to keep her strength up for the baby."

Rachel had survived a near-fatal infection after she'd given birth to Molly, still only a few weeks old. Owen had fallen hard and fast for the independent woman he'd married only for convenience's sake. Now Doc saw the worry lines bracketing his friend's mouth.

Doc brought over the nearest pail of fresh creek water so Owen wouldn't have to fetch it to add to the coffee pot. He looked as if a strong breeze might keel him over.

"Firewood's running low."

Doc saw Owen's glance at the woods a hundred yards to their north.

"We've been camped here too long," Doc said. "Folks have picked up what loose kindling and logs were freely available."

Owen frowned.

Doc knew what he must be thinking. Almost every single man in their smaller company had been hit hard by the typhoid—Doc was likely the only one left with the strength to use an ax, chop down a tree or split kindling.

Yet Doc was needed here. Even now, someone else moaned from a tent a dozen feet away.

"I've never been this sick before," Owen said. He pressed one hand against his stomach. He was nearly doubled over.

Doc had never suffered from typhoid, but the stomach cramps he witnessed in others were terrifying on their own.

"You've a strong constitution." But Doc's voice cracked as he said the words. He'd only known Owen for a matter of weeks, but the man had become a close friend.

Owen let out a blast of breath. "Check on Rachel for me, will you?"

Doc knew there was little he could do for his friend, knew that if Owen pushed too hard it wouldn't be good. But Doc was in desperate straits, the last man standing in this camp of gravely ill pioneers. If Owen wanted to make tea, he'd let him.

Inside the tent Owen and Rachel shared, Rachel was curled on her side on top of the quilt. The baby slept only inches away, and Rachel had placed one hand on the babe's diaper. Maybe reassuring herself even as she slept that the baby was there.

Rachel's color was better. Her cheeks were a healthy pink, not flushed with fever. She seemed to be sleeping peacefully, face slack and relaxed. She'd been one of the first to suffer from the ailment. Maybe she'd already turned a corner.

Doc was loath to wake her. He gently put one finger at the inside of her wrist where she touched the baby. Her skin was cool and dry.

Hoofbeats thudded from outside the tent. Doc knew that Owen's little sister Alice, along with another traveler, had left camp on horseback days ago. Owen had been furious.

Had they returned?

But this sounded like numerous horses—

Doc backed out of the tent and let the flap down gently, so as not to wake Rachel or the baby.

Owen had straightened to his full height but looked unsteady on his feet.

Ten or more soldiers on horseback appeared. With Alice. Hollis, their former wagon master, with his rich brown skin and muscular build, dark eyes watchful beneath the brim of his light-colored hat. Hollis's wife, Abigail, her tawny skin with a pale undertone as if she'd been ill.

And Maddie, riding close behind.

"You want me to see to them?" Doc asked Owen, who promptly sat down, pressing one hand to his temple.

"If you please."

By the time he reached the center of the wagons, Hollis was off his horse and quietly speaking to the soldiers. He glanced up at Doc. Nodded.

Maddie was at the wagon master's side. Doc kept his eyes off her and focused on the man.

"We're here to help. What's your most pressing need?" Hollis asked.

Doc drew up short. He'd been prepared for a fight. But judging by the grim set of Hollis's mouth, his half of the company hadn't fared any better than Owen's. And Jason was too tired—there were too many who needed help—to seek out a fight.

"We need to boil water. A lot of it, to purify it so it's fit to drink."

Hollis nodded.

"Firewood's scarce," Doc went on. "Been here too long."

A shadow passed through the wagon master's eyes. "We'll take care of it."

He turned away, giving directions to a gaggle of soldiers who hovered nearby. Some of the men had tied bandanas over their faces. Some looked askance at the wagons and tents. Afraid of getting infected themselves?

Maddie had stayed as Hollis turned away. Awareness of her stare made Doc's skin prickle.

It would be rude not to acknowledge her. She'd come back to lend aid. He needed help, needed her, even if he didn't want to. He braced himself and glanced at her.

She had her hands clasped in front of her. She wasn't smiling.

"How can I help?" she asked quietly. "You—you were right that I don't have an education like you do."

Something inside him twisted and coiled tight at the tremble in her words. Shadows chased behind her eyes.

"If you tell me how to help the company, I'll do my best."

This wasn't the same young woman who'd jutted her chin stubbornly and laughed when he'd found himself stitching up a dog.

What had happened in the days since he'd seen her last?

It didn't matter.

"I don't suppose you brought any peppermint from the fort."

She nodded. "Some."

"We can ration it. Do you know how to brew willow bark tea?"

Another nod.

He felt the brush of her gaze, the questions she held back. He hadn't asked for her help before, hadn't wanted it. But circumstances were dire. And she was here.

There was no other choice.

After rejoining the company, Maddie had been on her feet for nearly forty-eight hours. Now she toted pails of water from the creek to the roaring fire in the middle of camp.

It had been Hollis's idea to create one big communal fire, which meant more water could be boiled for drinking. Maddie and Jason had both been run ragged since Hollis,

Abigail, and Maddie had returned from the fort with a contingent of soldiers riding along.

Stella and Lily had both suffered from the typhoid but were on the mend. Lily was cross at Maddie for leaving. But so many people still needed help, so there wasn't time to beg her sister for forgiveness. It would have to wait. Maddie would give her sister a day or two, but then she'd do her best to make things right.

Life was too short.

She'd learned that over the past few days as she'd lost Mrs. Barrigan and Mr. Miller to the sickness.

Right now the camp was quiet as night fell. The soldiers had been given shifts. Two of the men followed Jason across the circled wagons. Jason looked as exhausted as she felt. If he held the same weight of grief that she did, he hid it well.

Her arms ached from the heavy water pails. She put them into the hot coals at the fire's edge. She'd gathered two empty buckets when Alex jogged up to her near the Fairfax wagon.

"Miss Maddie—" He stopped short and doubled over, one arm curling around his midsection. His face was still pale.

"Easy." She set both pails on the ground so she could go to him, one hand on his shoulder. "You're still sick."

She meant the words as a reprimand. She could feel the heat of his feverish skin through his shirt. He should be resting in his bedroll, not running around camp.

His breath caught. "Ma's awake." He panted the words.

Maddie went on alert. Mrs. Miller had fallen gravely ill while Maddie and the others had been separated. When Maddie had checked on her last night, she'd gotten a report from the boys that their mother hadn't been able to keep down any water or herbal tea. Maddie had been fearful this

30

morning when Mrs. Miller didn't waken but slept on restlessly.

The boys had already lost their father. She understood the sorrow and worry etched on Alex's face.

"I'll come now." Maddie left her pails behind and lifted her skirts. When Alex would've started running again, she held him back with a hand on his forearm. "If you push too hard, you'll fall more sick," she warned.

His eyes had a feverish sheen but also a new, brighter light in them. "If she's awake, that's good, right?"

Maddie hesitated. "It might be a good sign," she said carefully. "This sickness is very dangerous. Where's Jenny?" Maddie asked gently, hoping to redirect his thoughts. "Still with Mrs. Carter?"

The youngest member of the Miller family hadn't fallen sick at all. Thank heaven for small mercies. The Millers' neighbor, Mrs. Carter, had been caring for the young girl for the past two days, when Mrs. Miller had fallen so ill that she hadn't been able to get out of bed.

Alex nodded. "Paul's doing better too, like me. He ate some broth."

They neared the Millers' tent. Alex and Paul had moved outside this morning so they wouldn't disturb their mother. The boys' pallet was on the ground outside the tent. Paul knelt in the opening of the tent, speaking quietly, urgently to his mother inside.

"I brung Maddie," Alex called out as they drew close.

Maddie put her hand on his shoulder once more to stop him from joining his brother.

"Would you see if the Boyd family can spare a cup of milk? Maybe it would soothe your ma's stomach."

Alex nodded excitedly. "O' course!"

"Slowly!" Maddie called after him.

Paul had backed out of the tent during the exchange and now he looked at Maddie, expression stricken. He was two years older than Alex's ten years and had a maturity that Alex didn't. Maddie moved toward the tent as Paul sat on the pallet outside, head in his hands. She paused for a moment before ducking inside, reached out to put her hand on his shoulder. His shoulders hunched, and she sighed gently before going to help his mother.

The inside of the tent was still, the air heavy with the scent of sweat and sickness. Mrs. Miller was awake, her eyes glassy. She couldn't lift her head from the pillow. Her skin was nearly translucent, her cheeks sunken.

"Alex is fetching you something to drink," Maddie whispered as she knelt by the woman's side. She brushed Mrs. Miller's hair from her forehead and felt the heat of her skin through her fingertips. Mrs. Miller was still burning up.

Maddie grabbed the bowl of water and a damp rag near the foot of the tent and began dabbing Mrs. Miller's face and neck.

"We'll get you cooled off," she said soothingly. "I'll send Paul to fetch the doc."

But worry streaked through her like a jagged bolt of lightning. Mrs. Miller had suffered this fever for too long. Why hadn't it broken after such a long sleep?

Mrs. Miller grabbed Maddie's hand with a weak grip, pulled it away from her face.

"Where's Linus?" her ragged whisper seemed to sap her strength.

Maddie's eyes filled with tears.

Mrs. Miller seemed to read the truth even as Maddie pushed the words through her lips. "He's gone."

A light went out in Mrs. Miller's eyes.

Maddie rushed on. "But Jenny is healthy. The boys are recovering. It'll only be a day or two and you'll be out there with them, ready to pack up and continue on the trail."

Mrs. Miller's head twitched on the pillow. Had she meant to shake her head? Refuse Maddie's words?

Mrs. Miller's lips moved, but Maddie couldn't hear the near-silent whisper.

"What?" She leaned in close, so that her ear was near Mrs. Miller's mouth.

"Too weak," came the raspy whisper. "Strength fading." A breath against Maddie's cheek. "Promise you'll take care ... children."

Maddie gripped the other woman's hand. "You'll take care of them yourself," she whispered fiercely, aware of Paul right outside the tent. "You're going to drink something. Get stronger."

But Mrs. Miller was too weak to grasp her hand.

"They'll be... lost if... you don't." Mrs. Miller's breaths grew more shallow, her words weaker.

"Don't try to speak," Maddie said. A tear slipped free and fell down her cheek.

Mrs. Miller gripped her hand with a sudden and surprising show of strength. "Promise."

"I promise." The words left Maddie's mouth as a sob hiccuped from her throat.

"I got the milk!" Alex blocked the sunlight in the doorway, a tin cup bobbling in his hand.

"Here." Maddie took the cup and angled her body so that

Alex could come inside the tent. "Come and sit with your ma. Paul, you come too," she called out.

She slipped from the tent, changing places with Paul, who had a mulish set to his jaw but tears standing in his eyes. He knew, as Maddie did, that his mother was fading away.

Alex knelt beside his ma and finally seemed to understand the gravity of the situation.

Mrs. Miller held his hand, and he bent his head to listen to the words she whispered.

Maddie stayed with the boys as in far too short a time Mrs. Miller's whispers died out. As her breaths grew more shallow and more raspy.

And then she was gone.

Alex wailed as Paul stayed silent, both of them in the tent. Maddie sat just outside, her back to the tent, both hands over her face.

Promise you'll take care of my children.

Mrs. Miller had known her end was coming. Maddie hadn't wanted to face it.

Had she done everything she could for the woman? She'd tried her best, but been run ragged as their entire company battled the illness.

The children had lost their father and mother in quick succession. Hearing Alex's muffled cries threw her back into the moments when it'd been her beside her mother's bedside, sobbing into the quilt. Stella had stood beside her, stoic and silent. Lily had been too small to understand what was happening. And their father had been... probably lost in a bottle. Not there in Maddie's memories of those last few moments with Mama, the grief and the loss.

Promise you'll take care of my children.

What had she done, promising such a thing? Maddie had

said the words without thought, only reacted in the moment. But hadn't she wished someone would swoop in and take care of her and Stella and Lily? Yes, so many times in her shortened childhood.

And yet she didn't know if she could keep this promise.

Chapter Three

THEY'D LOST TOO MANY.

Doc knelt next to one of the deceased, gently wrapping a quilt to cover the old man's face. Owen had recovered, was almost at full strength, and he and Hollis had decided that the company would move out in the morning, after a funeral and burial for these unfortunate folks.

The line of wrapped bodies on the ground was cause for grief. Especially the two smaller ones. A ten-year-old girl and a fourteen-year-old boy who hadn't survived the illness. The pain was an echo of the past. Another company. Another time filled with so many lost.

Doc was on one knee, almost finished with ensuring this man had a proper and honorable covering, though they couldn't provide a casket out here in the wilds, when footsteps approached. He glanced up to see Maddie, accompanied by a soldier. The two of them carried another quilt-wrapped body between them and moved toward the opposite end of the row.

Doc was low to the ground and stationed near a wagon. It

was growing dusk, long shadows being thrown. They might not notice him here if he stayed quiet.

"...can fetch more firewood for ya." The soldier seemed to be more focused on Maddie than on the task at hand.

"That would be fine." She turned her face toward him. Was there a smile in her voice? At this distance, Doc couldn't quite tell. "You can leave it in the stack near the wagons."

Maddie tipped her head to indicate that they should set the wrapped body down on the prairie grass. The soldier followed suit. While Maddie remained kneeling by the body, the soldier shifted his feet.

"I could meet ya by the campfire for supper," the young man said. He took off his hat and passed it between his hands.

Maddie gave him her attention. "That's very kind. I'm not sure that I'll get a break. There are still a few folks who need care, or need help packing up to roll out tomorrow."

The soldier faded away with a murmured goodbye.

Doc watched Maddie tuck the fabric of the quilt beneath the body. She was whispering something... maybe a prayer? He should fade into the growing darkness, too. Losing a patient was difficult, and everyone had faced terrible loss over the past few days.

Yet her steady presence had been an unexpected blessing.

He found himself aware of her, even when she was across camp. It was more focused when they were in close proximity, though he'd tried to keep his distance from her. She had a gentle way with those who needed help, especially the children. He'd found himself listening to her lilting voice more often than he should.

He must've shifted slightly, because she glanced up, her gaze landing unerringly on him.

His knees complained of the long time on the hard

ground, so he stood. Hovered, when he should have walked away.

"Are you all right?" Had he really meant to ask the question? It should've been the young man who'd recognized the sorrow in the lines around her eyes, the droop of her shoulders.

She straightened, too, brushing her skirt. "As well as can be expected. Are you all right?" In this moment, she had a gravity that made her seem older than her years. Both of them had borne witness to too much death.

He felt her question like a blow, one that stole his breath. Folks looked to him for comfort. Not the other way around.

The recognition of shared pain was too much. He glanced away and nodded the same direction the soldier had disappeared.

"You didn't like the young man's company?"

She shook her head slightly, brows creased. She hadn't understood his question.

"He wanted an excuse to be near you," Doc explained. "The firewood, having supper together. He fancies you."

Even in the fading light, he easily read the surprise crossing her expressive face. She hadn't realized. If he'd needed a reminder of her youth and naivety, here it was. That moment of connection from before had been a dissonance—a blip of wrongness.

She shook her head, eyes now downcast. Started to say something. Closed her mouth. Opened it again.

"Good evening," she murmured. She hesitated and then skirted the outside of the circle of wagons, not heading back to where he knew her sisters were camped.

The last thing he should do was follow, but his feet carried him after her anyway.

She glanced at him as he fell into step with her, two yards still between them.

"Some people find comfort in each other in difficult circumstances," he said, the words bubbling out. "There's nothing wrong with it."

She didn't look at him directly, but he caught her wrinkled nose and the slight shake of her head. Kept trailing her at her side as she veered away from camp and toward the river.

"Don't you have tasks that require your attention in camp?" she asked.

Did she want him to stay behind? "I'm sure they can wait." Young Mrs. Donnigan had fallen ill most recently, but she'd been sleeping when he'd checked on her not an hour ago.

"It isn't safe for a young lady alone," he said.

Another hesitation. She darted a glance back toward camp. A shadow crossed her expression when she said, "I know." A pause. "I'm only going after some more willow bark. Alice said she'd seen a willow downstream—not far. I won't be long."

She'd given him the perfect excuse to return to camp and seemed frustrated that he followed.

He couldn't seem to stop his feet from accompanying her. "If you don't want me, you should've asked your soldier to accompany you."

"If you insist on being here," she snapped, "I see no reason for us to speak."

Beneath the canopy of trees near the water's edge, decayed leaves muffled their footsteps.

"There it is." She sounded relieved to see the willow, with its low hanging branches, not far ahead.

The moon was barely up over the horizon but with the

cover of the trees, it was nearly completely dark. He trailed her to the tree, then splashed across the narrow creek bed as she got out her knife and began scraping the bark into a small leather pouch.

He kicked a protruding root. Why should he care whether a soldier fancied her? He shouldn't.

"Jason—"

The quavering note in her voice snapped him back to the present. He heard a shuffling. Something big was moving through the woods—and close. It snorted.

Maddie. Where was—?

He saw the shadow of her standing up against the willow's trunk. Frozen.

Heart pounding in his ears, he crossed the creek as quietly as he could, wincing at each splash. She jumped when he reached out and placed his palm on her lower back. From just the simple touch, he could feel her rapid breaths. Knew that her pulse would be racing, her heartbeat elevated.

Whatever it was grew closer. A sort of huff-growl had Maddie trembling. Doc stood close enough to feel the vibrations in her body.

"Bear?" She barely breathed the word.

"Maybe."

A sudden wave of scent, like animal feces, something dead, and wet fur combined blasted him in the face. Surely that was a bear. A sudden big tearing noise accompanied the growling—as if the bear had ripped apart a fallen log. Maybe it had, with only one swipe of its claws.

They had to get out of here.

Maddie remained frozen with fear.

"Where's your gun?" he whispered into her hair. Trying not to notice the warmth of her standing so close.

"Where's yours?" she countered, voice trembling.

"You didn't bring one out here? Alone in the dark?" He went on before she could speak again. "I wasn't planning to leave camp—my revolver is in my saddlebag." And his rifle in its scabbard in his saddle.

Moonlight glinted on metal as she held up her small knife for him to see.

"That won't even penetrate its fur."

There was nothing for it. He let go of Maddie and put his arms over his head, stretching to his tallest height as he stepped out from behind the tree. "Ho, bear!" he shouted. He let loose a piercing whistle.

The grunting turned to a soft huffing, like the animal was sniffing the air.

He whistled again, already backing away. He grabbed Maddie's hand and pulled her along with him.

The bear rattled off into the woods, away from them.

Maddie clung to his hand as he backed through the woods, all the way into the prairie before he stopped. Moonlight spilled over her features. They both breathed hard, as if they'd run a great distance.

Her eyes were huge and round. "I can't believe that worked."

"I can't either," he admitted.

Something passed between them, a moment of connection. She seemed to gasp for breath—and then let go of him to press her hands to her face.

Only then did he realize she was giggling uncontrollably.

"Is this what happens when your life is in perilous danger?"

She nodded and dissolved into giggles again.

A beat, and his mouth wanted to respond in a smile.

The pull of muscles in his cheek felt foreign—and he yanked himself out of the moment to realize how close he stood to her.

Maddie's giggles turned into soft sobs. She bent in half, burying her face in her skirts.

He recognized this grief, felt it a mirror of his own. The terror and levity had unleashed the emotion, and now she couldn't contain it.

Instinctively, he touched her back, felt her freeze. Even her breathing stilled.

The crying jag only lasted a moment. One moment for the emotion of the past days to escape, like a tablet of medicine fizzing over the top of a glass.

She wiped her face quickly and then straightened, staring at him in the moonlight. All traces of a smile gone.

"How do you do it?" she whispered brokenly. "How do you heal from something like this? From watching someone take his last breath? Being helpless when a child loses her parent?"

The moment stretched long as he stared at her, an invisible thread connecting them. He'd watched her with the Miller children earlier today as their mother passed, seen Maddie's stoic expression, the gut-wrenching sorrow in her eyes. She might be young, but she understood loss in a way the other pioneers never would.

She went on, "When there should be something I can do but there is nothing. How do I heal from this?"

She looked at him with the light of hope in her eyes.

And here was the chasm between them. He would be the one to dash her hope.

"You don't."

Chapter Four

"LET'S put that crate right here," Maddie said.

Alex hefted the crate filled with odds and ends from the breakfast dishes they'd used and brought it to where Maddie stood at the back of the Miller family wagon. There was a spot cleared right in the back and between the two of them, they wedged in the crate.

Strong wind blew strands of her hair into her eyes and her skirt against her legs. She whisked her hair from her face. Over the past day and a half, no one had questioned her for caring for the Miller children, but she still needed to talk to Hollis to make it official.

Hours had passed since the sun had come up this morning. She'd spent a sleepless night remembering the interaction with Jason in the woods.

"You don't."

What deep losses had he faced that caused such certainty? She might never forget the sorrow and gravity in his expression.

A small brown blur ran underneath the wagon from outside the circled conveyances.

Alex's dog.

The dog darted to Paul to sniff his boots where the boy squatted beside the fire. When the dog turned to the quilt where Jenny lay, Paul cried out, "Hey!" The dog scampered away, bypassing Alex to put his paws on Maddie's knees.

"Hello, you little scoundrel." She patted its head. "Alex saved you some breakfast."

Alex moved to the front of the wagon where he'd stashed his plate with table scraps, clucking to the dog, who ran to him.

Maddie crossed to the space just beyond Paul, where the boy's bedroll was laid unrolled in the waving grass.

Jenny was a good natured baby, but this morning she was quiet, head craning all around. Looking for her Ma and Pa?

Maddie glanced at the Fairfax wagon, where Stella should be packing up, but her sister wasn't there. Belongings littered the campsite spanning between the Fairfaxes' wagon and the Millers' wagon.

Maddie bent to roll up Paul's bed as he played with a long reed, pushing the last of the fire's coals around before dragging its smoking end from the fire.

"Did you want to go to the funeral after all?" Maddie asked quietly, while Alex was distracted by the dog.

Paul stared at the barely-glowing coals. "Naw."

She'd discussed the matter with the boys over a quick breakfast, and both had been adamant that they hadn't wanted to attend the group funeral and burial. But something was obviously bothering Paul. He'd been quiet all morning, almost belligerent when she'd asked him to help load the wagon.

"I don't understand why we can't take them with us," he said.

Take them... He meant the bodies of his parents.

She picked up the bedroll under one arm and reached his side after a quick glance at Jenny, still lying quietly.

"They should be buried in Oregon—once we find our new land. Not—not out in the middle of the wilderness."

When she stretched out her hand to pat his shoulder, he sidestepped. Her hand fell back to her side.

"We can't." It would be too gruesome for the child to hear how the bodies would decompose, to try and describe how the corpses might spread the sickness.

"I know it's hard." She opened her mouth to tell him how she'd felt when Mama had died, but he sent her a scathing glance.

"You don't know anything," he muttered.

Maddie worked to keep her expression neutral as Alex, finished feeding the dog, glanced over at them.

Paul tossed his reed atop the coals and turned to her, arms crossed over his chest. "Jenny needs her diapers washed. Ma would've already done it." Said with a mulish tilt of his chin.

Oh. "You told me so last night, didn't you?"

Over the boy's head, Maddie saw Lily round the corner of the Fairfax wagon.

"Perhaps a distraction would be good for all of us," she suggested gently. "Why don't we walk to the creek together. I'll wash the diapers before the bugle calls."

Paul's expression softened the tiniest bit. His arms dropped to his sides. "I guess."

It wasn't the most rousing endorsement, but she would take it in this moment when his grief was so fresh.

She scooped Jenny into her arms. "Let me tell my sister

where we are going. Can you and Alex round up all of the soiled cloths? Grab the soap?"

Both boys wrinkled their noses almost identically but agreed with reluctant murmurs. The dog followed at Alex's heels.

Maddie carried the baby to where Lily was muttering under her breath as she picked up the cookpot and tins and utensils left behind after breakfast.

Lily glanced up at Maddie, who couldn't help but notice how peaked her sister still was. Typhoid had lasting effects.

"I'm going to walk down to the creek and help the boys wash out some diaper cloths."

Lily's nose wrinkled almost the same way the boys' had. Her gaze flicked to the boys standing near their family wagon.

"What are you doing with those children?" she asked, voice low.

Promise you'll take care of my children. Mrs. Miller's dying request slipped through Maddie's mind once more.

"They lost both their parents. Surely you don't expect them to make it to Oregon without help."

Lily's eyes took on a calculating gleam. She frowned. "Let someone else deal with those brats."

Maddie bristled. "Who?" She motioned to the young mother in camp with her three tiny ones. "Mrs. Kelly has her hands full already. Mr. Larson would work them to the bone." His own children were silent little worker bees. After her own childhood, Maddie wanted to cry every time she glanced in the family's direction. "Who in the company wouldn't appropriate the supplies that rightly belong to the children?"

Lily pointed her finger at Maddie. "You abandoned Stella and me—"

"I didn't abandon you." Exasperation leaked out in Maddie's voice, but Lily didn't listen to her interruption.

"—and now you're spending all your time minding those three? Look at this mess." She swept her hand around the campsite. "Not one thing packed."

"Where's Stella?" Maddie kept her voice as even as she could. There was no use arguing. Before she'd left with Hollis, she'd explained in detail why Hollis and the company needed her.

Lily was obviously still sore, though they'd been reunited. Maddie had been busy with patients and the Miller children all night and morning. Her bedroll had never even moved from its place packed inside the Fairfax wagon.

Lily looked like she would argue further, but then her angry gaze slipped past Maddie. She ducked her head. Maddie glanced over her shoulder to see a pair of wranglers walking near the edge of camp, yards away. The cowboys had been hired on to push Leo and his family's small herd of cattle across the plains—and for help with protection from beasts and man. One of the men tipped his hat in their direction.

When Maddie turned her head, intending to ignore the gesture, she caught sight of Lily's still-downturned face and a blush climbing in her cheeks.

"C'mon, Miss Maddie!" Alex's voice.

Torn, Maddie shifted on the balls of her feet. Lily glanced up at Maddie, gaze shifty. Something had passed between her and the cowboy.

The sound of voices singing carried on the wind, and Maddie realized Hollis must've begun the funeral. It wouldn't be long before the bugle would blast and the company would roll out. And she had to help the boys with those diapers.

"I have to go," she said.

Lily wore a mulish look and muttered to herself as she packed up with jerky movements.

There was a knot in Maddie's stomach as she left her sister and collected the boys. She should speak to Stella. Stella would know what to say to Lily.

As they walked toward the stream, Alex sent a pensive glance over his shoulder. Maddie held Jenny against her sternum and patted her back while she followed the boy's eyes to where most of the company had gathered in a huddle on the empty plain. Soon enough, the dozens of bodies of those they'd lost would be lowered into the ground and covered with soil.

"Your mother and father were good people," Maddie said quietly.

Paul looked forward, jaw set.

"Would you tell me one of your favorite memories with your mother?" she asked gently.

Paul shook his head, but Alex lit up. "Remember that one time she was mending one of pa's shirts, and she didn't have the right color thread?"

Paul flicked a glance at his brother.

"Pa was so embarrassed to wear that blue shirt to church, stitched with white thread all around the pocket—until she stitched both of our Sunday shirts to match. Remember?"

A tear slipped down Paul's cheek. He whisked it away with his sleeve, frowning fiercely. Maddie thought about reaching out again, but the way he'd stepped from her touch earlier made her hesitate.

"Do you still have that shirt?" she asked Alex gently.

"Sure do. Not much use for Sunday best out here, though." He squinted and looked to the horizon. Swallowed hard.

"Perhaps you could wear it tonight at supper, when all the chores are finished. To honor your mother."

He lit up. "Yeah! You should wear yours too, Paulie!"

Paul shrugged.

They'd come near enough to the creek for Alex to roll up the cuffs of his pants. "Can I wade?"

"If you'd like," she said. "Paul, will you hold Jenny while I wash the diaper cloths?"

A beat of relief passed over his expression. Had he thought she meant for him to do all the work to care for his baby sister?

Paul set the bundle of diapers and the bar of soap on the bank and reached for Jenny. Maddie handed over the baby, who screwed up her face to wail until her brother bounced her slightly.

Aware that their time was short—Maddie didn't want to get left behind when the wagon train pulled out—she knelt on the creek bank and reached for the first diaper.

Keeping her eyes on the water she said, "I don't know much about raising a baby, but what would you young men think about staying with me from now on? Going to Oregon together?"

Alex let out a whoop. "Yeah!"

But Paul was watching the horizon again, expression shuttered. He didn't answer for such a long time that Alex prompted, "What d'ya think, Paulie? Miss Maddie is smart and pretty and nice."

"I guess," Paul said finally, grudgingly. "Having Miss Maddie is better than nothing."

Not a rousing endorsement, but she knew how badly he hurt inside.

This would work. She would do everything so the children would be safe and loved.

* * *

"Fire!"

The cry rang out as Doc was checking his horse's back hoof, expecting the bugle call at any moment. His head came up, eyes scanning the horizon.

How had he missed the acrid scent of smoke carried on the wind? It seemed all he could smell now that he saw the dark gray trails spreading into the sky across the entire horizon. A flock of birds took flight from the woods two hundred yards to the north, their calls piercing the sudden stillness. And then chaos.

Women cried out.

Men shouted.

A dog barked and a horse whinnied in clear terror.

One man ran to his team of oxen, half hitched to the wagon, and fumbled with the buckles.

"You can't outrace that fire," Doc called out to him. "Not with the wind blowing like it is!"

The man glanced at Doc, letting him know that he had been heard even as he kept on working.

Not far away, two men tussled. One threw a punch and connected with the other's jaw, knocking his head back.

A woman staring at the rising smoke wept openly. Her young daughter tugged on her skirts, sobbing, too.

Where was Hollis? The wagon master needed to issue directions. Calm the company. If folks drove their wagons away willy-nilly, they'd likely get themselves killed.

Pounding hoofbeats approached. Doc only saw movement on the other side of two wagons parked close to each other, unable to make out who it was.

A shrill whistle rang out. "Every man gather here!"

Relief surged. Owen.

And he was calling the men to come to Hollis.

Doc joined the crowd, listened to Owen's quick instructions to create a small fire in a horizontal line between the company and the raging wildfire. If the smaller, controlled fire could burn up enough grass, the wildfire wouldn't have any fuel to sustain itself. It would die out.

Doc knew it was a risky move, but Hollis and his captains seemed determined. And giving the men specific directions had indeed calmed the company enough to take action.

He was peripherally aware of the women and older children hauling buckets and pails in a race toward the river as he wielded a shovel to tamp out furls of fire that crawled toward the wagons.

Where was Maddie? Frustration fired through him when he realized he was looking for her every time he twisted toward the wagons.

She's not your responsibility, he told himself. *Let her sisters worry about her.*

But he couldn't seem to keep from scanning every woman who came into his peripheral vision. None of them were Maddie.

Just this morning, Doc had stood at the graveside through Hollis's mournful words. Maddie hadn't attended. Over Hollis's shoulder, Doc had seen her and the two Miller boys walking away from camp, toward the woods and twisting creek that was an offshoot of the river.

That had been over an hour ago. Surely she'd returned to camp to prepare for pulling out.

"I need ya, Doc!"

A teen boy approached, one hand holding his forearm. Blood seeped through his fingers. Doc motioned him toward the wagons and his saddled horse. His medical supplies were in his saddlebag.

"What happened?" Doc demanded.

"Cut myself. I was reaching into the wagon for a quilt—"

That didn't matter now.

"Where's Maddie?" the female voice turned Doc's head.

Both of Maddie's sisters were throwing pails of water on the canvas of their wagon, drenching it until rivulets streamed toward the ground. Good. That would give it a fighting chance if the wildfire crossed the fire break.

But the younger sister shook her head. "She went to the creek with the Miller boys," Lily cried. "Isn't she back?"

"I haven't seen her!" Stella said.

Doc hurried to his saddlebag, now unable to quell the mass of writhing snakes in his stomach. Maddie was missing. The kids, too.

He tried to ignore it. She wasn't his to watch over.

But his fingers trembled as he pulled a bottle of disinfectant from his medical bag. He flexed his hand and tried to focus as he pried away the boy's other hand to see the injury.

The cut wasn't that deep. Would need stitches, but the teen wasn't going to bleed out in the next hour or two. Doc's breath sawed in and out of his lungs, the smoke in the air burning with each breath. He hesitated before he reached for the needle and catgut.

"I have to go," he blurted.

The teen's eyes went wide. "But—"

"I'll be back," he said. He quickly wrapped a bandage

around the cut. "It'll hold until I can stitch it later. Go help your family."

He stuffed the disinfectant back in his bag and vaulted into the saddle before the boy could protest. He'd kicked the horse into motion before he could even think. It wasn't rational, the fear that choked him. But he had to get to Maddie. Find her.

If the wildfire caught up to Maddie and the Miller children, they would die.

Soil kicked up from behind his horse's hooves as they raced through the wagons at the eastern edge of the camp. Doc sent up a prayer that Hollis's plan would work, that the company would be saved. He leaned into the canter the horse gave him, heading the same direction Maddie and the boys had gone earlier. *The creek*, her sister had said.

But when he reined in his horse near the edge of the woods, there was no shock of auburn hair, no children's voices chattering. There was only the trickling of the stream and the roar of the wind in Doc's ears.

He wheeled his mount. Had she gone back to camp after all?

The smoke had grown thicker, and when he looked back toward the company, he couldn't see the wagons any more. Only a wall of fire advancing from the horizon.

Where would Maddie have gone?

He shouted her name. Shouted for Alex and for Paul until he broke down coughing from the smoke.

Then he thought he heard the faint sound of a baby crying.

He strained his eyes to see through the blowing smoke and glimpsed movement. Maddie's blue dress, familiar to him now.

They were at an angle to him, a good hundred yards away. Out in the open, away from the creek. Too far away from the company and the activity that would hopefully save the camp. His horse gave him the speed he asked for and each stride ate up the ground until he reached them.

They were running, heading back toward the creek.

"Jason!" Maddie shouted when she saw him.

Drawing near, he scrambled off his horse, his boots hitting the ground while the animal was still in motion.

Her face was stricken, eyes wide with terror.

Thunder rolled, cutting off whatever she was trying to tell him.

"On the horse," he told the two boys when the thunder had abated. "Get to the creek and get in the water."

He boosted Alex into the saddle behind Paul, who had a bundle clasped to his chest. He slapped the horse's flank, and the animal jumped into motion. Probably as frightened as Jason was.

"C'mon," he shouted to Maddie over the roar edging closer. Only a scant dozen yards left between the fire and the two of them.

Maddie was already running, holding the wailing baby to her shoulder. Doc put his hand to the inside of Maddie's elbow and urged her to move faster.

His lungs burned, the urge to cough pressing hard.

He couldn't stop. They didn't have time, not even to take an extra breath.

The heat grew, warm air scouring the back of his neck beneath the brim of his hat.

The woods were close.

The creek was right there—

Maddie stumbled. Doc hauled her to her feet and pushed her forward.

"Almost there," he huffed, nostrils burning.

The two boys already stood in the creek when Doc and Maddie hit the woods. His horse was nowhere in sight. Had it run off?

Maddie screamed, and he realized a tongue of fire had jumped and caught the hem of her skirt. He let go of her to smother it between his hands.

"Get in the water!" he commanded.

Her boot slipped on the muddy bank, but she kept her feet as she stumbled into the creek.

Doc splashed in at her heels.

"Get down!" he shouted to the boys. "Hold your breath and go underwater as the fire passes over."

Maddie knelt in the foot-deep water, looked up at him, stricken.

"What about Jenny?" she cried.

Doc scooped water into his hat and dumped it over her and the baby both.

She gasped, and Jenny wailed louder.

Fire crackled only feet away now.

"Jason! Your arm," Maddie cried out.

A spark must've flown up. A tiny flame licked at the sleeve of his shoulder. He clamped his hand over it, felt a spark of pain before his wet skin doused the fire.

Feet away, Alex was coughing and couldn't seem to stop. Doc glanced over. Paul had one arm around his brother's shoulders. They were lying in the water, practically submerged. Only their heads showed above the waterline.

Would the fire pass over? Or were these moments their last?

Maddie reached for Jason at the same moment he reached for her. His arms came around her shoulders. He flattened both of them as much as he could into the water, the baby between them. The shock of cold water only lasted a second.

The tiny wails pressing into his shoulder reassured him. Jenny was breathing fine if she could scream. Maddie fisted the collar of his shirt in one hand, her entire body trembling.

He bent his head, his cheek pressed against hers as the roar of the fire deepened. Felt the blast of heat against the exposed skin of his jaw and the back of his neck.

A feeling of downward pressure, hot wind sinking against his skin—

And then it was over.

The fire skated away, skimming through the woods on the opposite bank.

He felt every trembling breath that escaped from Maddie, both where her shoulder pressed against his chest as he held her, and from the heat of her exhale on the sensitive skin beneath his jaw. Prickles of awareness skittered up his spine and raised the hair at the back of his nape. He was holding her.

Let her go. But he stood frozen, staring down into her eyes.

He'd never thought to feel anything like this again, not after losing his late wife.

Paul's whoop startled him. Doc became aware of Alex, still coughing nearby, of his own ragged breaths, the sting in his throat from the smoke.

"I think—we're all right," Maddie whispered, her words hot against his neck.

Doc made sure she was steady on her feet before he stepped back, one hand coming to the back of his neck. He half-turned away, trying to find equilibrium again. He felt as if he'd been burned all over. His skin raw and stretched too tight over his bones.

Another clap of thunder was the only warning they had before the sky opened up and a deluge of rain fell.

Jenny wailed louder, and Doc knew they needed to get back to the company. Maddie's family had probably sent out a search party by now.

Alex and Paul were dancing in the rain.

Maddie stared at Doc, bedraggled, rivulets of rain trickling down her skin. "You saved us."

He saw her mouth form the words more than heard them.

Gratefulness and admiration shone from her eyes.

He cut his gaze away, hands on his hips.

He'd helped them get to the creek all right—because he hadn't been able to stop worrying about Maddie. She plagued his thoughts constantly. There was no one else in camp who distracted him, infuriated him, challenged him, like she did.

And to harbor such feelings toward her felt completely, terribly wrong.

Chapter Five

"TOMMY!" A shrill whistle sounded just after the boy's cry. There was motion on the other side of the nearby wagon.

Doc knelt on one knee, his saddlebag on the ground in front of him, flap open. He stuffed a shirt into his saddlebag. Extra shirt. A journal he hadn't cracked in months. Pair of socks.

It was growing dark around Hollis's camp, the wagons circled outside the fort. Although no one had been seriously injured in the wildfire two days ago, every man and woman in the company was subdued. Earlier, groups of three or four folks had left to visit the fort and barter for supplies. Now that it was getting dark, most had returned.

These pioneers were worn down after difficult weeks on the trail and fear seemed to swamp the company. They'd survived the fire and made it to the fort, but a terribly long journey lay ahead.

It was time for Doc to leave. He'd made the decision last night, but even now, his stomach knotted.

He was alone in this part of camp, between two wagons, one

that belonged to Owen and Rachel. He'd taken every item out of his doctor's bag and laid them out on a clean quilt at his side.

Once he packed up, he'd be gone. It was for the best.

A hint of feminine laughter carried on the breeze. His head came up, gaze searching—

He blinked himself into the present, but the pain of the past sliced deep.

"What're you doin', Mister Jason?"

A boy's voice, followed by a cough. Doc glanced up to see Alex hovering at the rear of the nearest wagon.

Jason.

Maddie called him Jason. No one else.

"Packing my things." Doc went back to placing the items in his saddlebag. "Call me Doc."

Alex crept closer. "Are ya leaving or somethin'?"

"Something," Doc gruffed. He still needed to speak to Owen.

He reached for the square wooden board, painted on one side, and the small leather pouch. When Doc lifted the leather pouch, small wooden pieces flung across the blanket.

Alex quickly dropped to his knees at the edge of the quilt. "I'll help!"

Doc snatched up a few of the pieces, the boy's eagerness reminding him of another boy. Something inside him wanted to snap at Alex to go away, but he bit back the response.

Alex picked up several pieces, but then stopped and raised one to look at it. "By golly. I thought they was checkers, but lookit. It's a carving of a little horse." He examined another. "And this one's a castle. What're they for?"

Doc sighed and stuffed pieces into the pouch. "They're for a game."

"What kinda game? Like checkers?"

Alex held out the pieces, his eyes dancing with curiosity as he watched them drop into Doc's open palm.

"A game called chess. I learned from a Frenchman traveling the Trail last summer."

Alex's eyes grew wide. "You already been on the trail once? Why'd you come back to do it again?"

Doc felt the frown pulling at his expression. He'd never actually reached the Willamette Valley. And he never would.

"Where's M—"

A dog barked, followed by a chicken squawking, and Alex's head came up. "I gotta get 'im."

Alex scampered a few steps, and then had to stop as a cough overtook him. Doc listened for a moment, a sense of wrongness slithering through him, but then Alex's cough stopped and he ran off.

A shadow fell over Doc.

Owen. "You been quiet the past few days."

Doc kept packing.

"You all right?"

Are you all right? The memory of Maddie's words, her face in the moonlight hit him like a blow to the gut. He shoved the chess pieces, now wrapped, into his saddlebag and moved to pack up his medical supplies.

"I can't stay on." Doc glanced up to see Owen's arm drop. He'd motioned Hollis over.

The wagon master squatted across the blanket from Doc, his gaze taking everything in.

Doc sent a pointed look at Owen. "When I joined up with you and Rachel, I told you I wouldn't go all the way to Oregon."

No need to feel guilty. He'd been up front about his plans.

Hollis flicked a glance his way. "Shame. We need someone with your skills."

"There are a lot of folks in Oregon who need your help." Elizabeth's voice sliced through Doc's memories like a surgical blade. He stuffed the grief away.

"My wife thought the same." The words roughened in his throat. "It was my wife's dream to forge a new life there. After I lost her and my children—" He couldn't finish. Didn't have to.

There was a beat of understanding from Hollis. Owen listened thoughtfully. Doc had told him briefly about losing Elizabeth and the kids.

"We need you," Owen argued. "You saved Rachel's life. Molly's too."

"Rachel is strong. Her body fought off the infection—"

"With your medicine," Owen pushed.

"There's no more medicine to be had." That was true. Even so, the worry in Owen's expression made the knot in Doc's gut pull tighter. He tried to turn his insides to stone.

Hollis tilted a considering look into the darkness outside the circle of wagons. "Is there anything I can offer to get you to stay until the Rockies? We've still got some folks feeling poorly, and it'd be reassuring to them to have you on."

"We'd have lost more than we did without you and Maddie," Owen echoed.

"I can't have Maddie assist." The sharp words burst out of Doc before he could call them back.

He caught motion somewhere behind Owen, just outside the periphery of the campsite. The swish of someone's skirt, hurrying past. But Doc kept his stare aimed at Hollis.

He hadn't meant to tip his hand like he had. Hollis saw what he couldn't admit to aloud. Shame swelled.

"I can't guarantee you won't have to see her, but I think the company is big enough for both of you to keep your distance. I can speak to her."

"Please." Owen's voice was laced with emotion. "Rachel would've died if it wasn't for you. Molly wouldn't have survived without her ma. Stay on. As long as you can. We need you."

Doc had to look away from his friend's plaintive gaze. Owen wasn't someone to be overcome with emotion. That he would resort to near begging showed how serious he was—rightly worried about the dangers they would face ahead.

Hollis stood to his full height. "Let me know what you decide." He moved off into the darkness.

Owen waited. Apparently the man wouldn't leave until Jason gave an answer.

"I'll stay on until the foothills."

The words had a cost. Doc was rocked by the memory of JJ's excitement, Hildy's wonderment when they'd seen the mountain range at close proximity.

He couldn't face that crossing again.

Owen smiled warmly, clapping a hand on Jason's shoulder before he left.

Doc fought off a wave of regret, already wondering if he'd made the right choice.

* * *

"I already washed up." A string of coughs followed Alex's words from behind the Miller wagon, only a few yards from where Maddie was hanging damp laundry on a line she'd tied between the wagon and the Spencers' neighboring wagon. Night was falling around her.

"I can't have Maddie assist." The words she'd overheard Jason say when she'd been walking past shouldn't sting so much. Yet she'd been gnawing on them like a dog with a bone ever since last night.

He'd told Maddie his views on her education from the start, hadn't he? She was unschooled. But after they'd worked together for several days during the epidemic, she'd foolishly hoped they might become friends.

Hollis had come to speak to her today as she and the kids had walked alongside the wagon. Asked her in the politest way he could to keep her distance from Jason.

She'd coolly agreed. Why should she argue and humiliate herself?

But she was confused. Frustrated.

She hadn't imagined the moments of connection throughout the ordeal. They both knew the hardship of losing patients. The exhaustion of working into the night, lucky to fall into one's bedroll and catch a few hours of sleep. She'd thought perhaps she was starting to prove herself to him.

"Then why's there dirt behind your ears?" came Paul's impatient retort. The boys' argument from nearby broke into her thoughts.

Maddie glanced at the tent pitched nearby. Jenny was sleeping inside, though it had taken nearly an hour to get the girl to sleep. Every time Maddie laid the girl gently onto a pallet, those brown eyes would pop open.

"Go back to the creek and wash up for real," Paul ordered.

"I *said* I already did."

Maddie's fingers were pruny after washing up the large

load of laundry. Maybe that was why the next tiny dress slipped off the line as she tried to secure it. She caught it as it fluttered toward the ground—thank goodness—just as a sharp, ugly word was uttered on the other side of the wagon.

"Boys!" she called out, jogging around the wagon.

Only to find them tussling. Alex had thrown one shoulder into Paul's gut and was hanging on, while Paul pounded his fist against his brother's back and had his other arm around Alex's shoulders. Or maybe he was reaching for his brother's ear.

"That's enough!"

But they didn't hear her over their grunts and growls—or they ignored her.

She flapped the tiny dress, but that didn't catch their attention either.

"Stop this!" She closed in, getting her toe stepped on for good measure. She put a hand on Alex's shoulder, gave a push, and finally they separated.

They stood with only inches between them, breathing hard. Alex's hair was rumpled, face red. Paul crossed his arms over his chest, expression clearly showing his anger.

Was Alex wheezing a bit?

"We don't fight in this family," she said when the angry silence lengthened and it became clear neither one was going to apologize to the other.

"I heard you tell him to wash up, and he didn't." Paul's chin jutted out.

"I did, too!" Alex said.

"You didn't go down to the crik—"

"You ain't the boss of me—"

"Stop!"

Alex flinched at her strident tone, but Paul kept glaring, this time at her.

"We're all tired," she said. That much was true. Hollis had blown the bugle before dawn today and they'd left the fort behind, traveling almost twenty miles. "Why don't you go into the tent and go to sleep." She made it an order, not a question.

Alex stomped off, but Paul looked like he would refuse.

"Don't wake up your sister!" Maddie called after the younger boy.

But it was too late. She heard the plaintive cry that had become so familiar over the past few days.

Weariness sank deep into her bones.

"Go to bed," she said to Paul. "Please?" Maybe her exhaustion came out in her voice, because he stalked off after his brother.

She slipped her head and shoulders into the tent only long enough to pull Jenny into her arms—only realizing when dampness seeped through the shoulder of her shirt that the little dress remained over her arm.

Jenny swiveled her head, looking around the campsite in the growing darkness. Two cowboys passed by, one tipping his hat toward Maddie. A mother from a nearby wagon glanced over from where she was putting a toddler to bed inside the wagon. Compassion lit her features before she turned back.

"It's all right," Maddie murmured to the baby. But when she attempted to settle Jenny against her shoulder, she arched her back, crying even more loudly.

Jenny stuffed the fingers of one hand into her mouth, her anxious gaze scanning around as her little legs kicked against Maddie's side. Maddie hummed, the sound inaudible beneath the baby's crying, as she walked slowly around the campsite, bouncing slightly after each step.

When she and Mrs. Murphy had helped the neighbors in their tenement in Dublin, she'd held plenty of babies. Itty bitty ones that had come before their time. Hefty ones with rolls of fat on their legs and arms. She was good with babies. Mrs. Murphy had said so. But nothing she tried would calm Jenny.

By the fifth circuit, her legs were tired from traipsing around and around the campsite.

Paul peeked out of the tent. Maddie pretended not to see him, hoping he'd go to sleep by himself. Her own bedroll beckoned her, laid out near the children's tent. She'd been up before dawn, when she'd been whispered awake to see a young mother who had been having pain when she nursed her weeks-old baby.

But then Maddie paced past the damp laundry in the basket. She couldn't leave it crumpled and wrinkled. How musty it would smell in the morning. And Jenny needed those diapers to be dry.

"Yah, yah, yah," Jenny's cries now seemed to form a word, one that Maddie couldn't understand.

The girl *finally* laid her head on Maddie's shoulder. Maddie used the hand that wasn't holding Jenny to rub gentle circles on her back. It seemed the most natural thing to do to rest her cheek on top of Jenny's head. But Jenny popped up, her eyes wide and distressed. Her tear-streaked cheeks made Maddie's heart twist.

"We'll get through this together," she whispered, knowing that Jenny didn't understand.

The baby took one more look around the quiet campsite and wearily laid her head on Maddie's shoulder once again.

She snuffled, but her breaths finally calmed. She wasn't asleep yet, but she was worn out from looking for her parents.

Maddie's heart broke for her. Maddie herself had been very young when her mother had passed away—young enough that she couldn't remember the woman's face, only a vague emotion when she tried to picture her. But Maddie could remember with vivid clarity, a morning not long after Mum had died when she'd woke in the early morning, certain that all of it had been a bad dream. She'd searched the apartment looking for Mum, until she'd accidentally woken Da and received a swat and an order to go back to bed. She knew the emptiness Jenny must feel, though Jenny was far too young to understand *why*.

For the first time, Maddie felt a flicker of uncertainty. Jenny was grieving and Maddie didn't know how to help her. The boys were grieving too. That's what those angry words had been about.

Jenny drooped against Maddie's shoulder, but the occasional sniffling breath told Maddie she still wasn't asleep.

On the next turn, Maddie stopped near the basket of washed laundry. Tears pricked in her eyes as exhaustion swamped her. How was she supposed to do this all alone?

A shadow moved just past the wagon next to Maddie's in the circle. She waited a beat, expecting more movement. Perhaps one of the men going out to take his turn on watch? Or a woman gone to fetch something from her wagon as she prepared for bed?

But no one moved away from the wagon.

Something niggled at Maddie, the faintest tingling of something wrong. Memories tickled her consciousness, those terrifying moments when she'd been grabbed by two of the

Byrnes' men much earlier on this journey. Instinctively, she turned her shoulder so Jenny was more protected.

The flickering firelight from inside the circle of wagons cast shadows among the wagon wheels and a stack of crates nearby—

There.

The shadow shifted again, just a hint of movement.

Perhaps it was a dog.

But the fine hairs at the nape of Maddie's neck raised.

"Is someone there?" she called out. And then instantly regretted it. She glanced over her shoulder, aware of the empty campsite. Lily was out late tonight. Again. Collin and Stella had probably stolen away for some alone time.

Maddie was unarmed.

Someone was out there.

Her heart beat in her ears, drowning out the sounds of Jenny's snuffling breaths.

"Hard night?" The feminine voice turned her head. Alice approached, carrying two folded quilts over her arms.

Maddie glanced back at the shadows beneath that near wagon. Everything was still. No hint of movement. Had she imagined it?

She turned to Alice with one last glance over her shoulder, glad for the company.

"She looks for her mum everywhere," she admitted in a soft voice.

Jenny nuzzled into her shoulder slightly. Still awake. And Maddie was so very tired.

Alice's expression showed compassion. She carefully placed her bundle on the wagon tailgate and moved to the basket of waiting laundry.

"You don't have to—" Maddie started, but Alice was already lifting the first garment, reaching for the clothespins.

"It won't take but a minute," Alice said.

Maddie felt the hot prick of tears. It'd been less than a week since she'd assigned herself the task of caring for the children. Only two days since she'd informed Hollis she was to be their guardian. And she couldn't get everything done that needed to be done.

Alice clipped the first of several diapers to the line. "You're doing a good thing for those children," she said over her shoulder.

Maddie blinked, stopping in her tracks. She only started swaying again when Jenny shifted in her arms.

"I don't remember my real pa." Alice didn't look Maddie's way as she clipped a small boys' shirt to the line next. "But some of my earliest memories were my stepfather holding me on his knee at the supper table. Telling stories. Taking care of me and Leo."

There was a pause before Alice continued. "Sometimes family is the folks who stick around." A quiet note of sorrow tinged her voice. Was she thinking of her father? Or someone else?

"You should go lie down," Alice suggested. "Perhaps she'll sleep beside you."

"Thank you," Maddie murmured. Alice was almost finished with the basket now. One worry that Maddie wouldn't have tomorrow morning.

She stole into her bedroll, pulling her shawl over her shoulders so little Jenny had enough room on the blanket.

Alice's words were the bolster Maddie needed. She hadn't chosen this path because it would be easy. But the Miller children needed her. And she wouldn't let them down.

Not like she had their parents.

Chapter Six

DOC FINISHED DABBING disinfectant on the older woman's papery skin where an insect bite had grown infected, her forearm swelling.

"Won't this stop the itching?" Mrs. Kuss asked.

"This medicine is to treat the infection," he told her. "As the bite heals, the itching will grow less and less."

She pulled a sour face. "But I want it to stop itching." She sounded petulant, like a small child.

He'd known many patients like her.

"If you scratch the bite, it may turn into a wound," he warned her. Open wounds were a danger out here with the dust kicked up by the wagons and not always having clean water to wash with.

"My ma always made a little mud pack from our creek and used it to stop the itch," Mrs. Kuss grumbled.

"If you put dirt on this, the infection can spread," he told her.

Her mouth twisted into a frown. "Miss Maddie would make me a poultice."

Maddie.

Hollis had been true to his word. Maddie never came near Doc. But that didn't stop him from noticing when she crossed camp, or when she happened to be washing up nearby when he visited the creek.

He was twisting the cap on the disinfectant when he noticed his hands shaking.

With a quick motion, he ensured the cap was tight, but Mrs. Kuss must have the eyesight of a predator, because she said, "You all right, Doc?"

"Of course." His response came automatically. He tucked the bottle back in his black bag and straightened.

He and Mrs. Kuss stood to the side of the wagons rolling past, keeping to their route for the day. The sun was hot overhead and for a moment he removed his hat and used it to fan himself.

Not far away, several children ran and played. Tag? Delighted shrieks rang out.

"You sure?" Mrs. Kuss pressed.

Doc's smile turned tight. "I'm certain. Something to eat will fix me right up."

It was true that he hadn't slept well. He'd woken in the night from a nightmare of darkness and Hildy calling out his name. While awake, he saw one of the men on watch trail into camp, holding his wrist. He'd fallen asleep in the saddle, fallen from his horse, sprained his wrist.

The distraction was just what Doc needed.

If he could sleep through the night tonight, he'd be right as rain. Since the rockslide had stolen everything he held dear, it was easier to work than to sleep. Or think. Or remember. But when exhaustion became too heavy, he couldn't seem to steady his hands. Mostly, he was able to hide it. Except from the occasional sharp-eyed patient. Like Mrs. Kuss.

Who looked slightly skeptical as Doc mashed his hat back on his head and then doffed the brim.

He was securing his bag to his saddle when the shrieks from the children nearby changed pitch.

Something was wrong.

A voice from the nearest wagon called out to the kids, but Doc didn't look in that direction. The wagons kept rolling as he grabbed his bag and left his horse behind to run to a boy lying prone on the ground.

A few steps away, he recognized the familiar form.

Alex Miller.

"What happened?" Doc demanded of the two girls and a younger boy standing around Alex. One of the girls dropped to her knees beside him. Where was Paul?

"We was playing tag and he just fell down," the girl on her knees said. "Listen to 'im—it's like he cain't breathe."

She was right. Doc knelt beside the boy, who was pale and struggling to draw breath. Each inhale was loud and shallow.

"I'm going to look in your mouth." Doc used his fingers to check Alex's airways quickly. Nothing there.

"Did he get stung by something?" he asked.

A mumble among the friends, nothing coherent. Doc checked Alex's arms and legs, the back of his neck. Sometimes a bee sting could cause a bad reaction.

Alex shook his head. His skin was unblemished. But if anything, his breathing was becoming more rapid, more pained.

"Did he eat anything recently? Chew on a plant?" Doc demanded.

He reached for Alex's wrist, used two fingers to feel the flutter of his pulse. Too fast.

Alex wheezed. "Nothing since breakfast."

One of the little girls burst into noisy tears.

One of the wagons left the line of those marching west like little ants. This wagon pulled to one side of the trail and stopped.

A moment later, Maddie was almost flying in their direction, Paul on her heels.

Doc felt an instant awareness as she came near. He ignored it.

"What happened?" Maddie cried out when she got close.

To her credit, she didn't crowd in or try to push Doc away, but hovered at Alex's other shoulder.

The children repeated their story.

"Has this happened before?" Doc demanded of Paul.

"I—" Paul shook his head, his wide eyes focused on Alex, whose skin was turning blue around his lips.

He wasn't drawing enough oxygen.

"Sit up straight," Doc commanded gently, one hand beneath Alex's elbow to help. "Your body is telling you that you aren't getting enough air. It feels like panic, doesn't it?"

Alex's eyes revealed his terror.

Kneeling on Alex's other side, Maddie's grateful gaze pierced Doc for a moment before her focus returned to the boy. She put one hand at his back to support him.

Alex needed treatment. And there wasn't much time to figure out what would do the most good.

"Try to slow down your breaths. Like this." Doc breathed slowly and loudly, nodding his head when Alex began to follow.

"Has this happened before?" he demanded of Paul again, quietly. "Perhaps when Alex was small?"

Paul's expression lit with recognition. "I-I think so."

It could be an asthma episode. There would be time for figuring it out later—right now they needed to get Alex to breathe.

"We need boiling water. And a towel." He threw the words in Maddie's direction, but she didn't flinch.

"Cindy, run to the wagon," Maddie pointed to the stopped conveyance, "and fetch the water bucket and a pot. Callie, bring a towel."

At another time, he might've been impressed that she knew the children's names. But of course she did.

The two girls scampered off.

"Paul, will you fetch some firewood?"

He was running before she'd finished speaking. She moved several paces back and started ripping grasses out of the ground with her bare hands. She meant to boil water right here?

She did.

By the time Paul had returned with several sticks and twigs, Maddie had a small fire going with the flint and tinder she had hidden in a pocket.

"I need some cedar boughs," she mused. "Something that will spark hot and bright." Paul ran off again.

It seemed impossible, but only a few minutes passed before she had a small, hot fire and a pot of water close to boiling.

Alex's distress remained.

Doc dug through his bag until he found a packet.

"Boil this in the water." He handed it to the young boy, who handed it to Maddie, kneeling near the fire.

Wasn't she too close? What if she got burned?

"What is it?" she asked the question even as she ripped the paper and poured the powdered contents inside.

"Stramonium. It'll ease the constriction in his airways. He needs to breathe the vapor."

Understanding lit her expression. She was smart.

"You'd better go," she told the girls. "Catch up to the wagons."

Until this moment, Doc hadn't noticed that the noise from the wagons and oxen had died down. The company had already moved several hundred yards beyond Maddie's stopped wagon and made no sign of slowing.

The three other children ran off, though Paul hovered nearby.

"We'll catch up just as soon as he's breathing easier." She must've read Doc's thoughts. "It won't be long now." She smiled gently at Alex.

Her water was boiling merrily now and she grabbed the pot off the fire with her skirt around her hand to keep the handle from burning her. Then she sat behind Alex, draped the towel over his head as Doc helped him to lean over the water. Steam rose into the air but remained trapped by the towel.

"Breathe as deeply and as slowly as you can," Doc said.

Alex did as he'd ordered, Maddie coaching him through each breath.

What would Doc do if this didn't work? He'd read about this treatment but hadn't administered it personally. Steam by itself often helped young children with croup.

What if it wasn't asthma at all?

Alex's parents were no longer able to tell Doc about his

medical history. If Paul was wrong, Doc's treatment might not help at all.

But within a matter of minutes, Alex's breathing had eased. Paul looked immensely relieved as Alex's color returned.

"It worked," Maddie murmured softly.

It had helped. Alex still sounded raspy.

"Keep at it," Doc said. "A little longer. And don't throw out that water. You'll want to reheat the water and treat him again this evening before bed."

Alex wrinkled his face like he wanted to protest, but Maddie guided him through another breath.

When she glanced up, Doc was caught. Tears stood in her eyes, the warmth directed at him. A far cry from the way she'd looked at him the last time they'd been close enough to speak.

"Thank you," she said with a quiet fervor.

Now that Alex was steadier, Doc stood up.

Maddie followed suit. He should've braced for the up-close vision of the sweep of her lashes against her cheeks, the fiery wisps of hair curling around her temples.

As it was, he felt as if he'd been bludgeoned.

"Thank you for stopping to help him." An uncertainty in her words. It was on the tip of his tongue to reject her gratefulness. "You didn't have to stop, but I'm so glad you did."

She didn't seem to require an answer from him, because she knelt at Alex's side again.

Doc stared at her, but she didn't look up.

Of course he'd stopped.

But she hadn't expected it. That much was clear.

Did she really think him that cold? That heartless?

He couldn't allow himself to ask for an answer. He stumbled to his horse, running her words through his head.

Was he as heartless as she believed him to be?

Chapter Seven

ALICE TOOK one look at Maddie's face in the moments after the company had finished circling the wagons and shooed her off to the creek for a few moments alone. Alice had taken charge of all three children, with specific instructions to keep Alex still and quiet.

Maddie couldn't stop thinking about what might've gone wrong earlier today if Doc hadn't stopped. If the remedy he'd tried hadn't worked.

After she'd pushed the Millers' oxen to catch up to the wagon train, Hollis had required more miles today, making the afternoon and evening longer before he'd called for a halt.

Maddie's stomach had been twisted in knots ever since Alex's episode.

Hearing the screams of the children, finding Alex pale and struggling for breath... she'd been frightened she was going to lose him.

She'd hidden her feelings, stuffed them away deep inside her. Partly because Jason was there, handing out orders like an army general.

I can't have Maddie assist. I don't want her near me.

A part of her had been frantic to help Alex, while another part had wanted to prove just how capable she was.

And Paul had been hovering, listening to everything that was said.

"Alex is all right." She said the words aloud to give them more weight. Repeated them, as she forced herself to stand up, to turn toward camp. It was already growing dark.

A branch cracked, somewhere close.

She jumped as a shadow moved from only feet away. Maddie knew there were men on watch, others nearby doing their own washing up. The knowledge didn't stop her heart from pounding in her eardrums. The way the last rays of sunlight slanted through the trees reminded her of another evening. A jagged collection of moments when a hand had come out of the darkness to clasp over her mouth. When she'd been grabbed.

The light was fading fast and Maddie had been the only one to come in this direction—

"Who's there?" She hated the way her voice shook on the demand.

"I'm armed," she called out when there was no answer.

The shadow didn't move.

Maddie forced away her fear and took a step toward the shadow, now hovering behind a tree. She stepped wide—

And glimpsed a head of brown hair in a simple braid. A slip of a young woman was swallowed up in a drab gray shawl that went nearly to her knees. Fear and tension bled out of Maddie as she took in the other traveler.

"Hello," she said on a breath.

The young woman watched Maddie with wide blue eyes and looked as if she wanted to shrink inside herself. She ducked her head so her face was nearly buried in the shawl's folds.

Maddie felt a beat of familiarity. She recognized that shawl. She couldn't say from where, but she'd seen it among the wagon train before. And the weather had only just begun to cool so that a heavy shawl like this was needed.

"I'm sorry if I startled you," she said with a smile, trying to make peace. She motioned to the gloomy woods darkening around them. "It can be frightening out here when I'm alone. Do you want to walk back to camp together?"

The young woman shook her head, but a rustling in the brush from not far down the creek made both of them jump.

Maddie breathed through a smile. Extended her hand, and was gratified when the young woman joined her, though she kept several feet between them.

"I'm sorry I don't remember your name," Maddie said as their feet crunched through the dry underbrush. The canvas tops of the wagons were already in sight through the shadowed tree branches.

The young woman turned her face away instead of answering. Was she extremely shy?

"Did you join up with the caravan at the fort?" Maddie asked curiously.

There. A tentative nod.

A patch of sunlight angled through the trees behind them as they came out into the clearing. Maddie's companion lost her grip on the shawl and it slipped down her shoulder. Perhaps her dress was torn, Maddie couldn't see. But she did see an expanse of bare shoulder and a dark bruise in the shape of a hand.

Her shock was audible in her inhale. The young woman jerked the shawl back into place.

They neared the edge of the caravan now, and someone had put a plate of pan biscuits on the open tailgate of a wagon.

The young woman hung back. Maddie hesitated. Stopped walking.

"I've been nursing lots of folks in our company," she said quickly.

The young woman shot her a surly look and sidled close to the wagon. Her family's? Must be.

"If someone has hurt you, I can help," Maddie rushed to say.

People moved inside the circle of wagons. The young woman picked up two biscuits, stuffed one of them in her pocket, the other in her mouth.

"I want to help—" Maddie's words were cut off by the sharp shake of her head.

"I don't need no help."

The sharp words stung and Maddie glanced away. Only for a moment. She wasn't one to give up so easily. But when she'd turned her head back, the young woman had disappeared completely. Maddie blinked. Where had she gone?

Perhaps she'd slipped between two wagons.

Maddie sighed. She had no choice but to move on, but she wouldn't stop worrying for the girl. As Maddie passed into camp, sharp, questioning words came from behind.

Had the young woman gotten in trouble for taking the biscuits like she had? Maddie wished she knew her name. A glance over her shoulder showed an older woman with hands on her hips and no sign of the young woman Maddie had spoken with.

She was nearing her sisters' wagon, parked only two places

away from the Miller wagon, when the sound of voices from the other side of the conveyance slowed her.

"She looks tired." That was Stella's voice. Was she talking about Lily? She had been quiet since the epidemic, still cross with Maddie, that much was certain. It hadn't stopped Maddie from noticing how Lily slipped into her tent early every night.

But Stella kept speaking. "Why didn't she ask me about taking in those children?"

Those children.

Stella wasn't talking about Lily. She was talking about Maddie.

"Three children is a lot of responsibility." Lily's voice. Was Collin with the sisters, too?

She couldn't believe they were speaking of the children in this way. What would they have had her do? Leave Paul and Alex and Jenny to fend for themselves?

"You cannot let her do this," Lily insisted.

"I'm not sure you can stop her," Collin said quietly.

"What will she do once we reach Oregon?" Stella sounded genuinely concerned.

Maddie had planned to file for a homestead, like many of the other travelers. It wouldn't be easy. Especially with the children. But she couldn't help the stab of betrayal that her family was having this discussion without her. Why hadn't Stella or Lily brought up these concerns to her directly?

"There must be someone else who could take on the children," Lily said. "Anyone else. What does Maddie know of being a mother?"

The words battered at Maddie's confidence, already frayed and tattered by the events of the past week. She'd done everything she knew to do, had worked herself to exhaustion trying to help each traveler who had been hit by the typhoid.

Yet she hadn't been enough to save Mrs. Miller. Or Mrs. Barrigan.

Maybe her sisters were right.

Their mother had passed away when Lily had been tiny. Their father might've remarried if he hadn't fallen into a bottle, never to resurface. Stella had been the only mother figure Maddie had, until their neighbor Mrs. Murphy had taken Maddie under her wing under the guise of teaching her healing skills.

Maddie didn't know how to raise a child, how to be a mother.

Promise me. The echo of Mrs. Miller's dying plea flowed through her mind. *Promise you'll take care of my babies.*

"What about the ruby?" Lily said, voice so low it barely registered. "We could give it to her."

Maddie froze. She felt the same ice through her veins as she had moments ago when remembering being grabbed.

"It's worth a pretty penny," Collin said slowly.

"It isn't ours to sell," Stella said. Maddie could imagine the way her sister's eyes flashed. "The Byrne brothers sent paid mercenaries to follow us and find it—"

"And they are long gone, carted off to go to prison, remember?" Lily interrupted.

"What is it?" Stella demanded. "You know something."

Collin started speaking, slowly at first and then faster. "When Hollis and Abigail were separated from the company, Hollis came across a man who might be following the wagon train. We've kept it quiet. Don't want the travelers to get nervous and trigger happy."

Maddie's stomach roiled at the thought of someone out there watching, following them.

She couldn't stand here and listen any longer. Her sisters might want to plan her life, but Maddie was the one who had to live it. And right now, there were three children depending on her.

She skirted behind the wagons until she could slip between two. Alice was walking in slow circles with a crying Jenny in her arms. Alex sat on a crate near the front of the wagon, listlessly tapping a stick on the ground.

"Can you hold her for a minute more?" Maddie asked. "She may be ready to sleep for the night. I just need to get the tent pitched."

"Of course," Alice said.

Satisfied that the fussy little one was all right for the time being, Maddie wrestled the canvas out of the back of the wagon. Her hold slipped. The weight of it came tumbling down on her—

Or would've, if not for the large hand that stayed it.

She hadn't sensed someone nearby, but it was Jason who had stepped close. Jason whose shoulder pressed into hers.

"I've got it," she said.

The glance he gave her said more than his words could. The same coolness he'd shown this afternoon. He hadn't even accepted her thanks. But he didn't argue, just let her take the weight of the canvas. It dropped to the ground at her feet and she dragged it past the wagon to a patch of clear ground to pitch it.

He stood near the wagon, frowning.

"I came to check on Alex," he said finally, his words stiff as a starched shirt.

* * *

The baby's cries filled Jason's ears as Maddie abandoned her attempt to set up the tent alone and approached Alice Spencer. After some murmured words, Maddie took Jenny into her arms and Alice left the campsite, sending a look over her shoulder.

Maddie's shoulders carried an almost imperceptible line of tension. When he'd been standing nearly nose-to-nose with her, he couldn't ignore the lines of exhaustion around her mouth. The same kind of lines Elizabeth had worn when their babies had been teething and she'd been up all hours of the night.

Not that he should notice Maddie's tiredness.

Alex looked up from the crate where he sat. And there came Paul around the side of the wagon, his arms full of sticks for the fire. His gaze had zeroed in on the tent, and Jason saw the anxious expression that quickly disappeared when he caught sight of his brother.

Doc couldn't make out Maddie's soft murmurs to the baby as he crossed to Alex, bypassing the fire where supper bubbled in a pot.

He lifted his leather wrapped case for Alex to see. "I thought after sitting still all day, you might want something to occupy your mind. I can teach you to play."

Alex lit up.

Paul glanced over from where he'd placed the firewood in a neat pile a few feet from the blaze.

"I can teach you, too," Jason offered.

A spark of interest lit Paul's eyes, quickly banked. "I prob'ly got more chores to do," he mumbled with a glance at Maddie.

The baby arched in Maddie's arms. Something inside Jason reacted, remembering a time when he'd held a tiny JJ who'd been throwing a tantrum and arched away in a similar fashion, trying to get as far away from his father as possible.

The memory cut like a scalpel, and Jason quickly looked away.

"There'll be time for work in the morning," she told Paul. "You should play." And then with a chin lift to Alex, "We'll need to breathe your medicine again in a bit."

Alex pulled a face, but Jason lifted a serious eyebrow at him.

"Fine," the boy muttered. He hopped to the ground, making a beeline for Jason. "Here, we can use this!" He overturned a crate to create a table. He was quick to sit cross-legged beside it.

Jason squatted and unfurled the leather casing, showing the checkered board that had been stained into its inside. He took out the small cloth pouch that held the pieces and laid the board flat.

Jenny continued to cry, pushing away Maddie's hand when she offered a cup with milk in it.

"Ya got lotsa pieces," Alex said to Paul. "And the little ones just jump one space forward—mostly. But the other pieces move all different ways."

Paul scrunched his nose, sending a look at Maddie and Jenny. "Hard to concentrate with her crying like that."

Alex wilted a little. "She'll pro'lly cry all night."

They were right. Jenny's cries were distracting. Jason stole a glance and saw the tension increase in Maddie's shoulders. She sang softly as she took a meandering circuit around the campsite, swaying with each step.

Another bolt of memory, another cut. Elizabeth had

moved in a similar manner when she'd been up with one of the babies when they'd been ill.

Maddie's expression in the flickering shadows revealed a mix of desperation and worry.

Jason couldn't keep himself from straightening. "I'll be right back," he told Alex.

He left them to look at the pieces and moved toward the fire while digging in his pocket. He came up with his handkerchief. It hadn't been used since the last washing. It would have to do.

He took an inch by inch square chunk of meat from the pot. It was hot, a bit dried out from the heat. Tough. Good.

He sensed Maddie glancing his way as he put the meat in the center of the kerchief and carefully tied the material in a knot so the meat was enclosed inside it. Then he touched the little bundle to a bit of broth in the pot before going to Maddie.

She stared at him with a mix of curiosity and skepticism.

"See if she'll chew on this," he suggested quietly.

Jenny still wailed, wouldn't settle, struggled against Maddie's hold.

Maddie took the cloth from him, nose wrinkled. But he remembered an exhausted Elizabeth in the early days after Hildy had been born. His wife had been sleep deprived and exhausted. Willing to try anything for a few moments of rest.

Maddie must have felt the same, because she tried Doc's remedy without arguing. She lifted the kerchief to Jenny's lips, teasing when the baby tried to turn her head away.

Then the tiny lips smacked, an indrawn breath breaking the constant cries.

Maddie offered the kerchief again, and Jenny opened her mouth and began to gnaw on it.

Maddie seemed to be holding her breath, Jenny's snuffling breath the only thing audible in the small space between them. The baby's body relaxed slightly, her weight going heavy against Maddie's shoulder.

Maddie tipped her head, her gaze fixed on Doc. "How did you know that would work?"

"I didn't," he murmured. "I remembered—" He shook his head. Felt her curious gaze on him. He couldn't talk about his wife and children with her.

Her lips firmed a thin, white line when he didn't say anything else. She started toward the wagon.

"I think the efficacy of the stramonium water has diluted," she said over her shoulder, a touch too brightly. "Would you mind checking it?"

Doc trailed her.

At the wagon, she showed him the water left in the bowl. He took a sniff. It certainly wasn't as potent as it had been earlier.

"I've only got another two packets of the substance," he said in a low voice.

"Does the herb grow wild?" she asked as she tugged something forward on the tailgate, adjusting Jenny in one arm. A thick tome titled *Plantae Utiliores* he saw before she flipped it open. It showed an illustration of a plant on one page and text on the other.

"I borrowed this from Evangeline." She glanced his way and must've caught sight of his curiosity. "She has a veritable library in one of her wagons."

He stepped shoulder to shoulder with her, flipping pages until he found the right one.

"The common name is Jimson weed," he said. "Lobelia

has some of the same properties. Both may help relax his airways. But they may be difficult to find out here."

She pulled a piece of ribbon from her apron pocket and slipped it into the book. "Thank you. I'll record this in my journal after everyone is settled for the night."

"You keep a journal?"

He shouldn't care, shouldn't have asked the question.

She nodded, not quite looking at him. "Some of the native plants here are similar to what grew back home." In Ireland, she meant. "But some are very different. I met a woman not long after we set out from Independence who showed me a dozen herbs she used for her own healing. I was afraid I would forget them, so she let me sketch them."

Smart. Very smart.

The bolt of admiration came on the heels of the realization that he was staring at the apple of her cheek, watching the slight rise and fall of her breath, the way her lashes swept across her cheekbone.

He cut his gaze away, cleared his throat. "It's a fine idea," he murmured.

"Come see, Maddie!" Alex interrupted. "We want to play."

Maddie turned from the tailgate.

"Oh my," she said a touch too brightly. "This looks like a complicated game."

Paul glanced up at Doc. "How did you get Jenny to stop crying?"

"It's a trick that helps when a baby is teething."

He knelt between the two boys sitting opposite each other at the crate.

Maddie rubbed Jenny's back. "This whole time, I thought she was simply missing her ma and pa."

He gritted his teeth to keep the words inside but ended up blurting, "That's probably part of it. It can be both things."

For a moment, her gaze clashed with his. A tenuous connection hung in that breathless moment, until she ducked her head and said, "Thank you."

"Yeah, but how'd you know?" Alex pressed.

"My wife used that trick with our babies when they were teething." Doc didn't know how the words emerged.

Maddie went very still. Doc kept his focus on the board, pointing one finger to the space on Paul's side. "White moves first," he prompted.

Alex stared at him, nonplussed. "You got a family?" he asked incredulously.

Doc's insides screamed. He gritted his teeth to keep from letting the sounds escape.

"Hush," Maddie whispered, one hand on Alex's shoulder.

He didn't know how it was possible, but words tumbled out of Doc's own mouth in an orderly, matter-of-fact march. "I had a beautiful wife, two daughters, and a son. My son was about your age."

He saw the question in Alex's expression, saw the squeeze of Maddie's fingers on the boy's shoulder.

"They died." Now he had to force the words out. "Last year, on a crossing of the Rockies. In a rockslide that caught our company unawares." His gaze swept toward the mountains, invisible in the darkness. "I couldn't save them."

Before the terrible memories could overtake him, he stood. "Perhaps we'll try the game another time."

"But—"

Maddie's hand on Alex's shoulder quelled the boy's protest quickly, but he couldn't avoid the stares from all three. He strode away, leaving the board behind.

Chapter Eight

SOMEONE SKULKED around Doc's bedroll.

Evening was falling, but warm dusky light still shone on the western horizon when he caught sight of a swishing skirt where he'd left his saddle and bedroll before he'd gone to the creek for a much-needed wash.

Now his damp hair sent a drip down his collar as he neared his things. And whoever was waiting for him. He should've expected someone needing medical attention—he'd been woken from a dead sleep in the dark of morning to help a man in his mid-fifties who'd been experiencing chest pains. By the time he'd settled the patient, it had been too close to dawn for Doc to go back to his bedroll. The day had been a constant effort.

Of course someone would seek his help now.

He couldn't get a good glimpse as the person seemed to be crouched low, his vision blocked by a stack of crates someone had removed from a nearby wagon.

By the time he'd reached his things, the person had disappeared.

He turned a slow circle, trying to see which direction they'd gone, but the camp was busy with folks settling children and putting away things for the night.

Then he caught a metallic flash in the light thrown by a nearby fire. Someone had left a plate on his neatly-folded bedroll. Another upturned tin plate sat on top, no doubt to keep whatever was inside protected. Next to the plates was the leather pouch that kept his chess pieces contained.

He squatted and pulled away the top plate. Steaming hot grouse, along with some steamed vegetables.

He glanced up and there—a flash of pale gray skirt as Maddie scooted across the camp away from him. She didn't look back. She'd been the one to leave this?

As he picked up the plate, the savory scent of meat fresh from the pot made his mouth start watering. But it was the thoughtfulness of her gesture that made him feel as if he was reeling.

He didn't want for food. Owen and Rachel fed him more often than not. Sometimes it was Abigail, the wagon master's wife, who brought him a plate. But for those families, he was an afterthought. Often the food was cool, partially congealed. The leftovers. He didn't mind. What he received was enough to sustain him. And it wasn't easy to cook for himself or keep things warm out in the open. He didn't need anything more.

For Maddie to serve him hot, fresh food...

It was a kindness he didn't deserve. Not after the way he'd treated her. The coldness he'd shown her. He should've kept his distance—visiting her campsite last night was a mistake. But the vows he'd made as a physician warred with his nature. Alex still needed help.

He fell on the food, not realizing until his stomach rumbled halfway through the plate that he had missed the noon meal. Elizabeth had chided him when he'd become so caught up in his job that he had missed lunch.

He couldn't say how many times he'd skipped it during the past months.

How long had it been since someone had thought of his needs? Had sought to take care of him, even in such a small way?

As he sopped up the last of the gravy from the plate with the final bite of biscuit, he felt a warmth from more than the food he was digesting.

Because of Maddie.

His insides remained in a tangled knot as he took the two plates to return them to her. He slowed as he neared the Millers' wagon. The canvas cover had been rolled back on one side. Alex was in the wagon bed, while Paul stood at the side. The boys chattered and Jenny sat on a quilt spread on the ground, playing with two tin cans. Maddie moved between the quilt and the wagon itself. The little dog slept beneath the wagon.

Darkness was falling. Why weren't her sisters helping in whatever this endeavor was?

All the activity paused as Doc approached. He approached Alex in the wagon. "How was your breathing today?"

"Fine."

Doc raised one brow at the non-answer from the boy.

"Better," Maddie interjected. "He rode in the wagon all day."

"It was boring," Alex muttered.

He didn't seem bored now, shifting bottles and jars in the wagon.

"I brought this back." Doc lifted the plates.

She nodded and he saw that her hands were full of... dried leaves?... as she crossed to Alex in the wagon.

He needed to clear her from his thoughts. "Supper was a kindness, but it was unnecessary—" He cut himself off as his curiosity overtook him. "What are you doing?"

Paul seemed to be sorting a collection of empty jars, tins, and small boxes on the ground near Jenny's quilt, while Alex shifted things around inside the wagon bed.

Maddie moved to the tailgate. Doc registered her nearness and took a step back. He watched her hand Alex the dried leaves—coneflower, he thought. Then the boy tucked them inside a small tin in the wagon bed. Several other small boxes were lined up inside.

"We're making us our own thepoth—apoth—" He wrinkled his nose as his tongue twisted over the word.

"Apothecary," Maddie prompted quietly.

"We got a lot of tins and jars from other folks in the company," Alex said proudly. When Maddie pointed to a space in the back of the wagon, Alex moved to arrange several more empty jars there.

Doc followed Maddie's gaze to Paul. The boy hadn't spoken while Doc had been standing here, though he seemed to be moving awfully slowly if he was supposed to be sorting those wooden boxes by size.

Concern flickered over Maddie's expression. "Do you need any help?" she asked the boy.

Who shook his head silently.

Her gaze flicked to Doc and then back into the wagon as awkwardness settled between them. "I thought perhaps we'd stock up on the herbs we can find before everything dies off for the autumn," she murmured in explanation.

"To make your own apothecary," Doc said, because it seemed a big undertaking, and she already had charge of three children.

She must've picked up on his thoughts because her chin lifted in a stubborn way he'd come to recognize. "The boys inspired me."

Alex glanced over his shoulder with a grin. "We was having us a competition today. Who could find the most willow bark. I won."

Paul grunted even as Doc followed Alex's pointing finger to a pile of bark taking up one corner of the quilt.

Maddie's voice emerged a bit too brightly. "If the three of us spend some time each day foraging, we can have things on hand to help those who need it over the last months of our journey."

He'd thought her intelligent last night when she'd described her journal and how she'd learned of some of the remedies used here in the West. Here was more proof of her ingenuity. Everything about her drew him in.

But perhaps she took his silence for disdain, because she added in a low voice, "And we needed a change. With the wagon. It was time to put away some of their father and mother's clothing."

Doc noticed that Paul kept his head down, but his shoulders had gone tense.

Doc moved a step away, nearer to the fire, to put the plates down by a pile of other dirty dishes.

"Mayhap you think it's a bad idea—"

"I think it's a good idea," he said, surprising her into silence. It was dangerous to allow this vein of conversation, but he couldn't seem to stop himself.

One of Maddie's hands came around Jenny's back, resting gently there as her chin came up, her eyes stormy. He fell into step beside her as she moved around the wagon, away from the boys.

"I will happily shop from your wares," he found himself saying. "If you'll allow it."

"I'm surprised you'd want to." There was a chilly note to her voice. "Given my lack of education. I heard you tell Hollis you don't want me to assist you."

He saw the flash of hurt before her gaze cut away.

She'd heard? He'd been the one to demand space from the wagon master. Had needed to protect himself. But her hurt knocked the breath out of him in a way he hadn't felt in a very long time. It only increased the tangled knot inside him.

Aware of the boys nearby, he lowered his voice. "That's not why," he said.

She glanced back at him, brows drawn in confusion.

"Your education is not why I told Hollis I don't wish for your help."

"Then why?" she pressed.

He wasn't going to answer. But he couldn't keep his traitorous eyes from dropping to her lips and then back up to her eyes.

He saw the moment she recognized what he meant, felt rather than heard the catch in her breath.

There were too many things happening for the moment between them to be truly private. The baby between them, the boys murmuring from only feet away, another family arguing somewhere nearby. And yet an invisible cord seemed to bind them, pulling taut, stretching until it vibrated with fine tension. It would snap once he stepped forward, reached for her—

"Can I go to the creek to wash up?" Paul was suddenly there at her elbow and the moment was broken.

He couldn't be mistaken about the flash of relief he saw in her eyes as she turned to address the boy.

Doc half-turned away, shaking at the ferocity of the emotions rocketing through him.

Jenny wiggled, and a soft babbling cry rang out.

What was he thinking? He never should've admitted to his attraction.

He should go.

* * *

Maddie couldn't say how she answered Paul, and then Alex, who quickly joined his brother. They scampered off, and she regained her equilibrium enough to call out, "Stay together. And don't be long!"

Jason stood near the fire, half-turned away, staring into the darkness beyond the wagons. He looked as if one wrong word would send him fleeing. And in this moment she didn't know how to find any right words.

Part of her couldn't believe he had stayed in her campsite for this long.

Her face was flaming, no doubt her cheeks as red as an apple straight off the tree.

Surely he hadn't meant what she'd inferred from the intense look he'd given her just before Paul had interrupted. For a moment, she'd thought Jason would step forward and take her in his arms—

Jenny snuffled and jammed her tiny fist into her mouth. She looked up at Maddie with suspicious eyes. If she followed her usual pattern, it wouldn't be long before she started crying.

Jenny didn't want Maddie. She wanted her mother.

Right now, Maddie was grateful for the distraction.

She'd been unable to sleep last night thinking about Jason. *I couldn't save them.* Whatever mixed emotions she'd had about the doctor had been blasted away by the well of deep grief and guilt she'd witnessed in his broken words last night. She'd brought him supper as some kind of peace offering. She never expected him to come to her campsite. And the admission he'd just made came as an utter shock.

On autopilot, she moved to where Paul had abandoned the dozen small containers. She sighed as she steadied Jenny with one hand and bent to scoop up two of the jars with her other while trying to understand her spinning thoughts.

She'd known Jason was handsome from the very beginning. But his looks hadn't mattered because he'd disdained her from the first time they'd spoken. Hadn't he?

She was so distracted that she plopped the jars into the wagon bed with a thunk. And almost bumped into Jason when she turned to go back for more. His gaze bounced away from her.

"You don't have to help—" she started. "I should've realized it was too big an undertaking for one day. The boys and I will finish arranging the wagon later."

Now she was babbling.

"Ba, ba, ba," Jenny sang quietly, the nonsense word muffled by her fingers in her mouth. Jason had been right yesterday when he'd guessed she was teething. Maddie had felt the tiny knob beneath the gums in three places. Poor babe.

"It's inconvenient," he said in a low, matter-of-fact voice. As if she hadn't unleashed a torrent of unrelated words.

He made no move to fetch more of the boxes and she froze in place, angled between him and the wagon. What was inconvenient?

She hadn't realized she'd spoken aloud until he answered.

"I'm nearly old enough to be your father," he said bluntly. His gaze landed on her face again, and she saw the consternation and disdain—aimed inward, she now realized. Not at her.

Had she been mistaken about his motivations since the very beginning?

"Surely not. An uncle, maybe." She said the words in a teasing manner but his quick scowl made her wish to take them back. "How old are you?"

"Old enough to know better," he muttered. He raised one hand to rub the back of his neck.

"It isn't that unusual, surely. You're a handsome man, and —anyone would notice. You're certainly not *too* old." Her quick, rambling words cut off as she snapped her mouth closed.

Jason stared at her.

He couldn't be more than forty. Probably younger than that. There were several couples in their company alone—not to mention back in Ireland—where the husband was several years older than his wife. Did it matter so much?

Or maybe the gap in their ages bothered him more because of *her* age. Perhaps he thought her too young. Naive. Maddie had to turn her face away as she went cold and then hot all over again at the memory of Seán's words.

You act like a child.

Afraid Jason would see too much, she ducked her head and brushed past him to pick up more of the boxes. There weren't many left, but still too many for her to grab with one hand.

Jenny let out a cry of protest at Maddie's too-quick movements.

"I'm sorry," she said quickly. "Sometimes my mouth gets carried away."

She paused. "Or perhaps you are right." She jerked her chin up when her lips wanted to tremble. "My fiancé thought me too immature."

Jason went still, but she was already turning away, moving to gather the herbs still drying on the quilt. They would dry just as well in the bed of the wagon. Her nerves drove her actions.

She couldn't understand why Jason wasn't gone already, but he still stood at the rear corner of the wagon. And for some reason, the words kept tumbling out of her mouth.

"We'd been planning to marry for months, and I thought —" She'd thought his whispered words of love in her hair one night after he'd walked her home had meant forever.

You're too emotional. The words he'd thrown at her on the night Mrs. Murphy had been so desperately ill rang through her mind like a clear church bell.

Jenny was crying in earnest now, and Maddie didn't know what to do with the invisible tension between her and Jason. It was easier to focus on the baby.

"Mrs. Murphy used to rub whiskey on a baby's gums when they were teething—I'm not sure I dare do that for her," she murmured. "Your diagnosis was spot on."

He stood with hands in his pockets, staring into the darkness. "Licorice root might provide some relief. If you can find it," he offered quietly.

Uneasy quiet settled between them again.

"Perhaps it was a good thing that Seán changed his mind before we wed," she muttered as she strove to untangle Jenny from the wrap before the girl grew inconsolable. Agitation made Maddie fumble.

Of course it hadn't felt like a good thing in the days after Seán had told her in no uncertain terms that there would not be a wedding, that he didn't love her anymore. She could still feel the sharpness of that grief, the shock of having the very ground swept out from underneath her.

"I couldn't be what he wanted. He made it clear that he needed someone less emotional." The words sounded more jagged than she intended as those old feelings leaked out. She fought with the knot of the wrap with one hand, trying to get it undone as Jenny kicked, wiggling in her other arm and splitting Maddie's concentration.

"He was a fool."

Suddenly, Jason was there. At her side, his big fingers nudging her hand gently out of the way as he untied the knot with both hands.

She couldn't look at him as she swallowed back the ball of tears that had risen in her throat. Which meant she saw the way his fingers trembled.

"Jason?"

His fingers flexed wide and then he fisted his hand, dropping it to his side. "Did you know you're the only one who calls me that?" he said the words absently, head still ducked.

She didn't know what to say. Did he want her to stop?

"Are you all right?" she asked. "Do you need—?"

"I'm fine," he said abruptly, taking a step back. The tension she'd felt moments ago seemed to have magnified.

He was a fool.

Had she imagined the words? Everything that had

happened tonight felt like a fever dream. Fanciful happenings she'd conjured to explain away Jason's indifferent actions. But the ground beneath her feet was solid. And that fire in his eyes hadn't been her imagination.

Paul and Alex barreled back into camp, chattering about an opossum they'd seen.

And when Maddie looked up, Jason was gone.

"What kinda bug crawled into your brother's bedroll last night?" Rusty asked.

Coop glanced up from the cards in his hand. His eyes took a moment too long to focus on Rusty lounging against his saddle across the small fire burning in the evening light.

"No telling," he said easily. "I fold."

Were his words slurring?

Nearby, Gerry Bones glanced up from beneath his stained white ten-gallon hat. His dark brown eyes were curious in his brown-skinned face. He was whittling something Coop couldn't make out in the growing darkness.

Coop tossed his cards into the pile between him and Harry, another cowboy from the outfit. When Harry sent him a questioning look, asking whether Coop wanted to play another hand, Coop waved him off. He knew better than to play cards when he'd been in his cups this deeply.

He pocketed the few coins on the dusty ground in front of him.

"What'd he do this time?" Coop asked lazily, tipping his head back to look up into the star-studded sky.

"Bout bit my head off because I let a steer lag too far behind," Rusty said.

"He don't need a reason to gripe," Harry said. "I think he's like the rest of 'em. Look down on us because we do the dirty work. Herd owners treat us like manure under their boots."

Bitterness cloaked the man's words.

Coop swallowed back a defense of his brother. After Leo's father had left, Leo's mother had been destitute. It hadn't gotten better after she'd married Coop and Collin's pa because the twins had come soon after, and it'd been a difficult pregnancy for their ma.

Leo had grown up as poor as they came. He'd worked long hours with no days off for years, earning a place as a foreman at the powder mill. He'd been a fair boss. Been prideful about being able to buy Alice a new dress.

He'd married Evangeline, whose father was some kind of lumber tycoon from back East. She was the one made of money, the one paying the cowboys' salaries. Leo didn't think himself better than any of them.

But Coop kept his trap shut.

He didn't care what they said about Leo. It didn't touch him.

Since the night when everyone'd been recovering from the typhoid and he'd walked away from that campfire, Coop hadn't slept one night in Leo's camp. He rode out at dawn—no matter how late his time on watch was—and kept to the worst of it, usually riding drag. The farthest from the wagons. As much distance as he could put between him and his brothers.

The cowboys kept their own little camp, usually only a fire and their bedrolls, separate from the company itself. Coop unrolled his bedroll with the cowboys.

He did feel a mite guilty every day when Alice came to check on him, usually at supper time. He bore her judgment when she stared him in the eyes. But she didn't ask him to come back to camp. That was telling.

"Where you been?"

Coop let his head fall forward in time to see Matt slip into their circle and sit down by the fire.

"Around," mumbled the man. He accepted the flask Rusty passed him and took a slow swig.

Coop watched him do it, thoughts thick as molasses.

Sometimes he imagined Matt didn't slug from the flask—that he only took a sip even though he seemed to take a deep pull.

"He's got a girl," Harry muttered.

Rusty whistled. "You been out courtin' tonight?"

The teasing words made Matt frown. "There's no girl."

Coop couldn't figure him out. Matt had joined the company at the last fort. Leo'd hired him on, claiming they needed more manpower. All the other cowboys seemed like a band of brothers—maybe that's why Coop felt like he belonged with them. But Matt had stayed on the fringes from the very beginning. Sometimes he disappeared and a body didn't realize he'd gone missing until he showed back up—like he'd done just now.

What was he sneaking around for?

Matt cleared his throat and Coop realized he was holding out the flask. Coop took it but passed it on to Harry. Coop's stomach was sloshing. He hadn't felt back to normal since the typhoid had knocked him around.

"You ain't like them, Coop." It took a second for Harry's statement to make sense. He was talking about Leo and the others in the company again.

And he was right. Coop wasn't like them.

"Nope." He popped the P loudly. He really was deep in

his cups tonight. Good thing he wasn't supposed to go on watch until tomorrow.

Coop tuned out the conversation around him for several moments, finally coming back to himself to hear,

"...you heard what those soldiers from the fort said," Rusty said.

"Yeah, but I think they were joshin'." That was Lucky.

A sudden bodily urge pushed him to his feet as the two hired hands began arguing about a rumored ghost in the Rocky Mountains–the same mountains the company would cross in a few weeks.

Coop wobbled dizzily for a minute, to the chuckles of his friends, then started off for the woods and the creek where they'd washed off the trail dust earlier. He muttered to himself as he walked, stopping every so often to reorient himself to his surroundings.

He'd grown up idolizing his older brother. Wanting to be just like Leo. Strong. Admired. Unafraid. But it seemed no matter how hard he tried, he always fell short.

You need to learn to take after your older brother.

How many times had he heard the words from a school-room teacher, or his ma?

He'd started resenting Leo soon enough. Collin too, who seemed to easily copy Leo in mannerisms and intelligence.

Coop never could. He saw things differently. Couldn't behave, not when his legs itched to be moving and his thoughts whirled faster than a dervish. He'd given up about the time the teacher had asked him not to return to the schoolroom.

He'd been ten.

He leaned his shoulder against a sapling at the edge of the woods, taking care of his private business, realizing how maudlin his thoughts had become. He was really sloshed tonight. Usually the whiskey relaxed him. Helped him forget.

Not tonight.

He fastened his trousers and headed back toward camp.

But he'd only taken a few steps—hadn't he?—when he realized he'd become disoriented. It had grown darker, as if the night had fallen from the sky and engulfed him.

He stumbled, almost went to his knees. Realized he'd gone farther into the woods, not back out to the prairie, to the cowboys' camp.

The trickling of water reminded him of the stream. His throat was suddenly parched. Maybe a drink of water would help sober him up enough so he could make it back to his bedroll. He definitely needed to sleep this off.

He took two more steps. His brain felt heavier, his limbs weighted down. He must've drank a lot more than he'd thought. The whiskey was hitting him hard now.

A splash and he realized he'd stepped right into the stream. It wasn't deep here, just over the toes of his boots.

The shock of cold brought him to awareness.

A bit.

He dropped to his knees right there. Cupped his hands and took two deep draws from the bitingly cold stream. But when he tried to stand up again, his limbs wouldn't obey.

Darkness slipped over his eyes. He tipped forward, part of his brain strangely aware of what was happening as he fell into the water.

The coldness enveloped the entire front of his body. His nose and mouth submerged.

Get up.

His brain was so foggy.

He managed to get one pinky finger to wiggle, but he

couldn't find the wherewithal to use his arms to push himself out of the water or roll over.

The cold darkness was kinda nice.

The icy water numbed all those awful feelings from his childhood. Made his brother's words in his head go away.

He tried to inhale but his lungs filled with water.

He still couldn't wake up.

Sudden panic overtook him, or at least the part of his brain still functioning. With sudden clarity he realized he was going to die here. Alone. In the dark. Drunk. Drowning in a two-inch puddle of water.

He thought of the shadows in Alice's eyes. Imagined never seeing her smile again.

She'd be furious with him.

Would Collin miss him? He and his brother had been close until Collin had fallen in love and married Stella.

He didn't want to die.

His panic increased. He struggled to find one iota of his brain that would push him to an awakened state, get his muscles working.

Nothing.

His lungs burned.

Suddenly there was a splashing in the water at his shoulder. A voice, muffled. A pair of small hands tugging at his shoulder. Harder.

He rolled onto his back. Felt the firm ground of the creek bank beneath his left shoulder blade. His right half was still in the stream, his arm trailing in the pull downstream.

He coughed, his body hacking out the water he'd inhaled.

It took a moment before he could breathe again. That first breath of fresh air was life.

Who—?

He tried to force his eyes open. Only managed a crack. It was enough to see a shadowy form. A young woman.

In the darkness, he couldn't see her face but he inhaled the scent of rosewater.

And then she was gone, leaving him in the darkness.

Alive.

Breathing.

Whoever she was, she was his angel.

Chapter Nine

"WE'LL BE CIRCLING UP SOON." Jason said the words from where he'd climbed onto a spoke of the wheel so he could see Alex inside the wagon. Today had been difficult for the boy, the asthma flaring up. It hadn't been like right after the wildfire, but Doc had checked on him several times throughout the day and found his breath shallow and difficult each time.

"We'll boil some water with the stramonium and that should help," Doc said.

Alex wrinkled his nose. "That stuff stinks."

Maybe it did, but it would help ease the boy's airways.

"And sleep will help."

Alex flopped to his back in the narrow space inside the wagon. Glass jars rattled in the neat rows Maddie and the boys had made. "I'm tired of layin' around. This is boring!"

Doc couldn't blame the boy. He remembered a time when he'd been recovering from a bad fever and had been itching to go outside and run. Boys weren't meant to be still all day long.

"Maybe I can find you a book to read."

Alex only groaned and threw his arm over his eyes.

Doc snapped his bag closed. He patted the boy's leg and left the wagon behind. He'd left his horse grazing nearby. The horse whickered at his approach.

The poor animal had been responding to Doc's agitation all day as the company had edged nearer to the Rocky Mountains. The towering, craggy mountains now seemed almost close enough to touch.

And so did Doc's darkest memories.

The morning had dawned cold enough that most everyone in camp had donned slickers, shawls and scarves. Many of the pioneers had shed them as the sun warmed the travelers during the day. Now the sun was waning behind the mountain range and shadows stretched long. Jason pulled his slicker from his saddlebag to slide his arms into the sleeves.

The company had hit a slow-down late this afternoon as they'd reached a difficult uphill climb. Hollis had ridden back through the line of wagons snaking up the incline not long ago and said he wanted to circle up on a plateau a half mile farther. They just needed to get the wagons up and over. Using the ropes meant they could only take one wagon at a time. Doc figured half the wagons had made the crossing thus far.

He'd fought with himself all day. Standing at his horse's saddle and staring up at the peak towering overhead made him want to turn around and ride back.

Oh, it wasn't the same crossing where Elizabeth and the children, and so many others had lost their lives. He'd never dared to go back within a hundred miles of that evil place. It was the mountains themselves, dangerous and unpredictable. Age-old and cold.

If it weren't for the promise he'd made Owen, Doc wouldn't have come.

He was wintering on the prairie this year, he reminded himself. A few more weeks with Hollis's company, and then they would go their separate ways.

His gaze unerringly found Maddie, several dozen yards away where she was conferring with the young mother she'd helped during the epidemic. Jenny was in Maddie's arms, but the baby was fussy.

You're not too old.

Several days had passed since Doc had revealed his inappropriate attraction to her. Her genuine surprise and pragmatic acceptance shouldn't have surprised him. She'd been a surprise from the first day he'd met her. But he couldn't ignore the fact that she'd agreed he was handsome.

Not that she'd fancied him.

No matter whether she thought so or not, his attraction to her was inappropriate.

He'd dreamed of the interaction last night, of the surprise etched across her expression when she'd understood his words. Except instead of the shy way she'd ducked her head and moved away, the Maddie of his dreams had boldly admitted she felt the same way. In the jarring way of time in dreams, she'd been in his arms in an instant, his lips only a hairsbreadth from claiming hers.

He'd jerked awake in his bedroll, breathing hard, like he'd been chased by the wildfire all over again.

He forced his gaze away from Maddie now, focusing on the wagon having so much trouble getting up the gravel hill.

His feelings for Maddie were wrong. Not only was he far too old for her, dreaming about her felt like a betrayal of Elizabeth and the marriage vows they'd made to each other.

It didn't make sense. He knew that. Elizabeth was dead. Til death do us part.

But that knowledge didn't ease the conflict that boiled inside him.

He'd kept his distance the past few days.

It hadn't helped.

Sometimes he would catch her watching him from across camp. There was a new awareness in the air between them now, and it showed itself in that instant their gazes clashed. The thoughtful way she studied him.

Another reason he should leave the company.

A shout came from ahead, and Doc's gaze zeroed in on the wagon now tipping precariously to one side on that slope. About to crash onto its side.

He left his horse, ran at full speed.

He didn't recognize the man who'd been leading the oxen, now rounding the wagon to try and brace it. The man could be crushed beneath the wagon if it fell.

"No!" But Doc's cry didn't seem audible.

And now, without its owner's guidance, the pair of oxen veered left.

From over the lip of the slope, August Mason appeared, running to help the man. Two more men, some of the cowboys he recognized, left the wagons still on level ground at the bottom of the slope to help. Doc joined the two men at the rear corner of the wagon, the three of them pushing against what felt like a thousand pounds.

A jolting movement. Maybe the oxen trying to find their footing.

August's voice rose above the other shouts, giving orders to the oxen. He must've taken over for the wagon's owner.

Something shifted inside the wagon, a heavy object

sliding backward to thump against the closed tailgate. Doc felt the bump where his shoulder pressed against the buckboard side. He had a white-knuckled grip on the top edge of the wagon bed; the muscles of his legs strained as he and the others attempted to keep the wagon from going over.

And then, with a great heave from the oxen, the wagon pulled loose, tipped itself upright—though still angled on the slope. Relief flared. Doc stood where he was as the two other men followed the wagon's owner. August remained at the head of the oxen, though he looked back toward the wagon itself.

There it was again, the sound of something shifting inside the wagon, tumbling...

Time seemed to slow for a moment. A quick hiss, like a match striking. A breathless moment of stillness—

Light flashed.

A giant boom.

Doc's chest compressed from the sound.

The wagon splintered into pieces.

The ground shook beneath his feet.

For a moment, he was sucked back in time to when he'd awakened from a dead sleep to find the very ground being swept from underneath him—

And then a massive force tossed his body backward, as if he were nothing more than a ragdoll.

He might've blacked out for a few seconds.

Everything was quiet.

What had happened?

A rockslide!

Doc raised his head gingerly, a sharp pain emanating from the back of his skull. It took a moment for him to blink himself into consciousness, to force his aching body to sit up.

The chaos around him made no sense.

It was late afternoon, though his brain wanted to tell him the sun hadn't risen yet.

The air held an acrid scent of gunpowder, stronger than anything he'd ever smelled before.

People were running toward a crater in the side of the hill, where dust still hovered in the air.

Black scorch-marks marred the ground in a jagged pattern, like a starburst.

Where was Elizabeth? The children? His sister-in-law Sally?

Someone stopped a few feet away, bending with hands on their knees to speak to him—

Except he couldn't hear.

The ringing in his ears intensified, shutting out all other sound.

His head hurt.

But his thoughts cleared enough for the memories of the rockslide to retreat into place where they belonged. In the past.

He was traveling with Hollis's company. Something bad had happened with the wagon that had nearly toppled.

An explosion.

Doc still couldn't hear anything, and the man who'd come—maybe offering help?—faded from his focus as he took stock of himself.

He'd been thrown by the force of the blast. There was no bleeding, at least none that he could tell anyway. No broken bones, though he would be bruised and sore in a few hours. He touched the back of his head and winced as his fingers connected with the knot. He must've hit his head when he'd fallen.

He staggered to his feet. Steadied himself.

A lot of folks ran toward where the wagon had been. Men lay on the ground.

They'd been much closer than Doc when the blast happened. The wagon owner and two hired hands had been injured—he didn't even know their names.

August.

Doc moved toward the decimated wagon. Every step hurt. He must've bruised his ribs.

Someone was prone on the ground, two women kneeling over him. Beyond that, others tried to help.

One woman looked up, over her shoulder right at Doc, her expression panicked and blood on her hands.

He pulled up short. He needed his bag. Towels. For bad injuries like this, they'd need hot water. A lot of it.

Someone was at his side, he realized. A tall man. Doc knew his name but couldn't think it—

The ringing in his ears only intensified, and when the person grabbed Doc's arm to try to get his attention, pain pierced behind Doc's right eye.

He tried to breathe through it. Tried to explain that he couldn't hear anything. Didn't know whether his words made any sense or were completely garbled.

And then Maddie was there, taking the place of the man.

She gripped his hand—her steady touch a lifeline. She held his bag in her other hand, lifted it so he could see, quickly passed it to him. She must've fetched it once she'd realized there was a need.

Her eyes scanned his face, but her mouth wasn't moving. She wasn't trying to talk to him. Had she realized he couldn't hear her?

She let go of his hand only to lift hers. He couldn't help

flinching away from the brush of her fingers at his ear. She lifted her hand, palm toward him, and showed him the blood on her fingertips.

He was bleeding from the ears.

"Bad?" he tried to ask.

She shook her head slightly, eyes still watching him carefully.

"Are you all right?" She spoke slow enough for him to read her lips.

He didn't know how to answer, could only give her a grim smile.

She glanced over her shoulder toward the chaos and then back to him. *"We must help."*

But how could he, when he couldn't hear anything?

Maddie started toward the wreckage and wounded men, hoping Jason would follow. She missed a step when his hand closed around her wrist in an almost-punishing grip. She didn't stop moving, but when she shot a quick glance at him, his expression was both mulish and apologetic—a complete dichotomy.

If he needed to hold onto her for the moment, that was all right. She was still trying to shake off the terror of hearing the explosion and the helpless moment of watching Jason's body thrown through the air.

She'd frantically passed Jenny to Stella, who'd been nearby, and run to his side, arriving only moments later, but she wouldn't soon forget the stricken expression he wore.

Only as the debris and gravel shifted beneath her feet did she realize how this must be affecting him.

They died. Last year on a crossing of the Rockies.

This wasn't a rockslide. But it was an emergency. She guessed that something shifting in the back of the Kellers' wagon had caused a spark that somehow ignited a barrel of gunpowder. What else could've caused such an explosion?

The very ground had tilted and shaken, and it was entirely possible that Jason was disconcerted by the event.

And now he couldn't hear.

He'd been shouting the words at another man as she'd run to him. Seeing the blood at his ears made her fear the worst—what if it his loss was permanent?

But he still seemed determined to reach the others and help. If she knew him at all, she knew he wouldn't rest until anyone who needed doctoring received care.

As they neared the place where the wagon had once been, she heard moans of pain from more than one man.

August sat on the hillside several yards away with his head in his hands. Felicity knelt at his side, already reaching for him.

Maddie turned her attention to the disaster site.

Three men injured on the ground. A teen sat nearby, cradling one arm.

A woman walked around in circles yards away, muttering to herself.

A sudden scream brought Maddie's head up in time to see Lily running toward the injured men.

"Help my husband!" A woman kneeling over one of the men on the ground shouted.

Maddie knew they needed to quickly assess whose injuries were worst and prioritize which to address first.

Doc let go of Maddie. She quickly moved between the

three men on the ground. Doc did the same, moving in an opposite pattern from her.

"Maddie!" Lily shrieked.

The young man—Harry?— was awake but wore a wide-eyed look of shock. Blood bloomed from his stomach.

"Put pressure on the wound," Maddie told her sister urgently. "Hold down as tightly as you can."

Jason stood at her shoulder. They needed to move fast— two of the men seemed in danger of bleeding out. This man and the man nearby with a head wound. But how could she communicate with Jason, if he couldn't hear?

She looked up at him from where she still knelt over the hired hand and pointed to the man bleeding from his head. Raised her index finger.

Pointed to the cowboy lying in front of her. Two fingers.

And the man a bit farther away who seemed in need of stitches but not as bad off as the others. Three fingers.

And a jerk of her head toward the boy with the limp arm. Four.

Jason's eyes lit with recognition, and his mouth pulled in relief as he nodded.

"Water," he said.

Thank God the word was clear.

He waited a beat until she nodded. "Towels. Clean blankets."

She relayed the needs to Leo and Owen, who'd come running from the wagons already pulled ahead.

"Keep pressure on his wound," Maddie told Lily again.

"But he needs help," she cried. Tears streamed down her face. "You have to help him. Right now."

"Keep him awake." Maddie hesitated in the face of Lily's

genuine concern. Her fear and horror tore Maddie's heart in two. "We will work as fast as we can."

She was joining Jason when Leo jogged near. "Can the injured men be moved? We need to get the rest of the wagons up this hill."

Jason looked at her; she knew he hadn't heard Leo's words, but no doubt he understood the urgency.

She knew Leo was only being logical and responsible—having the wagons split up at night wasn't safe. But these men were in desperate condition.

She glanced around and caught sight of a clearing not far away. Out of the path of the wagons but close enough that they might not be jostled much in the move. She communicated what she could to Jason, stumbling over hand gestures. Told Leo to bring boards to carry the two most injured men and to help the others.

Blankets spread, she and Jason went to work. They quickly cleaned the wound at the man's temple, a furrow of broken flesh deep enough to require stitches. Likely where a piece of wood or metal from the wagon had caught him. She pulled his eyelids back. His eyes were clear, but his pupils were large. A concussion?

She was reaching for a piece of clean cloth someone had brought—there was water too, and more coming. She barely looked up to register it when she noticed Jason's hands shaking as he tied off a knot in the catgut, finished with his stitches.

She glanced at his face. His eyes met hers.

She'd seen his hands trembling the other night, but he'd brushed off her concern. Now there was no denying that something was wrong.

His mouth set in a grim line. She pressed a folded cloth to the man's head as Jason wound the bandage.

"Here?" she asked before she shook her head, realized he wouldn't hear.

He gently repositioned her hand and the cloth and finished winding the bandage. The man still hadn't awakened. Not a good sign.

Jason spent several moments lifting the man's shirt, examining and pressing on his stomach before he shook his head and stood. Was it possible the man had internal injuries?

Leo and his men had moved Lily's cowboy onto a quilt only feet away. Maddie's sister was crying, wiping her face with her shoulder.

"Can you step back?" Maddie asked her sister gently.

She took Lily's place as Jason knelt on the man's other side.

"More water!" she called out even as she peeled back the blood-soaked cloth covering the wound. It'd only been a few minutes—they'd worked as quickly as they could—but the man had gone pale and quiet, though he was still awake.

"Can you take Lily away?" Maddie murmured to Alice, who'd brought two pails of still-warm water.

"Where's the blood coming from?" Jason muttered as he leaned over the man.

The shadows grew longer, the light more golden. On this side of the mountains, they'd lose the sunlight fast.

"Bring lanterns!" Maddie called to whoever might be hovering nearby. "As many as you can find!"

She didn't know how he managed, but a few moments later he used what looked like a small pair of silver scissors but was actually a metal clamp from his bag to stop the bleeding.

She didn't even know how he could see what he was doing amidst the blood and tissue.

When someone edged a lantern as close as they dared, Jason glanced up gratefully.

"We need to clean the wound," he said.

She understood at once. Whatever force or object had hit Harry, there were tiny flecks of dirt and threads of fabric in the wound.

Jason quickly doused the man with laudanum, and Harry breathed easier as he went unconscious. Jason lifted a pair of small tweezers but frowned and pulled his hand back before he'd neared the wound. His hand hovered in the air between them. It was shaking.

When he looked at her, she saw the desperation and self-disgust in his eyes.

He offered her the tool. "Please."

She didn't hesitate. They worked quickly as the light faded. He pointed to tiny specks of dirt and debris when she would've missed them. Helped her navigate the wound.

And then he handed her the surgical needle and catgut.

When she would've refused, his lips flattened and he nodded. He was trusting her to do this?

She worked in the stitches—more difficult than on an external wound—aware of the lines of pain around Jason's mouth as they worked.

When the last stitch went in, Maddie was the one whose hands were shaking. She dropped the needle and fisted her hands in her lap, dropping her head and closing her eyes.

She'd made countless poultices and even helped women birth babies, but this had been the most frightening hour of her life.

And she knew it wasn't over.

An open wound like this one would be at risk of infection —especially out here in the wild. What might've blown into the wound on the breeze? Dust particles, smoke and ash still floated in the air.

What if she'd missed a stitch? What if the man was still bleeding inside?

She jumped when a hand closed over the bloodied fingers of her right hand. Her eyes flew open to see Jason reaching across the man's body.

It was there in his gaze. He understood all of it. The elation, the fear, the worry.

"You did well," he said in a low voice. "Now only God knows what will happen."

Chapter Ten

EVENING HAD FALLEN and Maddie's energy was flagging.

Surely Jason had to be worse off, though the doctor hadn't complained once, even though she'd seen him moving gingerly.

"He can't be moved," Maddie said firmly.

Hollis frowned in the lamplight.

She glanced past the wagon master to where Jason knelt near Harry's shoulder, one hand on the man's upper chest as if to feel the hired hand's labored breathing.

When she glanced back at the wagon master, his expression was grim. "You're certain?"

"The surgery on his abdomen was extensive. He needs to stay still."

Her gaze flicked behind Hollis to see the tilt of Jason's head, one cheek turned slightly toward her.

If she didn't know better, she'd think he was eavesdropping. But there'd been clear indications as the evening had worn on that the hearing loss he'd sustained from the explosion persisted. Only a half hour ago, he'd startled when she'd approached from behind and touched his arm.

"Will Doc stay with him?" Hollis asked.

"I don't know—"

"He'll need constant observation," Jason said, the sound of his clothing rustling as he moved toward the two of them.

She felt a beat of relief, something big that flowed through her at the knowledge that he'd heard them—he must've if he'd responded to their conversation.

On the heels of relief was a deep concern. There was still a stain at his collar from the blood that had come from his ears earlier. Lines of exhaustion and pain bracketed his mouth.

"You should be checked over yourself," she murmured as he joined her and Hollis.

His eyes flicked to hers, a shadow flitting through the depths. For a moment, it looked as if he might protest.

She quickly rushed on, "There's no one else to examine."

"She's right," Hollis said. "Everyone else has been moved to camp."

Jason cringed, but she could see by the set of his shoulders that he would submit to an examination. That was perhaps more worrisome than anything else. Was he worried over the head injury? Something else?

"Will it hurt too badly to sit down on the blanket?" she asked quietly, trying to keep Hollis from overhearing even though he still stood nearby.

A flash of surprise in Jason's expression. Surely he hadn't imagined that she hadn't noticed how he'd favored his left side as he'd doctored the patients they'd seen all afternoon and well into the evening.

He didn't deny it as he let himself down to his knees on the blanket.

"Ribs?" she asked softly as she came near.

He nodded, and she reached out to prod his midsection the way she'd seen him check the others. Beneath the gentle press of her fingers, the muscles of his abdomen were tense and firm.

"Hearing is coming back?"

"Yes. The ringing is fading. It started out so loud that I couldn't hear anything else."

"If your patient needs constant attention, I'll talk to Leo and see if he can spare some men to set a watch out here." At Hollis's words, Maddie became aware for the first time of how quiet it was away from the noise and bustle of camp. Out here the only quiet noise was insects and the occasional chirp of a bird.

Terror sliced through her, a memory of two arms around her like iron bands, a hand clapping over her mouth.

Jason shifted, throwing her back into the present from those terrifying moments when she'd been snatched by Byrne's henchmen.

As if he'd known where her mind had gone, one side of his lips ticked in a sort of smile. "I'm armed," he said, voice low.

"And you've a head injury," she retorted. "I'm fine."

But it was a bit of a relief to straighten and step behind him. She was careful not to step on his feet as she edged to the back of his head, one hand on his shoulder.

"Can he be moved tomorrow?" Hollis pressed. "We'll be fighting to avoid the heavy snow as it is."

"I don't know," Jason said. "His injury is extensive."

Maddie thought of the expression on Lily's face as she'd hovered, watching the surgery as it happened. The cowboy meant something to her sister.

"What if we can get him into a wagon?" Hollis pressed. "He can lie still and ride along."

But Jason shook his head. "I'll need a day at least to make sure he's stable enough to bear it."

Hollis sighed heavily and muttered that he was returning to camp to send them help. He disappeared into the night.

"I'll need to check on the children." She bent close to Jason again.

"You should—" Whatever he'd been going to say was lost when her fingers gently tunneled into his hair. He froze completely.

"Can you tip your head forward?" she whispered, the moment suddenly fraught with tension.

He let his head fall forward. With the two lanterns remaining, she could see the bump at the back of his skull. With tentative fingers she lifted his hair, trying to see the size and shape of the lump. Whether there was any blood. But he was incredibly tense, and it seemed as if he was barely breathing.

"Look at me," she ordered quietly, rounding to the front of him.

She let her palms frame his cheeks. His stubble abraded her skin, and she worked to hide the shiver that traced down her spine.

"I think I would've noticed if you had a concussion," she said. "It's been hours. But I'm concerned about the goose egg on your scalp." She dropped her hands.

He cleared his throat and turned his face away. "You should return to the company and get some rest."

"What if it *is* a concussion?" she asked.

Jason sent her a skeptical look before he carefully rose to his feet. "I trust your diagnosis," he said gruffly. He moved off into the brush, bending to reach for something on the ground, and then putting one hand on his knee at an indrawn breath.

Her face warmed at his words.

"Our father died when I was fifteen," she said.

His head tipped in her direction, but she couldn't quite look at him. Why had she brought up her father? She carefully built up the fire one stick at a time.

"Stella took it upon herself to feed us—she hid her true identity, dressed as a man, worked in a factory."

He made a small noise of surprise.

"Someone had to look after Lily, but I also made friends with a woman from down the hall in our tenement."

Memories of the warring herbal scents that always followed Mrs. Murphy swept over Maddie, along with a wave of homesickness. "She saw how curious I was and started teaching me. It was a good thing for Lily and me." She raised her chin slightly, remembering. "I came to know all of the families in our apartment block. They'd watch out for us, when they could." She shrugged. "And I loved it. Helping folks. Holding babies."

"And when you needed rest?" he prodded. *Like now?*

She wrinkled her nose at the words he insinuated instead of spoke. A quick memory snuck through her mind—being woken up after several late nights with different families suffering from a fever that had swept through their building. Protesting that she herself needed rest, but being begged—and even threatened—by the suffering ones.

She hadn't thought about that in a long time.

"I can put aside my needs for others." She said the words quickly.

A shadow crossed his expression.

A movement flickered amongst the shadows outside the circle of firelight. She hadn't realized she'd stiffened until Jason turned in that direction.

"Why'd you jump before?" he asked, voice low. He was staring into the darkness as whoever was out there approached. "When Hollis—"

"I was abducted. Weeks ago. Collin and Stella rescued me. Nothing happened," she added quickly.

When she registered how tense he'd gone, she added, "I'm fine."

Felicity appeared out of the darkness, her arm threaded through August's. "Maddie? We need you and Doc."

"Of course." She jumped up and joined Jason where he met them.

August had a scrape on the back of one hand, she registered quickly. But other than that, he looked completely unharmed.

"You were close to the wagon when the blast happened," Jason said slowly. He was watching August's face closely.

Oh no. Maddie had been distracted by the children and hadn't seen.

"Why didn't you come sooner?" she asked.

Felicity's face was creased with worry. "I told him we should come—"

"Those other folks needed help more urgently," August said quietly. There was a note in his voice she couldn't read. "And I thought it might pass."

What might pass?

She didn't understand until Jason, face to face with August, lifted one finger and moved it back and forth in front of August's eyes.

The other man didn't blink. Nor did his eyes follow Jason's finger.

"What happened when the blast went off?" Jason asked.

"I heard the noise—looked right at it," August said. "I don't know whether dust got blown into my eyes or if it was the flash—"

Felicity bit her lip, and Maddie realized tears stood in her friend's eyes.

Jason gave her a grim look. "He's been blinded."

* * *

Jason woke in the hazy place between dreams and reality. It was entirely dark—the quiet of morning.

What had awoken him?

The skin on his left hand, the left side of his neck and face was chilled. He was sitting up, not lying in his bedroll.

He registered her there in an instant. Maddie, tucked into his side, a shawl draped around her shoulders, both of them leaning on a fallen log someone had dragged close to the fire earlier in the evening.

The fire had died down to a clump of red hot coals. He should get up and stoke it. Harry was lying caddy-corner, the soft rise and fall of his breath even. He would need the warmth. But Jason's eyes slipped closed again, his cheek nestling against the crown of Maddie's head. She fit against his shoulder just so, and she felt so good against him. His arm curled tighter around her shoulder.

He would get up and stoke the fire in a moment.

Just a moment...

He startled awake on a breath. It could've been only

moments later, but dawn's light was creeping over the eastern horizon now.

He still held Maddie cuddled to his side. He blinked more fully awake. Someone had stoked the fire. A large log popped, burning slowly. Someone must've noticed it and helped out.

How had Jason slept through it?

Harry was resting, though as Jason watched, he shifted restlessly and then winced. But he still didn't wake.

Something registered when Maddie came awake. A sudden stillness? A change in the rhythm of each indrawn breath? His burst eardrums must've healed as he slept, because everything that had been muted last night was crystal clear.

"We must've fallen asleep," she whispered into the stillness.

He hummed acknowledgement. They'd stayed awake far into the night, in whispered conversation. At first she'd been tense and alert, jumping at every crack of the fire, every leaf blown by the breeze. But the longer they'd talked, the more calm she'd grown. She'd even confessed that she trusted him.

And that felt dangerous.

After she'd opened up about her life back in Ireland, he found himself talking in fits and spurts about Elizabeth. About the children. Memories that were both poignant and painful as they'd sat shoulder-to-shoulder and stared out into the darkness. He hadn't consciously moved closer to her, but somehow, in the cool of the night, they'd snuggled together.

He should let her go. Get up and move away.

But somehow he couldn't.

His breath fogged in front of his face. "It won't be long until winter sets in."

"I want to be settled in the Willamette Valley before then," she whispered, seemingly content to stay close.

His stomach twisted. He wouldn't be there with her.

Now she shifted. His hand fell away from her shoulder, but instead of moving away, she tipped her head so there was only a breath between them. His hand settled at her lower back.

"How is your poor contused head this morning?" she whispered. Her eyes scanned his face. "Any dizziness?" Her words blew a warm breath against his chin.

He couldn't find the strength to look away. "My head isn't the reason for the vertigo I feel right now." His gaze fell to her lips.

Stand up.

Kiss her.

Two conflicting desires at war within him.

He should—

He did what he'd wanted to do for weeks. He leaned in to close the scant distance between them and brushed his lips over hers. Moved back a breath. Would she push him away?

He felt more than heard the catch of her breath. His hand at her back urged her forward again. She came willingly. This time his lips closed over hers fully.

She was so, so sweet. There was a moment when the turn of her head was slightly wrong and her nose bumped his cheek. He felt the puff of breath that would've been laughter and the curve of her smile before her hand moved to rest against his jaw. Her head tipped and—

He felt just as knocked off his feet as he had yesterday in the blast.

Her hand slipped behind his head, her fingers brushing

against the hair at his nape. She was careful not to get close to his wound.

He wanted to hold onto this moment, hold onto *her*, forever.

He broke the kiss.

"Jason," she whispered against his lips. And he *was* Jason again.

Not Doc.

Not his calling.

Only Jason.

The man.

The man who wanted this—

A voice carried on the wind at the very moment he would've drawn her close again. Someone was coming. Several someones. Young voices.

It was still dark enough that he doubted whoever it was— the Miller children, if he had to guess—had seen. But he still pulled away.

When Maddie's brows drew together, he tipped his head to the west, where the crunch of footsteps in the dry prairie grasses could be heard.

The low grade pain in his head intensified as he pushed up off the ground to stand. His ribs pulled, and he barely suppressed a groan. It would be weeks before his bruised ribs healed completely.

His heart pounded. The rush of blood pulsed through his face. His hands shook, but not from exhaustion.

What had he done?

He was aware of Maddie behind him, speaking softly. His pulse in his ears drowning out the sound of her words.

And Alex, running ahead toward them. Paul, carrying little Jenny as he walked next to Maddie's younger sister, Lily.

Jason had the presence of mind to step away from the fire, away from their vulnerable patient as the group approached.

And it was a good thing, as Alex rushed in like a buffalo into a dress shop. Jason expected him to go straight to Maddie, but the boy made a beeline straight toward Jason.

"Wait—!" Maddie called out softly.

Alex didn't wait. He reached Jason, arms outstretched for a hug.

It'd been eons—more than a year—since Jason had received a hug from his preteen son, but his body remembered, and he found himself holding a shuddering Alex in his arms. He barely felt the bruise in his ribs as emotion crashed into him.

Jason met Maddie's gaze above the boy's head, the feeling of being off-kilter still pulling him underwater so that he couldn't breathe.

She must've seen in his expression how shaken he felt. Not only from Alex's hug.

Alex pushed back, rubbing his cheek with the back of one hand. "I was worried about ya."

"How is he?" Lily said the words quietly to Maddie, and Jason couldn't make out Maddie's response as the two women moved toward the still-sleeping cowboy.

"I'm all right," Jason told Alex, whose gaze seemed shadowed. Worried. "Bruised and banged up, but all right."

Alex's brows drew tight and then smoothed. "Good. Cause ya gotta finish teaching me chess."

Maddie was with Paul, who hung back slightly at the edge of the clearing. "Did you have supper last night? Want me to take her?"

Paul handed over the baby, who pushed against Maddie's shoulder but then reluctantly settled in her arms.

"Alice 'n Abigail fed us supper," Paul said, nudging his toe into the dirt.

Lily looked at the cowboy, but said, "Paul was a great help with Jenny. He tucked her in bed himself."

"Well done," Maddie said softly.

But Paul frowned, his expression a mix of anger and something else.

Alex had wandered to where the scorch marks marred the earth. Paul slowly followed him. And Maddie came close to Jason.

He couldn't look her in the eye. Stared at a lone freckle on her neck above her collar. "I shouldn't have—"

"Kissed me?" she asked with a furtive glance over her shoulder at Lily kneeling at Harry's side. If he wasn't mistaken, the man was feigning sleep now.

When Maddie looked back at him, her chin tipped up. He felt the question she wouldn't voice.

"I can't open my heart again," he said firmly, though he felt as if the ground trembled beneath his feet. It wasn't fair to lead her on. Not when there was no future for them. "It's my fault that my family died."

The words fell in the quiet morning air between them like a stone into a still pond. Was it the first time he'd said the words aloud? He'd known it since the disaster had happened.

"How?" she asked gravely.

"I should've known better than to camp where we did— right in the path of the rockslide. I should've woken when the ground started to shake. I should've done more—"

She watched him with eyes that saw too much, so he turned to give her his profile. Ran one hand through his hair, relished the pain in his ribs. He deserved the pain. Deserved more.

"I shouldn't have lived." More words he'd never said aloud. But their truth fell quickly from his lips. "I shouldn't have survived. I don't understand why—"

Why God let me live.

"I promised myself I would spend the rest of my life helping those taking this journey in the wilderness."

He'd also vowed he'd never go to Oregon. That had been Elizabeth's dream. He couldn't make it his.

A deep sadness colored Maddie's expression. As she opened her mouth to respond, Lily called out for her. She pinched her lips together.

"It's better this way." The words tumbled from his lips as she turned away.

Chapter Eleven

"WHY ISN'T HE WAKING UP?" Lily's demanding question pulled Maddie's attention from where she watched Paul and Alex, with Tommy trailing on their heels, weave through the moving wagons ahead. Mrs. Duncan gave chase when they passed by her wagon, even though they hadn't come within five yards.

Lily walked next to the wagon Hollis had appropriated for Jason's patient—Lily had been a frequent visitor. Maddie wished she had better news to deliver.

"A wound like his will take time to heal," Maddie said with as much patience as she could muster. Hadn't she had this very conversation with Lily this morning? And yesterday evening?

The canvas flap on this wagon had been tied back so that, while his body remained shaded from the sun, Maddie—or Jason when he came near—had a clear view of his upper half in the back of the moving wagon.

Two days had passed since the explosion. Yesterday afternoon, Hollis had pushed them for a decision. Jason hadn't been happy, but putting Harry in an empty wagon where he'd ride as smoothly as they could manage seemed the only option. The company needed to keep moving. Maddie understood that much.

Jenny made a soft cooing sound from her wrap against Maddie's front. After a chilly morning, the day had warmed, and Maddie was sweating. But the moments of sleep were a blessing. Jenny had been terribly fussy all day.

Things weren't getting better.

Maddie would never be the girl's mother, her real mother. And the boys had a loud argument over breakfast that earned them glares from their nearest neighbors.

"Maddie—are you even listening?"

Maddie blinked away the thoughts that had been plaguing her since last night when Jenny had refused to settle for sleep.

Lily stared pointedly at her. "*When* will he wake up?"

Irritation crawled under Maddie's skin. "I didn't realize you even knew him."

A shadow passed through Lily's eyes before she cut them away. "We've formed a friendship—of a sort."

Maddie was certain she'd never seen the two together.

Lily nudged her chin up. "You didn't answer my question. When will he wake?"

Maddie shook her head. She sidestepped a pile of manure a pair of oxen had left behind. "There's no way to know. He's got a mild infection. At least that's what Jason said when he checked his wound this morning."

"An infection?" Lily bit her lip.

Maddie had seen the slight swelling and redness surrounding where she'd put the stitches in and felt a beat of terror until Jason had told her that was normal for a wound like Harry's.

"Every time he wakes, we—Jason or I—ply him with water and broth. All we can do is let his body work on healing."

Lily stared at the man sleeping in the wagon. Something was going on with her. But in the moment that a vulnerable expression crossed her sister's face, Maddie looked away. If Lily fancied the cowboy, she was stubborn enough that a word from Maddie, meant to discourage, might make her *more* interested.

She caught sight of Alex scampering through the wagons with Tommy at his side. Where was Paul—?

There. Walking at a more sedate pace, talking with a friend.

Paul had been quiet for the past several days. Not like the boy she remembered when his parents had been alive. She didn't know how to reach him.

"You've been spending a lot of time with the doctor," Lily said quietly.

Maddie's attention snapped back to her sister. Her face heated under Lily's glittering gaze.

"Enough that people are talking."

"What people?" Maddie demanded.

Lily didn't answer directly. "Isn't he rather old?"

"No older than Mr. Johnson to Mrs." Perhaps it was a slight exaggeration. There might be twenty years between the man and his younger wife. But they seemed happy enough when Maddie saw them in passing.

She caught the rise of Lily's eyebrows and realized that she had been staring at Jason as he rode past, tall and confident, on his horse.

She was struck again with a moment of terror that she'd felt when he'd been thrown by the blast. Perhaps Jason wouldn't open his heart again, but Maddie's emotions were already entangled.

That wasn't good.

"It doesn't matter anyway," she told her sister quietly. "It's better that I focus on the children and providing for their needs."

I won't open my heart again.

Maddie wouldn't soon forget the stricken, panicked expression on Jason's face after the kiss they'd shared.

Jenny woke with a fussy noise, and Lily slipped away in the chaos of wagons parking for the night. Dusk hovered around them. Maddie gave Jenny to Alice at her insistence. Maddie's stomach rumbled with hunger as she rounded the Miller's wagon and almost bowled over a teenaged—

No. It was the young woman she'd met in the woods days ago.

The woman shrank back before Lily could greet her. But she didn't disappear into the growing darkness.

"I need help," she whispered.

"All righ—" Maddie's words stopped as the young woman revealed a wound on the underside of her forearm.

"It's awfully hard to see here," Maddie said with a smile. "Come into the light—" She moved to the side, extended her arm in a clear invitation, but the woman shrank back even farther, turning so she was half hidden against the wagon itself.

Concern lanced through Maddie. She tried to slow her whirling thoughts, but one thing was clear: this young woman didn't want to come into camp.

"The doctor should look at your wound—"

The woman was shaking her head before Maddie finished her sentence, panic written on her expression in the growing dark.

"I know you got healing. I just want you." The words were barely loud enough to hear. She looked ready to bolt.

"All right."

If this woman needed help, Maddie was determined to give it.

The woman stayed put while Maddie approached one cautious step at a time. When Maddie gestured for her to show the arm again, the woman lifted it.

What might've once been a small cut was swollen and hot to the touch. A hiss of breath escaped when Maddie's prodding fingers got too close.

The young woman couldn't be more than seventeen or eighteen. She was slight, her wrist beneath Maddie's hand felt fragile to the touch. She was far too thin. The shawl wrapped around her was dirty, one corner in need of repair, snagged on something and unraveling. Beneath the shawl, her dark-colored dress was far more low cut than Maddie recognized from among the travelers. There was a bit of lace at the neckline. The material looked like satin, once shiny, though now torn and stained.

Her feet were bare.

"What's your name?" Maddie murmured.

There was a long pause. The young woman pulled her arm to press against her midsection. "I don't think I should say." Another whisper.

When a voice rang out from inside camp, the woman jumped. Her anxious gaze flicked to the canvas top blocking them from view, though Maddie knew she couldn't see past it.

"Who are your people?"

Maddie had found herself scanning faces among the company in search of the girl she'd seen only in the shadows. She'd started to think she'd imagined the interaction.

"Who are you staying with?" she asked patiently when the girl didn't answer.

The girl drew back, her panicked expression sparking an instant realization.

She was a stowaway.

The hand-shaped bruise at her neckline... the dress...

The girl wasn't a pioneer.

And right now she looked as if she was about to run off into the darkness.

"Your arm needs tending," Maddie said quickly. "A poultice would help draw the infection out."

The young woman melted back a step, but didn't leave.

She knew. She'd sought out Maddie, caught her in this moment where no one else would see them.

"It will only take me a moment to mix up the dressing," Maddie said with a quick gesture at camp. "I won't tell anyone you're out here. I promise."

The young woman glanced into the darkness on both sides. Finally, she nodded.

She obviously needed more help than a simple poultice.

How could Maddie convince her to accept it?

"I can't stop thinking about her." Doc looked away from the damp cloth he was holding to Coop Spencer's brow as the words burst out of his mouth.

He hadn't meant to say them.

But Owen was pacing in the darkness behind him and some weakness inside Jason had given in and there the words were. Out in the open.

He caught the flash of curiosity in Coop's quick glance and gritted his teeth to keep any more words from pouring out. His ribs ached.

Owen was his friend. Coop wasn't. He'd do well to remember that.

Evening was falling, and the first watch had been set.

Owen cast a furious look at Coop as Jason lifted the cloth to inspect the wound. The cut was right on the edge of the bone at Coop's eye socket.

"I think two stitches will seal it up," Jason said quietly, directing the words more to Owen than Coop. "The scar will be so close to his eyebrow that it'll barely be noticeable."

"Leo will notice, though," Owen muttered.

Jason had been filled in on the family dynamics before he'd arrived at Hollis's company with Owen and Rachel. Owen and August were Leo and Alice Spencer's half brothers. They shared the same father. After their parents had divorced and their father had gone after his fortune in the mines of California, Leo's mother had wed again and had the twins, Collin and Coop. As far as Jason could tell, the twins were complete opposites. Patient and short-tempered. Light and dark.

"I ain't gonna see Leo," Coop said with a mulish lift of his chin.

"Hold this," Jason ordered quietly. He left Coop to press the cloth to the wound while he twisted to his black bag, open on the ground next to him.

"You need to spend less time with the hired hands," Owen groused.

At the sound of a fist smacking flesh, both Owen's and Jason's heads turned toward the lone lantern on the ground, a good hundred yards away from camp.

"Whose idea was this boxing match anyway?" Owen demanded.

Coop's lips flattened in a line. He didn't flinch when Jason knocked his hand out of the way, lifted the needle and catgut very close to his eye.

"Be still," Jason said. He could see that the command, meant to protect his eye and the skin of his face, rankled the young man. It showed in the stubborn set of his lips that he wanted to protest but thought better of it.

The man absolutely hated being ordered around. That much was clear.

"Sixteen hours a day in the saddle." Coop pointed the words to Owen. "Men're bored. You think of a better way to blow off steam?"

"I can think of several," Owen countered, his pacing bringing him within a few feet of Jason and Coop.

The catgut tugged. Jason heard the quick intake of breath, but Coop didn't move a muscle. He only said, "What Leo don't know won't kill him."

Owen parked his hands on his hips. "How do you know he isn't already aware of the matches? Your brother isn't stupid. You show up with a collection of bruises and a black eye and he knows something's going on."

Jason put in the second stitch.

"And I'll be willing to bet there's money jingling in your pocket," Owen said low. "Hollis wouldn't be happy to know there's gambling happening in the company."

"You tell him and Leo will be out the men he needs to

watch his cattle and guard his wife's fortune." But an uncertainty skittered through Coop's eyes, quickly shuttered.

They were beyond the circled wagons. Another muffled punch and grunt as two men danced toward each other and away in that far-off lantern light. Would Jason have another patient soon?

Jason clipped away the excess catgut and handed Coop a different cloth, this one soaked with disinfectant. "Hold that on the wound for a moment."

Coop inhaled at the sting as he pressed the cloth to his brow. Jason was already tucking away his needle in the bag.

He moved a few feet away from Coop to stand beside Owen and stare into the darkness at the men now grappling with each other. Neither of them seemed particularly vicious fighters. Or maybe the distance and the darkness disguised that.

"Did you ever think maybe God brought you to this company to meet Maddie?" Owen asked.

Jason had hoped his friend was distracted enough by Coop that he'd forgotten Jason's blurted words. He smiled grimly. "You brought me to the company."

"You'd feel better if you took a swing at him."

Both Jason and Owen sent looks over their shoulder at Coop's intrusive words. Jason turned away first, aware of his friend's slow stare into the darkness.

"What happened to your family wasn't your fault."

Jason scowled. Owen knew how he felt about this. He'd told Maddie the truth of it. If he'd been awake, if he'd sensed the danger. If he'd chosen a different route...

It was his fault. He knew it in his bones. He'd forever bear the guilt of his family's death. He'd never understand why he'd been left alive.

So why couldn't he stop thinking about Maddie? What he'd told Owen was true. She was on his mind in those fuzzy moments between sleep and wakefulness—he'd reached for her only this morning, found empty air outside his bedroll. He looked for her in the crowd while riding alongside the company. Couldn't rest at night until he knew she was safe, bedded down with the Miller kids.

It wasn't right.

But he couldn't seem to stop.

"You told me that it wasn't a weakness to love someone," Owen said, voice low. He sent a look over his shoulder.

Jason heard rustling, but not enough to indicate that Coop had stood.

"It's not," Jason said reluctantly. He remembered the conversation. The hours when Owen had thought he would lose Rachel when she'd been very, very sick after birthing her baby, Molly. "I loved Elizabeth. Loved my children with everything in me."

Another thoughtful pause from Owen. "So you don't want to fall in love again?"

More rustling behind them. Jason turned to see Coop clamber to his feet.

"He doesn't deserve it." Coop said the words in a calm and matter-of-fact manner as he dropped the cloth on top of Jason's bag. His eyes glittered when he stepped toward Jason and Owen. "He's broken."

Something in his words agitated Jason—and yet there was an element of understanding. Something that resonated. Coop wasn't guessing.

"Bet he's punishing himself—"

Jason didn't consciously throw the punch, but it landed, hard, against Coop's lower stomach. Coop buckled, though he didn't double over.

"Hey—" Owen stepped between them.

But Coop straightened.

He was laughing.

Jason stood in stunned silence, blood pulsing through the fisted hand at his side. What had he done?

He strode off into the darkness, away from the far-off lantern, away from the camp.

He'd made an oath when he'd become a doctor. Not to do harm. But he'd let Coop's words get to him, let his temper fly.

Steps behind startled him. He half expected Owen to throw a punch of his own, to take up for Leo's brother.

But Owen just stood by Jason, his face in shadow, backlit by the dim fire from inside the circled wagons.

"He deserved that," Owen said quietly.

Maybe so. But Jason had a choice whether or not to react.

He stood in the darkness, chest rising and falling as he fought to control his rioting emotions. He should've left the company back at the fort.

"What if you traveled to Oregon?" Owen asked after a moment of silence.

Jason started to shake his head. That had been Elizabeth's dream. She'd spun stories of what it would be like in the West until Jason had itched for the adventure of it. Of doing it together.

Before he could voice his refusal, Owen said, "Lots of people out there now. Not a lot of doctors. Lots of folks who need doctoring."

The words hit hard. Elizabeth had said much the same thing.

The idea settled inside him again. Somehow right, even though he'd fought against it ever since Elizabeth's death. He didn't deserve to live their dream, not without her by his side.

"Even if I go, I can't be with Maddie," he said.

But ...

If he settled in the Willamette Valley... If Maddie settled there, too... Maybe eventually something could come of the tangle of feelings inside him.

He looked toward the company. Campfires from within the circled wagons lit up the prairie, highlighted the white canvases. Flickered.

Maddie was inside that circle, probably getting the children ready for bed.

"You talk to August today?" Owen asked after the silence stretched long.

"Yes." He'd checked on Owen's brother every morning since the explosion. Today, August thought he could make out some light through the darkness that had persisted.

Jason had been quiet in the face of August's excitement. There was so much uncertainty to an injury like his. And it'd been days without any real improvement.

"You ever thought maybe you haven't finished healing yet?" Owen asked.

Jason stared at the white canvases as Owen's question settled in the quiet night around them. He hadn't thought he ever would heal. The grief had been so powerful, so raw and strong...

But what if Owen was right? What if he *did* travel to Oregon? What if his healing was there?

Maybe he could become himself again. Be better than the Jason who hadn't been enough to save his family.

Be the kind of man Maddie needed by her side.

Chapter Twelve

"CAN I SPEAK WITH HARRY?"

For a moment, Jason thought the softly lilted voice belonged to Maddie.

But no, Lily hovered near the back corner of the wagon Jason had been using as a sickbed.

"He was awake for a bit earlier, but drifted off."

She frowned. Was she a bit pale tonight?

Jason sat on a large, sturdy stump that happened to be in the center of his camp. After so long on the trail, where dust and dirt flew into the air and settled everywhere, he needed to go through his medical bag and clean things out. Right now, he had a soft cloth in hand to clean each tool and bottle of medicine from his bag. He added each finished item to a clean quilt spread at his feet.

"Can I sit with him?" she pressed.

Jason thought about the way Harry feigned sleep when Lily had walked near the wagon earlier in the day. The younger man wasn't playacting now. His body was exhausted from healing such a terrible wound.

"I don't suppose it could hurt..." He was speaking to himself by the end of the sentence as she'd already clambered into the wagon.

The canvas remained pulled back, so most of the inside of the wagon was exposed. Jason watched her move slowly and carefully, not jostling his patient.

In the camps around him, the company rejoiced over reaching Independence Rock, even though the Fourth of July was far behind them. The landmark was roughly the halfway point in their journey, and Hollis had called for an early halt to celebrate.

Dinner consumed, folks stoked campfires so high that the interior of the circled wagons was bright. Owen and Leo and Collin had unpacked musical instruments, and other neighbors had joined them for dancing. Jason had seen August sitting away from the edge of their campsite.

Maddie was over there. Jason glimpsed Paul, hanging back near the edge of the crowd, and Alex dancing wildly through the couples moving more sedately.

Beyond the canvas tops of the wagons, the Rockies loomed dark and imposing.

Hollis allowed the pioneers to celebrate tonight, but there would be difficult and dangerous travels ahead.

It'd been days since Owen had offered his advice. Jason had wrestled with it since.

He'd barely seen Maddie. She watched over Harry when Jason was called away to help someone else and during the day when Jason rode horseback.

Where before the kiss, she'd been open and warm and nearly always present, there was a noticeable distance between them now. When in his presence, she was reserved. She gave him as much physical space as she could.

He missed her quick smiles.

It was his own fault. There was no one else to blame. He'd drawn her close because he couldn't seem to resist her, and he'd been the one to push her away.

Now he found himself staring as she approached Paul at the edge of the crowd and pulled him in for a dance. Jason couldn't make out anything save the musical notes rising into the night, but he saw her head tip back, saw the laughter in her expression.

When he came to himself, he was already on his feet, had taken two steps in that direction.

He forced his gaze away, turned, ran one hand through his hair in agitation. Only to meet Lily's eyes where she'd glanced up from inside the wagon bed.

He strode to the wagon. Harry was asleep. Lily sat at his side in the cramped space, her legs folded beneath her.

"I need to—" Jason cut himself off, not really wanting to explain to Maddie's sister. "Would you sit with him? For a bit? I want to go—" He gestured over his shoulder.

Lily's eyes narrowed slightly, but she nodded. "Of course."

Halfway between his campsite and the merriment, someone called out to him.

Mrs. Strathurst, a young widow. He'd doctored her ten-year-old daughter's spider bite this morning as the company had moved out for the day.

"I'm sorry. You must want to visit and such."

He glanced over her shoulder to the lively activity, saw a flash of Maddie's skirt as she danced.

"Olivia was complaining that the poultice made her skin itch even more than the bite."

There was a tilt to the woman's head and a certain way that she smiled—he remembered the signs of flirtation from when he'd been a medical student. He'd already been married to Elizabeth, but it hadn't stopped other young ladies from attempting to make his acquaintance.

Maddie had never tipped her head at him in such a coquettish way. Not even after he'd admitted he was drawn to her.

There was a frankness to Maddie. A genuineness that couldn't be imitated. And after he'd kissed her, after he'd pushed her away, she'd accepted that was what he needed.

He saw to Mrs. Strathurst's concerns, promised to check on her daughter first thing in the morning. And while he was polite and professional as he helped her, his awareness remained on Maddie.

He broke away as soon as he could and approached the gathering.

Alex was playing checkers with Ben. Paul had Jenny on his knee, sitting with Stella and Collin.

Where was Maddie?

There.

He turned his steps to meet her at the outer edge of the gathering, where Owen's wagon and Leo's wagon were stationed head-to-head. Maddie held a plate full of food in hand and walked as if to slip out into the darkness.

When he stepped in front of her, she drew up short.

"Surely you aren't finished celebrating yet," he teased quietly.

Her gaze glanced off of his. She lifted the plate, but if he'd expected her to say she was sneaking off to have a bite to eat, she didn't. "I thought I'd take a moment and get some fresh air."

The polite thing to do would be to step out of her way

and allow her past. Perhaps even the smart thing. What he *should* do.

But he didn't feel polite. Not tonight.

"The boys look like they are having fun," he said. "I saw you dancing with Paul."

Her eyes came to his face, and he saw the minute drawing together of her brow. "It is lovely to have something to celebrate after the hardships they've faced. Paul has taken it upon himself to watch over Jenny more."

Just this morning Jason had seen the hurt expression on Maddie's face when the baby girl had pushed her away after the breakfast meal.

Maddie looked over Jason's shoulder, but when he turned his head, he saw only the darkness beyond the wagons. Maddie's tent had been pitched on the very edge of camp, barely inside the circled conveyances.

When she smiled tightly and shifted as if she might brush past him, something inside him twisted.

He didn't want this Maddie. This veiled politeness and the distance between them.

He didn't know what he wanted.

"Are you finished dancing, then?" he demanded.

Her eyes flashed at the note of sharpness in his tone.

She set the plate on the back tailgate of Leo's wagon. When she looked back at him, her hands went to her hips. "Do you need someone to sit with Harry?"

"Your sister is with him."

Another flash of her eyes, one he couldn't decipher.

"I saw you speaking with Mrs. Strathurst," she blurted. A flush rose in her cheeks and her lips pinched together momentarily, but then she went on. "She's made no secret of the fact that she is looking for a husband. And she's beautiful."

He didn't care about Mrs. Strathurst. He was opening his mouth to tell her so when she said, "And she must be closer to your own 'advanced' age. Perhaps you should ask her to dance."

"The only woman I want to dance with is you." The words were out before he'd thought through them.

Even as he registered the flash of surprise cross her expression, he realized he didn't want to call the words back. Especially not when her surprise faded, replaced by a glimmer of uncertainty.

"I thought..."

Whatever she'd been about to say drifted away as he shifted closer and clasped her hand in his. "Dance with me."

It was more a demand than a question, but for the first time in the length of their acquaintance, she didn't argue with him.

He tugged at her hand, pulled her into the melee of other dancing couples, young and old.

When she faced him in the flickering firelight, something inside him came to life.

Part of Maddie understood that being here—Jason's hands at her waist, grasping hers as the song changed tempo—was foolish. Yet she couldn't seem to tear her gaze away from the intent look in his eyes.

She could lie to herself and say that she'd allowed him to draw her into the dancers to keep him—or anyone else—from noticing when Belle crept to the wagon and grabbed the plate of food Maddie had left for her. She'd intended to sneak away and deliver it to Belle, who'd hidden in the Miller's wagon the entire day. Lord knew Belle needed fattening up. From what Maddie could gather in stilted, quick conversations, the young woman had hidden in one of the wagons as they'd pulled out from the fort, running away from someone chasing her.

Judging by the now-faded bruises at her wrist and low on her neckline, and the way Belle jumped when a loud male voice rang out nearby, Maddie could guess.

Her thoughts of the young woman drifted away like smoke on the wind as the music of a reel swirled around them. Jason spun her out and then tugged her back, catching her in the crook of his arm. She heard Alex's whoop from somewhere nearby and couldn't keep a laugh from escaping.

Jason's eyes glittered, and one corner of his mouth twitched. "Surprised?"

"That you're a fine dancer? Yes." She had to count the steps for the next part of the song, but as they came face to face again, she said, "I imagined you as a medical student, too busy reading textbooks to have any fun."

His smile widened as he shook his head. "I'm afraid the only socials I attended were those my wife dragged me to." A flicker of surprise in his expression.

She worked to keep her face neutral, glad that he could mention Elizabeth in such an affectionate, fond way.

"My mother taught me to dance," he admitted. "I'm afraid I am quite rusty."

"It doesn't show."

He spun her out and back again, but this time the toe of her shoe caught on a rock and she stumbled. He steadied her, both of his hands at her waist. Even so, she landed squarely against his chest.

For a moment, time seemed to slow down. The music

muted, and dancers only a blur of motion as she stared up into Jason's face. She couldn't seem to catch her breath, couldn't seem to look away from his intensity as he watched her face.

They were almost as close as they'd been the morning they'd woke snuggled together. The morning he'd kissed her.

Her stomach swooped low, remembering the tender way he'd held her, the press of his lips.

Recognition flared in his eyes. Was he remembering, too?

I won't open my heart again. The words that had followed so closely after those stolen moments swept through her mind. She blinked, discombobulated.

And then a smattering of applause broke out when the song stopped, and the moment was broken. She stepped back from Jason as Collin's fiddle pulled a new note from its strings. Her gaze dropped, aware of Stella nearby. She had told her sister nothing of Jason's confessions, of the closeness they'd experienced. Stella had been too caught up in her own worries to notice.

But dancing in front of much of the company—confusion swamped Maddie.

Jason's fingers clasped her wrist, the touch searing for one second and then gone. "Take a walk with me?"

She moved out of the flow of dancing bodies, and he followed.

She pressed the back of one hand to her suddenly-hot face. "I should try and settle the children. They're my responsibility."

She knew at once that he'd registered her uncertainty.

"They won't sleep until the music stops," he said quietly. "Shall I ask your sister if she can watch over them for a bit?"

He was giving her a way out. All she had to do was say no.

She should say no.

I won't open my heart again.

But her heart was in her throat, her pulse beating in her ears. And she nodded.

A pleased spark lit his eyes before he strode around the dancers and approached first Paul, and then Stella. She couldn't hear what was said over the music, but Stella's eyes flicked to Maddie and back to Jason before she said something and nodded. Handed him Maddie's shawl from where it sat on an empty crate next to her.

And then Jason was there, wrapping the shawl around Maddie's shoulders with a warm clasp, gesturing that she should precede him between two wagons and out into the darkness.

She hugged the knitted fabric to her with both arms crossed over her middle, glad for something to do with her hands. When Jason fell into step beside her, it was she who put a half-step more distance between them.

What was she doing? Jason was still grieving the wife he'd lost. Maddie didn't want to set herself up for heartbreak.

Maybe he recognized her fear in the darkness, or maybe he felt the same uncertainty. He kept at a slow, meandering pace and didn't push closer.

"Have you always been close with your sisters?" His voice was quiet and calm.

Stella and Lily seemed a safe topic. She let her eyes adjust to the darkness outside the circled wagons, without the flickering firelight. There was no moon above them, only a blanket of stars.

"Growing up, I thought myself a lot closer to Lily than to Stella. But over the past months, Lily and I have grown apart..."

She still hadn't found the courage to confront her sister about the cowboy. And perhaps that was all right, because Maddie was keeping secrets, too. She cared far too much for the man walking beside her.

Since she couldn't talk about her current strained relationship with Lily, she rushed on, "Our mother died when I was small. I don't remember her, only flashes of what I think must be her sitting on the edge of the bed, brushing out her long hair or cooking supper. I do remember Lily being inconsolable. She wasn't much older than Jenny is now."

Maddie hadn't thought about those days after Mum's death in a very long time. Hadn't made the connection of why Jenny's cries seemed to echo a deeper hurt inside Maddie, not until this moment.

"Stella did the best she could, suddenly overwhelmed with chores that a little girl shouldn't have to be in charge of. I did my best to comfort Lily. I can't tell you how many times I sang to her when she didn't want to go to sleep at night. Or how many times I had to eat a spoonful of mashed food to show her that it tasted good before she'd try it."

She shuddered anew at the memory.

He was so quiet. Just listening. Her nerves skittered, and she babbled on. "My father was happier when Lily didn't cry so much. And Stella was happier too."

"Perhaps their happiness shouldn't have been expected of a little girl."

His sudden words jarred the memories she'd looked back on with fondness. Another remembrance surged, one where Maddie had cried herself to sleep silently, so that neither Papa nor Stella would hear.

"Families should help each other," she said with a stubborn lilt of her chin, even though she knew he couldn't see her.

He was only a shadow in the darkness, but she sensed him step closer when they stopped walking. Now they faced each other.

"Why should their happiness be more important than yours?" He towered over her in the darkness, but she wasn't frightened. Only discomfited by the question.

And then he asked, "What about your happiness, Maddie?"

A deeper meaning hid behind the words, something she couldn't face outright.

"Would you have given it up for your fiancé, too?" There was an edge to this one.

Jason pushed too hard, his questions felt too big and unwieldy.

"What are we doing?" she blurted. "Dancing together. Walking alone. What do you want from me?"

The quiet between them went so deep that she couldn't even hear him breathing.

"I don't know what I'm doing," he admitted.

Whatever sluggish hope had been building since he'd demanded his dance shattered.

"What I do know is that you are on my mind every moment of the day."

She might've expected him to sound resentful, but the words were simple and matter-of-fact.

And she didn't know what to do with them.

"You said—you said I was too young for you," she challenged.

"It was an excuse."

She wished she could see his face. Wished she could read

whether or not the chagrin in his voice matched his expression.

"One I was using to try and keep myself from growing close to you. Not that it worked."

Her heart beat wildly, so loudly she felt sure he must be able to hear it in the quiet night air. She reached out. Her fingers brushed his sleeve. She gripped the fabric, needing a way to ground herself.

"I'm afraid," she admitted in a near-whisper. "Of my heart being broken again."

He let her hold on to him, even as his other hand cupped her cheek gently.

A tremble shuddered through her. When he drew her closer, she went into his embrace.

He didn't lift her chin for a kiss, but tucked her head to his chest and simply held her.

Like she was precious.

"I don't want to make you afraid." His arms tightened around her, as if he could make the words real.

* * *

Lily barely registered the music nearby as she focused on the sound of Harry's even breathing. Her left foot had fallen asleep, but she didn't want to move. Not yet.

He was alive. That's what each breath meant, even though the pallor of his face frightened her.

Maddie's assurances had been weak, at best. Was it really normal for someone to sleep so much? Every time Lily came to check on him, he was sleeping.

But then, his wound had been awful.

She would not soon forget the screams from those

walking or riding close to the explosion. The moment she'd realized Harry had been involved, she felt a terrible coldness descend on her, trickling like ice through every inch of her insides.

Only the morning of the explosion had she realized she'd missed her monthly time. And that the nauseated feeling she had every morning wasn't a remnant of the typhoid.

She feared she was carrying his child.

And he didn't even know.

She registered a minute change in his breathing, though he didn't so much as twitch.

"Harry?" she whispered.

He seemed to be holding his breath. Pretending to sleep? Or maybe he hadn't heard her.

"Do you need some water?" A bit louder, after she sent a glance to the doctor dancing with Maddie in the throng of people. "Are you hungry? People are celebrating. We've made it halfway to Oregon. Isn't that exciting?"

Her rambling words trailed off as his fingers on one hand tightened into a fist.

We're going to have a baby. The words were there, trapped in her throat, heart beating like a caged bird.

"Go away," he said quietly. He didn't even turn his head to look at her. Her heart stuttered.

"I need to talk to you." She couldn't stop her voice from trembling.

She could only see the side of his face, the tiny beads of sweat that had popped out at his temple. Not his eyes.

"I got nothin' to say. Leave me be."

Now her heart jammed up her throat, cutting off any speech. Her pulse fluttered wildly. She wanted nothing more than to run away. Humiliation choked her as she imagined the expressions of her sisters when she told them she was pregnant. That there was no husband to be the father poured shame down her spine like burning hot molasses.

She couldn't give up. Not without telling him. Surely he would want to talk to her then.

"When we—were together," she stumbled over the words, "you said you cherished me. Was that a lie?"

She watched a muscle in his jaw tick and experienced a visceral memory of his face pressing against hers, his whispered words telling her how he felt about her.

Had he simply been using her? Had she been so blind, been so utterly enamored with him that she'd made such a terrible mistake?

"Were those words a trick? To get me to share your bedroll?" Her voice broke as she pressed on when he still refused to answer. "Do you—do you want me to tell Mr. Spencer that you seduced me?"

This wasn't how she'd meant the conversation to go. She'd thought the man who had pursued her with such intensity, who had spoken such adoring words, would at least look at her.

She had real feelings for him. She'd given him her heart. Foolishly, it seemed.

"Do what you need to do," he growled. "Jest go away."

She climbed out of the wagon, shaking. The nauseated feeling from this morning overtook her with no warning, and she bent over and emptied her stomach. Would the humiliation never end? She held onto her knees to keep from crumbling to the ground. Stood up with her wrist pressed against her mouth to keep from getting sick again.

She heard movement inside the wagon and turned her back, face flaring with heat and new tears flowing. Stood there like a dolt, not knowing whether she should stay or walk away. Wanting to run into the darkness.

She had to blink tears from her eyes to be able to see the faces in the gathering. There was no sign of Maddie, or the doctor.

She couldn't bear this.

She turned and rushed away from the wagons. Tears blurred her vision, and she fell to her knees just outside the camp, happy for the darkness to hide her emotion and shame.

How could she have made such a terrible mistake? Given herself to a man who held her in such contempt, as Harry seemed to? Why else would he ignore her? Avoid her?

Whatever promises he'd made, whatever whispered endearments he'd said, they had all been lies. A trick so that she would choose to be with him instead of holding to the morals Stella had instilled in her from a young age.

Stella would never forgive her.

Chapter Thirteen

"HAW!" The Millers' two oxen edged closer to where Maddie walked alongside them and then gave the command again, louder.

Perhaps the poor animals were having as much trouble traversing this mountainside as she was.

The mountain itself towered above her, craggy and gray with a sprinkling of snow on its peak. She couldn't look at it for very long without feeling dizzy. Surely the wagon train wouldn't climb to the very top.

Her lungs burned under each labored draw. But when Jenny turned her head from where she was wrapped against Maddie's midsection, Maddie found enough breath to sing quietly. "Twinkle, twinkle little star..."

Her legs burned with each step. The path wasn't much of a path at all, with jutting rocks and an angle that seemed more vertical than horizontal. Maddie was splitting her attention between keeping the oxen following the wagon in front of her and keeping the little girl she held occupied.

Alex and Paul had gone off with Jason this morning,

leaving Maddie to mind the wagon and keep Tommy from bothering Mrs. Duncan's chickens. She'd seen snatches of them as the company wound its way around the side of the mountain. There was something reassuring in knowing that Jason would make sure they were safe even as he watched over Harry, who was still healing.

It'd been two days since Jason had asked her to dance, and it felt as if everything had changed. Jason had become a fixture at her campfire. Not only sharing meals with her and the children, and conversation with Stella, Collin, and Lily, but often helping prepare the meals. There to clean up as Maddie tucked the children into bed.

He hadn't kissed her again. But just last night, he'd sat shoulder-to-shoulder with her after the children had been tucked into their tent. They'd talked until she couldn't keep her eyes open any longer. She'd been fighting off sleep so diligently that she couldn't be sure if the soft touch on the crown of her head had been him pressing a kiss there or not, but soon after he'd chuckled and pulled her to her feet and sent her to bed.

Something had changed with Lily, too. She was withdrawn and quietly angry. Still not speaking to Maddie.

The wagon rolled over a protruding stone, jostling the conveyance badly. A soft noise came from inside.

Belle.

As Jason had been around more, it had become difficult to keep her new friend hidden. Today, with a landscape where woods and brush were sparse and the wagons were spread apart, the safest place to hide Belle was inside the medicine wagon. Maddie had rigged her a spot at the front inside the wagon box, hidden behind two large crates and covered with a woolen blanket. It must be cramped in the small space, but Belle hadn't complained one whit over the past days.

She'd slept a lot. Ate like she was ravenous, like she was afraid the food would disappear right off her plate before she could put it in her mouth. Maddie had never met anyone so jumpy. But Belle had expressed her gratitude for the help nearly every time Maddie came within hearing distance.

Belle was scared. And Maddie hadn't earned her trust to know why. Not yet.

The wagon jostled. Maddie had let her thoughts distract her, and the oxen had veered off course slightly, the wagon tilting an inch or so. The nearest wheel had crept dangerously close to Maddie's feet.

"Haw!" Maddie cried as she was pushed to the side—right toward the drop off where the mountain fell away in a not-insignificant hill. She scrambled for a foothold.

She couldn't fall, not with Jenny strapped to her—

She stumbled. Momentum threw her forward—

She twisted her shoulders, intending to hit hard on her side rather than risk crushing Jenny—

But she didn't hit the ground.

A strong hand caught her beneath the elbow, another beneath her right armpit.

Jason!

Over his breathy grunt she heard the creak of the wagon wheel far too close to pushing them off the side of the mountain. Then the wagon was past, and Jason hauled her to her feet proper.

"Are you all right?" he asked.

She was breathing hard at the near-mishap. He brushed back a hank of hair as they stood face-to-face.

"Thanks to you," she answered.

He quickly tugged her elbow so she and Jenny were pulled away from the edge of the trail. A few long-legged strides put them in line with the oxen. At Jason's sharp whistle, the lead ox got back on the trail.

"That one is a troublemaker."

She was too shaken to do anything other than nod in agreement.

"Are you sure you're all right?" He hadn't let go of her. Still had her hand tucked in the crook of his arm as if they were strolling down the street in a big city. The concern in his eyes made her heart thump hard in reaction.

"I'm fine." She tipped her head forward to peer into Jenny's face. The girl seemed unfazed by what had happened, quiet for the moment.

"I hadn't realized until we got to this narrower part of the trail how ornery he is." She tipped her head toward the ox. "He wants to carve his own path."

The next obstacle on Maddie's side of the path was a two-foot high boulder. Jason let go of her to climb it with one long-legged stride. He turned and offered his hand.

"I heard you singing," he said. "Don't feel you have to stop on my account."

Her hand slipped in to his easily. He pulled her atop the boulder as if she were as light as a feather. Standing close for a moment, his eyes sparked with warmth. He left her breathless when he broke away to walk again.

"I'm sure your musical tastes are far more refined than the nursery rhymes I've been singing," she finally managed to respond to his earlier comment.

"Jenny likes them," he said. "I'm sure I do, too."

She shook her head at his antics. Bit her lip. "I'm sure you've got better things to do than listen to my singing."

His eyes shadowed for a brief second. They were both worried about August. The scout's initial bout of blindness seemed to have resolved, but then he claimed cloudy spots covered most of his field of vision.

Harry had burned off his fever last night. He was still weak, terribly sore from the rudimentary surgery, but Jason believed the infection might be past.

"Hollis called for a halt just ahead," Jason said. "Said everyone will have a few minutes to eat lunch and rest before we carry on. I'll help you find a stable place to park the wagon."

Warmth infused her. Surely he had more important things to do, but he had come to her to help.

"The boys are riding my mare," he said. "I didn't know Paul was so good with horses or I would've offered it sooner."

Neither had she. There was so much she didn't know about the boys yet.

A flat area ahead caught her eye, wide enough for her wagon to stop, not far from the wagon ahead of her. Mr. and Mrs. Pettigrew weren't the kindest couple, and they were awfully nosy. It was so much easier having Jason helping to stop the oxen, secure the wagon for the short break.

Jason had managed to get the stubborn ox to stop going off-trail. In the midst of the noise and bustle, Jenny slipped off to sleep against Maddie in her wrap.

Maddie felt the brush of his intent look and guessed that if the oxen weren't between them, if Jenny wasn't bundled to her he'd have crossed the space and drawn her into his arms.

His lips pursed slightly, like he was hiding a smile. Maybe he'd guessed her thoughts.

He tapped the ox's back and stepped toward the wagon. "I

stowed this morning's biscuits behind the seat. Boy, you've got the canvas battened down—"

Belle.

If he loosed the canvas and lifted the flap, he'd be face to face with the woman Maddie was hiding.

"Wait—"

She hurried around the oxen, one hand at Jenny's back.

But it was too late.

Jason pulled back the cover only slightly and then dropped it and jumped back. One hand went to the gun strapped to his waist.

"Jason—"

"Stay back," he ordered, his left arm held out to stop her approach. "There's someone there."

Rustling sounded from inside the wagon. Was Belle frightened? Maddie could only guess what she might do if she felt cornered.

"Jason, please—"

He didn't even seem to hear her as he rounded the wagon toward the back. She hurried after him, grasped his left arm in both hands as he reached for the canvas flap—at the same moment it flicked back and Belle's frightened, pale face came into view.

* * *

Everything went still.

Jason stared at the young woman clearly cowering in Maddie's wagon. He noticed the purple beneath her sunken eyes—a sign she wasn't sleeping enough. The way her gaze darted left and right—looking for escape.

She didn't find it, not with him blocking the rear of the wagon.

Jenny still asleep in her wrap, Maddie's hands gently tugged Jason's arm, as if she could simply sweep him away and he would forget what he'd seen.

Coals of anger stirred inside him. She was clearly keeping secrets. But the gaunt, frightened young woman in front of him banked the fire inside.

"What is going on?" he demanded of Maddie, though he didn't take his eyes off the young woman.

"Would you put the flap down? Please?" she returned.

Another wagon was rolling in behind Maddie's and the interior of her wagon would be visible within a few moments.

Jason let the flap down. "She armed?"

"No," Maddie said firmly.

He dropped his gun hand to his side. Turned so he was facing Maddie, his shoulder still close to the tailgate. If the woman jumped out of the wagon, he'd take the brunt of her attack, not Maddie.

Maddie's eyes were clear, and he'd seen that determined set of her chin on numerous occasions. "My... uh, friend came to me for treatment several days ago. I doctored her infected cut, and she's been staying with me."

With me. Not with me and the children.

"You're hiding her. Is that what you meant?" He couldn't help the challenge in his words. Had Maddie thought to wonder whether or not this girl posed a threat?

"I offered her a place to stay. A wagon to ride in."

"And the plate of food you were trying to sneak away the other night."

Her eyes flashed at him. Chagrined. Stubborn. Part of

him wanted to shake her. The other part wanted to draw her to him and kiss her.

Her compassionate heart was something to admire. He just didn't want it to put her in harm's way.

"Does this friend have a name?" he demanded.

When Maddie pinched her lips stubbornly closed, he waited. After a long moment, the canvas cover behind them shifted subtly.

"Belle," came the near-whisper.

"I suppose neither one of you notified Hollis that a stranger had joined his wagon train?" If he had to guess, this was the thief who'd stolen small amounts of food from multiple families in the company. Hollis wouldn't be happy to know they had a stowaway.

Maddie shook her head slightly, eyes narrowed dangerously at him. She motioned to her collarbone. *"Bruises,"* she mouthed. And made a circle around her wrist with one hand.

Bruises? Bruises happened under normal working conditions. But at a woman's throat and wrists?

Suspicion bubbled up inside him.

"What are you running from?"

"Jason," Maddie murmured. "She can't—"

"She's frightened enough to hide in your wagon all day long. You deserve to know what—or who—is chasing her."

He saw the words hit. He went on, "You wouldn't want the children in danger, would you?"

Doubt chased through Maddie's expressive eyes before she turned her head and bit her bottom lip.

There was a long pause. And then a sigh so quiet he almost didn't hear it.

"You're right," the girl—Belle—whispered. "I shouldna stayed so close to you, Maddie. I'll leave—"

"I won't hear of it," Maddie said. Her eyes flashed at Jason. She might have blasted him if they weren't trying to keep such a big secret.

He reached out and clasped her hand. She squeezed just to the point where it became painful. He wouldn't apologize for this need to protect her. She mattered.

"I been working at a saloon back at the fort—fer a long time." The words came broken, quiet.

A long silence.

Belle couldn't be more than eighteen or twenty. If she'd worked as a saloon girl for years, she must've been only a teenager when she'd come to the job.

Questions swirled inside him, mirrored by the horror in Maddie's expression. Who had convinced Belle to work there? Had she been forced? Had no other options?

"I saw him—saw someone," her voice trembled, "He killed her. Killed Em'rie. One of the other girls." Now Belle's voice shook like she was on the verge of tears. "I saw him. And I think he saw me. I had to get away—"

"Would no one at the fort help you?" Maddie breathed the question.

No reply.

Jason remembered the men in the fort. Young, most of them. Missing home.

"He's a sergeant," she whispered. "Who'd believe me over him? If'n he found me, I know'd he'd kill me."

"We won't let that happen," Maddie said firmly.

It was his turn to shake his head. "You can't promise that," he murmured.

This time when she squeezed his hand, it felt like determination.

"If he's stationed at the fort, he's meant to stay there,"

Jason said. "At least in the surrounding area." Surely she'd be safe the farther away from the fort they traveled.

"I don't know," came the jagged whisper. "Sometimes the soldiers travel between the forts. Or take long scouting missions."

He jerked his head to the side, asking Maddie to come with him, several steps away from the wagon. Her eyes darted to Belle, but she nodded and moved with him when he tugged her hand.

She was already whispering furiously before he stopped walking. "She jumps at every little thing. Flinches away when I touch her—and she had an infected cut," Maddie explained at his raised eyebrows. "I can't imagine what her life must've been like."

He'd been called to doctor some of the fallen women from saloons back home before he and his family had come west. Seen how they were treated. Compassion stirred. But—

"She could be in danger," he said, voice low. "Or she could be dangerous herself. Most of the women I've met like her— they have questionable morals."

Maddie frowned. "She still needs help."

Her chin jutted up like she was ready to argue with him all over again.

He squeezed her hand this time. "What do you want to do?"

All the fire in her dimmed in the flash of surprise, the beat of relief.

"I want to help her," she said firmly.

He nodded. "All right."

Another brief flare of surprise. Did she think him so callous that he'd leave a young woman alone out in the wilds?

"But you need to tell Hollis what's going on. He deserves to know."

She started to argue.

He held up one hand. "If someone does come after her for what she's seen, he won't want to be surprised. And you can't keep her hidden in a wagon forever."

Maddie wore a mulish look but finally nodded. "Soon."

He leaned forward to brush a kiss to her cheek. "I wish I'd had someone to look after me the way you're looking after her."

She looked up at him with a mix of curiosity and surprise. "What do you mean?"

"I left home at fifteen," he said. The words hadn't come so easily when he'd revealed his past to Elizabeth, but something about Maddie made him want to pour himself out to her. "My father lost control of himself in a drunken rage and I—" He shook his head. "I couldn't stay anymore."

He'd vowed, as he walked away from the only home he'd known, that he would never grow up to lose control like his father did.

"I got a job apprenticing with a blacksmith. I found a room." After several nights curled in a ball on the ground in an alleyway.

Maddie's arm curved around his back as she hugged herself to his side. "I'm sorry."

He dipped his head and rested his jaw against her temple. "For a long time, I thought I should have been stronger. Should have tried harder to convince him to give up the bottle."

"The bottle is an insidious enemy," she whispered. "My father would have periods where he didn't drink at all. Very good days where we felt like a true family again."

He absorbed the hit. She'd hinted at her father's addiction, hadn't she?

She tipped her face up. "You were plenty strong enough. To change things for yourself. You didn't follow in his footsteps."

He stared at the horizon. "I left my ma behind."

"Sometimes things are beyond our control."

Her words clung like a sticky poultice as someone called him away.

The older he'd grown, with distance from his father, he'd seen other men lose their battles with addiction. He hated it. Felt helpless.

But wrestling with *what ifs* didn't change anything.

Chapter Fourteen

JASON WOKE FROM A DEEP SLEEP, heart pounding and sweat pouring down his back. He fought against the bedroll that had somehow become wrapped around him until his arms were free. He sat up, pushing the covering to his waist.

Silence surrounded him, save for soft snoring coming from somewhere nearby. His gaze swung wildly, taking in Maddie's tent and wagon not far away. Leo and Evangeline's on the other side of her. The starry sky above. The way his breath puffed out in front of him.

The fire a few feet away had burned down to coals. The night was chilly, and the sweat cooling on his skin made him shiver.

Or maybe it was the nightmare that had woken him.

It felt so real. If he closed his eyes, he'd be back there. Hear the roar of thunder from the ground beneath him. A far-off cry, quickly muffled. The sense of wrongness, of being carried, bombarded, suffocated by soil and rock. Reaching for Elizabeth. For JJ, for Hildy and Edith.

He wrenched his eyes open when they tried to close and send him back into the nightmare. Or the memory. Tried to steady his breathing when it wanted to saw in and out of his chest.

Elizabeth was gone.

His children were gone.

He was the only piece of his family left.

Something moved in the darkness nearby. A soft shuffling and then an uncertain footstep. Like someone feeling their way in the dark.

He knelt and reached for several sticks to feed into the fire as August approached.

"You all right?" Jason asked in a low voice.

August hesitated a few feet from the fire and made a sound that could've been interpreted as good or bad.

From what he'd told Jason about his vision yesterday evening, the blurriness continued and some spots were completely dark. Like seeing through a cloth blindfold, August had told him yesterday.

"Do you have anything for a headache?" August asked haltingly.

"I can prepare a tea," Jason answered. "Sit for a moment while I make some." He had left his medical bag close, in case of a need like this. He twisted to the other side of his bedroll to open it up.

August shuffled forward and sat a good three feet from the small fire. Likely he could barely feel its heat from there. But Jason had treated many patients over the years and knew the importance of a man's pride. He didn't offer to help August any closer.

He found the coffee pot that had been left out for the morning, gave it a quick rinse with water from a nearby pail, and then filled it and placed it on the fire to heat.

All the while, he marveled that his hands were completely steady. Even with only an hour or two of sleep. Even when weariness swamped him.

How?

He cleared his throat. "How long has the headache been plaguing you?"

August shrugged. The man was known around camp for his quiet nature. He was an excellent scout. He noticed everything. So when he didn't elaborate further on his headache, but asked, "Nightmare?" Jason shouldn't have been surprised.

A rustling came from nearby. Owen slipped out of the wagon he shared with Rachel and little Molly.

August's head turned slightly, as if his ear had picked up the quiet sound.

"Did I make noise?" Jason asked August. It wouldn't be the first time he'd bitten off a cry as he'd woken in the tangled web of the nightmare.

"No," August said. "It was the change in your breathing. Like you were in pain."

In pain. Jason pressed one hand against what should be the open wound in his chest.

Owen came alongside August, rubbing a hand down his sleepy face. "Don't you want to be closer to the fire?" he asked his brother, voice deep with sleep.

August waved off the question.

Owen sat beside August, then cut a look at Jason. "You in pain?"

"Nightmare," Jason muttered.

The fire popped and sparks flew into the sky.

"I thought they would stop—or become less frequent," he

said absently as water bubbled in the pot, "when Maddie and I got closer. That my—" he cleared his throat. "My interest in her meant I was healing from the grief."

What he meant was he fancied her. But even that was such a weak expression of what he truly felt. He was falling hard for her. Every moment together solidified his deepening emotions. He loved her fiery stubbornness, the way she cared for Paul, Alex, and Jenny at the cost of her own sleep, how she listened, the curve of her smile. He wasn't certain he could contain his feelings, not when he wanted to be near her every moment of the day.

August had picked up a twig. He tapped it on the ground, expression thoughtful. "When one of your patients heals from a bad wound—like Harry or someone with a badly broken leg—do you expect it to heal without pain?"

Of course not. The words stalled in his throat as August's meaning became clear. Jason's pain meant he was healing.

Agitation pushed him up off the ground and to the fire, where the tea had boiled long enough. He poured it into a tin mug and brought it to August, tapping his hand before putting the cup in his fingers.

"It's hot," he cautioned.

August kept the mug at his knee, heeding the warning.

Jason felt Owen's intense stare as he sat on his bedroll again. He clasped one knee loosely in his hands and extended his other leg on the ground. Leaned his head back to look up into the vastness of the sky. The stars went a little unfocused as his thoughts spun.

After Elizabeth and the children died, he'd lived in what he thought was an eternity of deserved pain. Thought it should never end. Would never end. But meeting Maddie, being forced to work together, coming to know her... he'd discovered he wasn't dead inside after all.

He'd thought healing had come, but he hadn't considered that healing was often painful.

The fire popped again.

"Did you cause that rockslide?" Owen asked quietly.

They both knew the answer. No.

"As far as I can see, the only thing you're guilty of is surviving."

The words battered Jason on the inside.

"Don't you think I'm too old for her?" he asked.

Owen considered for a long moment. "She's an old soul," he finally said. "Stella said she's been awfully responsible since she was a kid. Do *you* think you're too old for her?"

"Too broken," Doc said into the stillness. He didn't know whether he *could* be healed enough to be a true partner to Maddie.

August suddenly blurted, "The real question is, how can you be with someone if you aren't whole?"

Jason's head snapped up, and he instantly saw that Owen had registered the words the same way Jason had. August had meant more than Jason being broken. His gaze had turned inward.

"You are whole," Owen muttered. "Tell him, Doc. His eyes are gonna heal."

Jason couldn't promise that. He'd told August yesterday when he'd examined him that the vision loss could be permanent. Miracles happened. Perhaps the eyes could still heal themselves. But there was no way of knowing. No guarantee.

"Leave off," August growled at his brother.

"I won't," Owen said, voice rising.

"Hush," August said, and at least Owen seemed to realize

his surroundings, that everyone around was asleep except the three of them.

"I don't accept it," Owen said furiously, quietly. "You aren't going to be blind."

August stayed silent, a muscle in his cheek ticking.

Owen stood over his brother and stared down at him. "You can't give up," he said with a gruff note to his voice.

"It isn't giving up to accept reality," August said.

"I don't accept it," Owen repeated. Then he stalked off into the night. Jason saw him climb back into his wagon, which rocked slightly.

August sipped his tea, silent.

Jason laid back in his bedroll, praying the tea would give August some relief from the pain in his head.

He stared at the night sky, emotions roiling.

Was August right? Could Jason truly be a good partner to Maddie if he carried this guilty burden? But how could he give it up when the guilt was deserved?

He'd lived when he shouldn't have. Lost everyone that mattered to him.

The fire crackled and popped again, but there was no answer for August.

Or for Jason.

* * *

Bark. Bark, bark.

Inside the wagon, a single candle flickered as Maddie lifted the coffeepot lid to check the water she'd boiled a few minutes ago. Still half full.

"Steady," she said quietly to Alex, who had his head

buried underneath a blanket while sitting over a bowl of steaming Jimson weed water.

They'd made slow progress through the mountain pass today. Poor Belle had ridden inside the wagon with the canvas pulled tight. She'd probably been jostled and shaken until her teeth rattled. After the wagons had circled up as darkness fell, Belle slipped into the darkness outside the circle of wagons to stretch her legs.

Shortly after that, Alex's asthma had kicked up. He'd hunched over with hands on his knees, barely able to draw breath.

Maddie had handed Jenny off to Paul and made quick work of boiling water, finding the lobelia, and getting Alex inside the wagon to give him the treatment.

Jason had traveled with them much of the day but had been called away to check on the heavily pregnant Mrs. Johnson in the late afternoon and hadn't been back since.

Bark! Bark! Bark!

"Stop it, Tommy!" Paul's exclamation and the dog's barks were audible, as was the sound of feet scuffling against rocky soil nearby.

A grunt. And Jenny wailed.

Maddie flinched.

She'd come to know the tenor of each of Jenny's cries after these weeks on the trail together. The little one was hungry. Paul must be hungry too.

As she strained her ears, she heard a soft gurgle from Alex's stomach, too.

Maddie was supposed to be cooking supper. But each breath Alex drew underneath the steam-filled blanket was raspy and shallow. He needed her. Supper would have to wait.

One corner of the blanket flipped, as if he'd made an agitated motion with one hand.

"Tommy's gettin' in trouble." Alex's words were muffled beneath the blanket.

She pressed one hand against his back. "He'll be all right until we can join Paul and Jenny."

She felt the next breath that shuddered through him.

"Mrs. Duncan already don't like him."

Oh, Mrs. Duncan hated Tommy. All because he wouldn't leave her chickens alone. If Maddie and the kids had already been settled in a stationary home, she'd have figured out some way to pen the dog when they couldn't watch him. But on the trail, Maddie was in a difficult spot. It seemed dangerous to tie the dog to the wagon while it was moving—what if the animal got caught underneath? They'd tried keeping Tommy inside the wagon with Belle during the day, but he'd simply jumped out.

Alex had been tasked with keeping the dog at his side during evening hours in camp—but tonight had to be an exception, didn't it? The boy was struggling to breathe, even after several minutes of the treatment.

Maddie tried to keep her worry contained. The treatment would work. She herself felt the change in the air as they climbed through the mountain passes. It felt thinner somehow. Alex just needed more of the treatment.

But she still felt torn in two at the sounds of frantic motion outside the wagon, the grunt and scuffling, as if Paul had given chase to the little dog.

Jenny's wail tapered off with a soft sob and then a snuffle.

At least that was a blessing, though she couldn't guess what Paul had done to calm her.

Maddie didn't need their neighbors complaining about a

baby crying. She'd already heard the whispers of gossip spreading through camp. *She ain't capable of keeping up with those kids.*

"Is the scent strong enough?" she asked Alex softly. "Should I add more medicine to the water?"

He took a breath. This one deeper. "The hair inside my nostrils is right burnin' off. I think there's enough medicine."

She tucked a smile into her shoulder. There'd been so many moments with the two boys where she'd realized growing up with two sisters meant a certain lack in her knowledge of child rearing. Raising boys was another animal entirely.

Another deep breath beneath her hand. And another.

The medicine was working. Alex was going to be all right.

Everything had gone quiet outside the wagon. No barking, no scuffling. Was everyone all right?

Her stomach rumbled, giving a reminder that everyone was hungry. Exhaustion slipped over her like a blanket. Wouldn't it be nice to simply eat and slide beneath the covers and sleep?

But there was still the tent to raise for the children, supper to cook and then clean up, and it'd been days since any of the children had had a bath.

"Feeling better?" she asked.

Alex nodded exaggeratedly beneath the blanket, the motion making her smile again at his antics.

"I'm going to step out and start supper." She rustled around in the corner of the wagon until she came up with a small bell. She'd found it among Stella's things in their wagon and appropriated it. Now she nudged it against Alex's knee on the wagon floor. "Ring this if you need me, and I'll be right back."

"All right."

Her knees protested being huddled in the small space as she clambered down from the wagon bed and straightened her spine. How did Belle stay cramped all day long? She slept there at night, too. But every time Maddie saw her long enough to exchange words, Belle was overflowing with gratefulness.

Maddie glimpsed a shadow hovering in the woods nearby and waved. As soon as Alex vacated the wagon, she'd signal Belle to come back. She hadn't meant to involve the children, but Paul had stumbled on a sleeping Belle early one morning, and Maddie had rushed to explain. Now the two boys were proud to be a part of the secret mission of keeping Belle hidden.

Maddie hadn't found time to tell Hollis yet.

Maddie rounded the wagon, mentally preparing herself for a long evening of chores, only to stop short.

Jason crouched over the fire, poking at something in the pot with a long-handled spoon. He held Jenny against his chest and side with his other arm, angling the baby away from the fire. She seemed to be chewing on his shirt or her fist, content for the moment.

A neat stack of firewood stood beside the wagon wheel. The tent canvas had been laid out, though the poles weren't up yet.

Paul was setting tin plates in a neat row on three crates stationed around the fire.

Tommy was lying next to the wagon wheel, gnawing on something. Calm.

Jason glanced up and one corner of his mouth quirked.

If she looked half as flabbergasted as she felt, she must be a sight indeed.

"I—what?" she asked.

"Paul and I thought we'd take care of supper, since you were helping Alex." A simple answer, but the intent look he sent her was anything but simple. Her stomach swooped and shimmied.

"I can see that," she murmured as she joined them. "Thank you."

She reached out her arms for the girl, and he handed Jenny to her.

He tipped his head toward the wagon. "He all right?"

"Breathing easier now. Did you want to check for yourself?"

His eyes warmed. "You're capable."

She wasn't prepared for the joy that spread through her like sun-warmed honey, flooding through every part of her. His quiet praise meant everything. She knew he wouldn't say it if he didn't mean it.

"This pheasant will be cooked through in no time." He stood, and it seemed as if there were sparks swirling between them the same as those that rose from the fire.

They hadn't shared a kiss since that day.

She'd seen his uncertainty in quiet moments, when he thought no one was watching. His gaze often straying to the mountains, the grief that still gripped him.

When he was with her and the children, he kept it hidden. Locked away.

And there was a part of her afraid that if she pushed, he'd snap and walk away.

But now his eyes, intent and purposeful, dipped to her mouth and then back up.

He wanted to kiss her.

And she wanted his kiss.

But when Jenny pounded on Maddie's shoulder and Alex called out, "Dinner ready?" she knew this wasn't the moment.

She took a step away from Jason and caught Paul's pensive look.

She smiled at him, still feeling those sparks swirling inside her. "I wish we'd found some more of those wild potatoes like you found two days ago. Weren't those tasty?"

He shrugged and added a tin fork to the plate in front of him.

"I'm hungry," Paul muttered.

She and Jason exchanged a look.

Alex had opened up to her, though Jenny remained unhappy. And Paul kept his walls up. Maddie didn't know whether to talk to him. Or wait.

Slowly, the noise from other travelers faded as they ate their supper. Alex joined them soon enough. After they finished, Jason played chess with the boys until both could barely keep their eyes open.

As Maddie put a sleepy Jenny to bed, she couldn't help feeling as if they'd become a family.

Chapter Fifteen

"THAT'S THE LAST... ONE."

Jason gently tugged the final catgut stitch from Harry's
wound. The younger man tried to hide his flinch. Jason gave a
few firm prods to the man's stomach. Only a small amount of
remaining tenderness, likely from the infection. But there'd
been no sign of fever in two days. Harry's coloring was good.

The man had rarely spoken over the past few days, though
Jason had caught him sending angst-filled glances in Lily's
direction.

She hadn't been back to check on him since the night of
the dance.

"Been eating?" Jason asked.

"Enough," Harry said with a sideways glance.

Not telling the full truth?

Leo stood over the two of them sitting on a quilt spread
on the ground. Was Harry being evasive because of his boss?

Jason put the small knife back in his medical bag. For a
moment, he stared at his hands on the bag. No shakes.

Even here in the shadow of the rockies, his hands were

steady. Was it because of Maddie? Because he was opening his heart, falling in love again?

Terror streaked through him on the heels of the thought. He shut it down immediately. This wasn't the time.

"When can I sit a horse?" Harry demanded as he buttoned up his shirt.

"We put a lot of stitching on the inside," Jason said carefully. "Sitting a horse isn't the problem. It's the movement. If your animal gets spooked and you get thrown—"

"Getting thrown is always a risk," the cowboy grumbled.

Jason exchanged a glance with Leo, who was watching with a calculating gaze.

Harry straightened his shoulders. Jason glimpsed Lily passing several yards away. She didn't look in their direction, but the cowboy had gone on high alert, his gaze trailing her. When she disappeared without so much as a glance, his lips tightened in a frown.

"I need ta get back to work." This was said with a sideways glance at Leo's boots.

Ah. There was the rub. Harry wouldn't be paid if he wasn't working. Jason knew that most of the men who took such a job needed funds. Many were loners, drifters.

Owen crossed paths with Lily, speaking something that Jason couldn't hear. Then he came toward Leo. Jason nodded to Owen.

Owen had pushed Jason to face his fears. He didn't know what would happen with Maddie. He knew what he hoped for. But first, they had to traverse these treacherous mountains.

A gun fired. The sound wasn't close, probably off in the woods somewhere. Jason knew some of the men had gone early-morning hunting. But he couldn't help the way he responded. A split-second memory of another boom—a different boom, though just as loud—flashed through him. He went hot, and then cold.

The three men nearby stilled. Jason ducked his head over the medical bag and snapped it closed. A moment passed before he felt steady again.

"You look like you've seen a ghost," Leo said quietly. "You all right?"

"Fine." Jason stood, bag clasped loosely in his hands.

"I heard some soldiers talking about a ghost in these parts," Harry said. "Don't know if she comes out during the day."

Leo's brows rose.

"There ain't no such thing as ghosts," Owen scoffed.

Harry struggled to his feet. "These two soldiers seemed pretty certain." His mouth had a stubborn set Jason had come to recognize. "They was sitting around a campfire and jawin' while me 'n the other cowboys was sufferin' from the typhoid."

Curiosity piqued, Jason asked, "What did they say?"

Harry jutted his chin up and mashed his hat on his head. "One of 'em said they'd been tasked to ride to the next fort over the mountains. Deliver some message. They went in pairs. And they wasn't the only ones who saw her."

A sudden cold draft slithered down Jason's spine. "Her?"

"A woman alone—from far off. She was wearing a white dress. Like a bride or somethin'. Howlin' a name. Edith."

Edith?

Everything seemed to disappear around Jason. He could feel his heart beating in the lobes of his ears as a rushing sound filled his hearing.

"Stop," he demanded as the cowboy made to walk off.

"Edith? You're sure it was Edith?" Jason noted Owen's expression of concern.

Harry nodded slowly. "I ain't never gonna forget. The way they told the story sent shivers down my spine."

"Did they try to find her?" Jason demanded. "The woman?"

"Course they did. By the time they approached, callin' out and tryin' not to mess themselves, she was gone. Disappeared. Not so much as a footprint. That's how they knew she was a ghost."

Jason trembled now, couldn't seem to draw a breath. "You said a white dress. Could it have been a nightdress?" Even his voice shook.

Owen took a step closer; Jason couldn't look at his friend, couldn't look away from Harry.

"Whatever you're thinking, it can't be true," Owen said quietly.

Leo shook his head. "I don't understand—"

"Edith," Jason said to Leo. "My daughter. Who else would be calling her name but my wife?" His mind flashed through those who'd traveled with them. His sister-in-law Sally. Theresa, the wagon master's wife who'd had a special place for Edith in her heart.

"It has to be her. It has to be Elizabeth," he whispered.

Harry's face had gone pale.

Leo stood next to him, reached for his shoulder. "There's no such thing as ghosts."

"You're right," Jason swallowed hard. "I think my wife is alive. Somewhere out there."

He gestured to the north, where the company had made the disastrous crossing a year ago. And as he turned his head, he caught a flash of motion.

Maddie, a basket of laundry in her hands. Close enough to hear.

Her eyes wide and distressed.

Jason couldn't look away from Maddie's stricken expression as he heard Owen's aside to Leo. "She's been gone over a year."

Owen's strident words broke the fragile connection with Maddie.

Owen stared at him. "Over a year," he repeated. "She can't still be alive. Not on her own, with no supplies. No shelter."

"Someone is out there," Jason said. The ghost-woman had called for *Edith*. It had to be Elizabeth.

As Leo and Harry walked off, speaking quietly, emotion rushed over him leaving him as tossed and crushed by the rockslide as before.

Memories of searching through the rubble, digging with shovels, with his bare hands. The rockslide had been huge and powerful, thousands of pounds of rock and dirt crushing wagons and bodies alike.

They'd never recovered Elizabeth or Sally or Edith. The earth had claimed the bodies of Jason's loved ones, had given them a burial he'd raged against.

Or so he'd believed.

Maddie came near, but he couldn't bear to look at her. Not until he had no other choice. Then he saw the echo of his own realizations in the depths of her eyes.

He was falling in love with her. If he was any judge of character, she was falling in love with him too.

And if Elizabeth was alive, that meant he was still married.

His heart wasn't free to love Maddie.

Maddie hadn't come close. She clutched the basket to her

middle as if she was holding on to the edge of a cliff. He saw her hands trembling.

If he was breaking apart inside, she must be too.

"You have to go find her," she said quietly.

"Jason—" Owen started.

"She's right." His voice emerged flat and hard as he fought the waves of emotion that threatened to overpower him. He'd only begun to heal from the grief drowning him. "If Elizabeth is out there, alone and terrified—"

Drowning in her own grief? Crying out for his daughter. Maybe crying out for him? Did she think him dead? Did she know that he'd gone on without her?

Did she feel betrayed?

Maddie ducked her head. "We've leftover biscuits and a venison steak from breakfast. I'll wrap it for you. I know you'll want to leave in a hurry."

She was gone before he could call her back. Maybe it was for the best. He saw the hurt she tried valiantly to hide. He wanted to pull her to him, comfort her in his embrace.

Yet how could he, when it would be a betrayal of the vows he'd spoken to Elizabeth?

He'd kissed Maddie. Wasn't that betrayal enough? How could he explain to Elizabeth, beg for forgiveness?

He ran a hand down his face, aware of Owen still standing nearby. Watching everything.

"If you're insisting on going on this fool's mission, I'll ride with you."

Jason shook his head. "Rachel and Molly need you. The company needs you."

Owen's face showed his dilemma. This man had become a dear friend. And perhaps Jason would never see him again.

He couldn't know where he would find Elizabeth or what condition she would be in.

"I need to talk to Harry again," he said. The cowboy might remember details about exactly where Elizabeth had been seen. The Rockies were expansive, but Jason knew where the rockslide had happened. A two-day ride from here, if he used every minute of daylight.

He rode out of camp a half hour later, leaving his heart behind.

Jason was really gone.

Maddie had done her best to distract herself throughout the day as the wagons had fought the difficult incline and rocky terrain.

It hadn't worked.

Now she'd burned the biscuits, and her thumb for good measure.

Dark had fallen. She'd sent the boys to make certain the oxen were picketed. She blinked back tears, but that wasn't anything new.

She'd known he'd leave the moment she'd heard the words uttered from his lips—*Elizabeth alive, lost somewhere in the wilds*. Jason was an honorable man. He wouldn't forsake the marriage vows he'd spoken. Rightly so.

She'd wanted to rage. Wanted to toss down the basket she'd held, the responsibilities binding her, and pound her fists against his chest. Sob and beg him not to go. She hadn't done any of that.

And nothing could stop the waves of guilt and sorrow

that had plagued her every moment since he'd left the company.

She'd fallen in love with a married man.

Oh, she hadn't known. He hadn't known—so how could Maddie? But now her world had turned upside down. The hopes she'd clung to these past days as they'd grown closer and closer shattered into dust.

You're a child. Seán's cruel words battered her. Was she naive to have fallen for Jason in such a short time?

Jenny began wailing from inside the tent, startling Maddie away from where she'd been hovering over the fire holding the pan of burned biscuits. She'd thought the girl was down for the night, having fed her earlier.

She tossed the pan onto the wagon tailgate with a clatter and moved toward the tent. Every step felt as if she were swimming in sludge.

Where were the boys? Shouldn't they be back by now?

She ducked into the tent and hefted a teary Jenny into her arms. "What's wrong, darling?"

The memory of Jason holding the little girl two nights ago, warm and happy, hit her hard.

Jenny wailed louder. Maddie couldn't stem the tears that filled her own eyes. How was she supposed to live with this emptiness inside? With the memory of Jason haunting her?

"Everything all right?" Mrs. MacGuire popped into the campsite. Maddie quickly brushed away her tears with the sleeve of her dress.

"She woke up crying."

"You look exhausted," Mrs. MacGuire said. "Here, let me take her."

Maddie was too tired and heartsick to argue. Or care about the rude comment. She'd become aware of the whispers going around camp at midday. Everyone knew she and Jason had been growing close. And somehow everyone seemed to have learned that he'd left because his wife was rumored to be alive.

She's far too young for him. So naive.

Maddie had received her share of snide looks as they'd made camp tonight. Yet Mrs. MacGuire hadn't been one of the women judging her.

Jenny quieted in the woman's arms immediately. "You poor dear," Mrs. MacGuire crooned.

A moment of quiet. Then shrieks from nearby.

"That menace killed one of my chickens," Mrs. Duncan screeched.

Oh no.

Feet pounded the ground, and Alex and Paul skidded into the campsite, both of them red-faced and panting. Alex held a squirming Tommy in his arms.

"What happened?" Maddie crossed to them as Paul leaned over, hands on his knees, shaking his head.

Mrs. Duncan stormed into camp, looking more angry than Maddie had ever seen her. Her face was mottled red, and her eyes flashed fire.

Maddie put herself between the boys and the irate woman.

"His dog killed my chicken!" Mrs. Duncan shouted, spittle flying from her mouth.

"No, he didn't!" Alex cried.

"I've told you to keep that dog away from my birds, you little cuss!" Mrs. Duncan's volume only seemed to increase.

"There's no need for name calling," Maddie said, her own temper barely contained.

Over Mrs. Duncan's head, Maddie saw Hollis approaching. Several other folks had stopped their work to watch the tableau unfold.

"I shoulda shot that mongrel back at the fort," Mrs. Duncan huffed.

Paul bristled near Maddie's left elbow. "You cain't kill our dog."

Hollis joined them, arms folded over his chest. "What's going on?"

Alex quailed behind Maddie, cowering in her shadow. "Tommy ain't done what she said," he whispered.

Mrs. Duncan was already rambling to Hollis, who listened.

Maddie glanced to Mrs. MacGuire. She held Jenny, who quietly chewed on her fist, wide eyes watching.

"Is that true?" Hollis demanded quietly, his gaze encompassing Maddie and both of the boys.

Mrs. Duncan wouldn't come at Alex or Paul, not while Hollis was watching, so Maddie took a step backwards and came even with Alex. She put one hand on his upper back. "Tell us what happened."

"He didn't touch her chickens," Alex said, his hands waving. "Me 'n Paul was walking back from washing up at the crik, and Tommy was runnin' ahead. I called him back as soon as I saw her chickens was out."

"Did he come right back?" Hollis asked.

Alex ducked his chin. "He barked at them." His chin came up. "But he didn't touch none of them. It ain't his fault one of 'em dropped dead from the fright."

Oh, Alex.

Maybe the dog hadn't touched the chicken, but if it'd scared the chicken and it had died—Mrs. Duncan had a right to be angry.

"We'll make restitution," Maddie said. "Surely we can come to an agreement on an amount—"

"That chicken was laying," Mrs. Duncan snapped. "How are you going to make restitution when my little girls won't have breakfast to eat tomorrow."

Maddie swallowed back the retort that wanted to escape. Mrs. Duncan had ten chickens. Surely some of the others were laying, too.

A tall figure pressed between the bodies watching the unfolding drama and for one moment, Maddie's heart leapt.

Jason!

But of course it wasn't the doctor.

Jason had left.

Mr. Larson shouldered through the ring of spectators, Stella and Collin just behind him. Had someone gone to fetch her sister?

"I want that dog put down," Mrs. Duncan said.

"That girl ain't fit to parent those kids," Mr. Larson interjected. "She's obviously too young to discipline 'em like she needs to."

Maddie felt the words like a blow to her midsection. They stole her breath.

You're a child.

Hollis's expression turned severe. "I didn't invite you to this discussion, Larson."

Mr. Larson didn't quail. "I ain't the only one who should be a part of it." He pointed to Paul. "That one got in a scuffle with my boy a few days ago. Gave him a black eye."

Shocked, Maddie turned to Paul, who looked vaguely guilty. Why hadn't she heard about the encounter? Had it been the same day Alex had had such difficulty breathing?

She'd been anxious when the treatment hadn't seemed to work at first.

"Those two run around camp like hooligans. Knocked down a clothesline and got the clean clothes all dirty. Mrs. Duncan's right that the dog is a menace, too."

"Poor little Jenny needs a mother," Mrs. MacGuire added into the beat of silence following Larson's words.

Maddie's breath stilled. The woman held Jenny, rubbing the girl's back with one hand. "Miss Maddie's too busy to see to the children, especially with the doc gone. And maybe she isn't fit to be their guardian, not after falling for a married man." The last was said in a low voice, for only Maddie to hear.

Each statement felt like a cut slicing through her heart. Was this really what everyone thought of her?

"I—"

Stella stepped through the crowd. Maddie felt one beat of hope. Stella would set everyone straight.

Stella came to stand at Maddie's side, but she didn't look at Hollis. She kept her gaze on Maddie.

"Maybe they're right," she said. "Raising three children is an enormous task. You aren't ready. Look at you. You've run yourself ragged."

Ice sluiced through Maddie's veins. Betrayed by her own sister.

Alex wrapped one arm around Maddie's arm, the dog pressed between them. "They cain't take us away, can they, Miss Maddie?"

"Those boys would be a welcome addition to my family," Mr. Larson said. Maddie knew why he wanted them. Alex and Paul were healthy. Hard workers. Mr. Larson had made no secret of his plans for a prosperous farm, how his own children would till the fields for long hours.

"I promised their mother I would look after them." Maddie's voice quavered.

She caught Paul's glance, his fierce frown.

Hollis sighed as someone shouted his name from somewhere else in camp. "Give me the dog," he said.

"No!" Alex shouted.

"Alex—" Maddie started.

He jerked his elbow when she reached for him, landing a blow to her midsection.

She bent over, pain radiating through her as everyone around them fell silent. She felt their judgment against Alex. Against her.

Hollis stepped close. "Give me the dog," he commanded.

Alex did as he said, then flew to the wagon.

Maddie could hear his quiet sobs as Hollis leveled a gaze on her. "We'll talk in a bit."

Chapter Sixteen

MADDIE RECOGNIZED the slight snuffling that usually preceded a wail from Jenny from where she stood behind the MacGuire's wagon.

The sound went straight to Maddie's heart, still bruised from the interaction this morning, and her eyes filled with tears. She pressed her palm to her mouth and closed her eyes to stem the moisture.

Two shaky breaths, and she forced her eyes open again.

Jenny let out a tiny wail.

Mrs. MacGuire cooed at her.

There was no use standing here choked with tears. Maddie'd left the boys at Stella's campfire with Collin, but she didn't want to be away long. Not with everything so precarious.

She wished Jason were here. But he wasn't, and so she rounded the wagon and forced a smile for Mrs. MacGuire, who looked hesitant to see her.

She held up the small rag doll she'd spent hours sewing

after the children had gone to sleep, straining her eyes by the fireside.

"I forgot to give you this. Sometimes it calms her."

Tension eased out of Mrs. MacGuire's shoulders. Had she thought Maddie was here to cause trouble? It wasn't Mrs. MacGuire's fault that Hollis had asked her to watch after Jenny. Maddie had felt an empty spot where she usually held Jenny as they herded the oxen along today.

When Maddie held out the cloth doll, Jenny reached for Maddie with two chubby arms. Maddie pretended not to notice and gently put the doll in Jenny's hands instead. "Here you are, darling."

Jenny buried her face in the doll, happily chattering nonsense words.

Maddie's smile was slipping, so she quickly said goodbye and left.

Stumbling around the wagon and out of sight, she couldn't seem to breath around the vice squeezing her chest. Was Jenny truly better off with Mrs. MacGuire and her husband? The woman had no children, though she must be in her thirties. She seemed kind enough, looked at Jenny with affection.

Maybe Lily was right. And Hollis. And Mr. Larson.

Maybe Maddie wasn't fit to be a guardian.

Back at camp, Alex and Paul were stacking firewood, uncharacteristically subdued. They'd been so all day, though Maddie had witnessed them whispering fiercely to each other when they'd thought she wasn't watching.

Tommy had remained tied up inside Hollis and Abigail's wagon all day. Hollis hadn't made a final decision about the dog's fate, and Maddie hadn't known how to reassure the boys. If Hollis decided the dog was a menace, Maddie couldn't go against his decision. He was the wagon master. But if Alex lost that dog, he'd be devastated.

She tried to put on a happy expression when Collin and the boys looked up at her approach. Stella rounded the wagon, dabbing her face with a towel. She looked peaked.

"Miss Maddie, can we go to the creek and wash up?" Alex asked the words with almost no inflection.

"We promise to go right there and come back," Paul added. He stood next to Alex and put a hand on his shoulder. He jumped, as if Paul had jabbed him in the side or squeezed him. Maddie couldn't understand it but she was too tired and heartsick to argue.

"We'll be good," Alex said.

"Ten minutes," she warned. "I don't have to tell you what'll happen if you cause trouble tonight, do I?"

Alex's expression shifted, but Paul's seemed to harden. His mouth moved. She didn't hear what he said under his breath to Alex.

"No, ma'am," they both mumbled. They were gone a moment later.

"You shouldn't let them go off alone," Stella said.

The sharpness in her voice reminded Maddie too much of moments from their childhood when Stella had been forced to be father, mother, and sister all in one.

But Maddie wasn't a child anymore. She was old enough to run her own household.

And she just felt tired.

"It won't do them any good to be under lock and key all the time," she said as evenly as she could muster. "They are old enough to take responsibility for themselves—at least in this."

Paul and Alex were good boys. Ornery at times, and liable

to argue with each other. Grieving their parents. But good at heart.

Stella appeared to have more to say, but Collin spoke to her in an aside that Maddie couldn't make out.

Maddie saw Belle slip from the Miller wagon and into the shadows outside camp.

She knew she should start supper for the boys. But all of the hurt and shock she'd felt last night burst out of her. "Why didn't you stand up for me?" she demanded of Stella. "In front of Hollis and the others. You know I've been caring for those children. That we've become a family."

Stella frowned. "You took on that responsibility without asking me or Lily—"

"Because there was no one else to help—"

"There are others now," Stella said with finality. As if Maddie hadn't spent the past weeks learning to love Paul and Alex and Jenny. She felt as if the family they'd formed was being ripped apart.

"They are too much—" Stella started.

But Maddie interrupted, hands flying into the air.

"Were we too much?" she demanded. "Lily and me, when we were barely more than babies? Mrs. Murphy had no responsibility to take us in, but she did. If she hadn't, we'd have had no one."

Collin tried to say something but a storm of anger broiled in Stella's expression.

"Mrs. Murphy was a matron. You're young. You've got an entire life ahead of you. And you're a woman alone."

"I'm not alone. I have you and Lily." Or she thought she had.

Stella shook her head. "I can't help you—not the way I

could've before." Collin looked chagrined when she glanced at him.

"This isn't the way I wanted to tell you, but we're going to have a baby. I've been sick—"

"I know," Maddie said. The words hovered in the sudden silence between the three of them.

Stella's mouth opened and closed.

"You're my sister. I know you better than anyone else. Of course I suspected." She suspected that Lily was hiding a big secret, too, but that information wasn't for this moment.

"I thought you knew me, too." Maybe Maddie had been wrong. She'd thought Stella would understand why she'd made that promise to Mrs. Miller. But the Stella watching her now with a sadness dawning in her expression was something of a stranger to Maddie.

Mr. Duncan stormed into their camp, interrupting any further talk. "Where's that mutt?" he shouted.

Collin edged between the man and Maddie, causing him to pull up short.

"Where is he?" Duncan demanded.

"What—?"

Abigail hustled into camp, her skirts in her hands. "The dog isn't in our wagon," she panted. "He was there just a bit ago, but—"

Foreboding crawled up Maddie's spine. Stella's gaze locked on hers for a moment—but Maddie couldn't bear to see the judgment in her sister's look, so she started off in the direction the boys had gone.

"Alex! Paul!" she called out.

They weren't at the creek. Where had they gone?

It wasn't long before most of the camp had mobilized.

Maddie's heart pounded with fear as her feet carried her

through the entire company, bending to look under wagons, behind crates.

Neither boy answered numerous calls of their names.

"She should never have been given custody of those boys." Mr. Duncan's voice carried from yards away as Maddie ducked into her own campsite.

She brushed tears from her face.

Belle was there, hidden in the shadows. Maddie thought she would've been in the woods, though men walked with lanterns.

"I think I know which way they went."

Jason had grown too used to the noise of Hollis's company. The quiet of being alone in the woods felt too raw. Each muffled thud of his horse's hooves on the leaf-strewn ground reminded him of everything he'd left behind.

He hated himself a little for feeling as if he'd left his heart with Maddie. And Paul, Alex, and Jenny.

Were the children faring well? Was Alex's asthma under control? Had Jenny cried herself to sleep last night?

The silent woods held no answers. Everything around him seemed to be holding its breath. Even the birds were quiet.

He'd traveled all day and well into the night, barely slept on the hard, cold ground, and pushed his horse more miles today. He had begun to recognize some of the rock formations. The stands of aspens in this part of the mountain range seemed familiar.

He passed a small stream and got off the horse long

enough to stretch his back and let the animal drink. He glimpsed something and leaned over to look closer.

That wasn't an animal track—

He squatted to be certain, but he couldn't deny a perfect print of what looked to be a woman's bare heel in the soft mud at the creek bank.

Heart thrumming, feeling torn in two, he took the reins and started out on foot, clucking so that his horse would follow.

He wasn't prepared to round the stand of aspens and see the jagged cut of rock, black and imposing, the hillside of boulders and soil, still stark and treeless. He was still a ways off, but the cliff and rockslide were just as they'd been when he'd ridden away over a year ago.

"Elizabeth!" he shouted. His voice quaked, but he couldn't help it.

How could he have failed so badly? Have missed rescuing her after the disaster?

Anger rolled over him, tinged with grief. And a cascade of memories.

Waking with a terrible pain in his head, legs buried beneath soft soil. Realizing that the avalanche of rocks and soil had swept away his wagon, his family. That he'd somehow been thrown free of the debris.

"Elizabeth?" he cried out to no one. "Hildy! JJ! Edith!"

He screamed until his voice was raw.

Scrambled over rocks and dug until his fingers were scraped and bleeding.

He heard others calling out, voices full of fear and pain. "Doc, we need ya!"

Why couldn't he find his family?

Surely he failed his calling over and over in those hours as he searched fruitlessly.

Then found the broken bodies of JJ and Hildy.

Elizabeth, Edith, Sally were simply gone.

The days following were hazy. Empty in places. He bandaged a broken arm. Waved away others with scrapes and bruises. Spent hours digging, searching. To no avail.

A crack like a branch breaking broke him from the memories. His glance went unerringly to a ridge not far away.

A ghostly figure seemed to float between two trees, a white garment blowing against her legs. Her dark hair flowed long, down her back, lifting like a flag in the wind.

He was too far away to make out her features or any details, but her form seemed so familiar to him.

"Elizabeth." He whispered her name. Until this moment, he hadn't believed it. Not really.

She disappeared behind the ridge before he could get into the saddle. He nudged his mount into a trot, and they climbed the ridge. At its apex, he reined in.

The woman was gone.

"Elizabeth!" he shouted. Surely she couldn't have gone far. Not barefoot on this treacherous terrain.

Questions whirled through his mind. How had she survived? What had happened after the company had left? Would she recognize him?

"Elizabeth!" he called. "Where are you?"

He scanned the area. The ground was covered in fallen leaves, new and old. They would hide any tracks. But this hillside had no ground covering, and the tree trunks were sparse. Where could she have gone?

He noticed a jut in the hillside behind a stand of three trees growing close together. A long, jagged shadow. A cave.

He slipped from the saddle and approached warily.

"It's Jason." His voice broke on the words. "I'm here—I'm finally here."

Still yards away from the cave, he took it in. The blackness disappeared into the earth, a cut almost as tall as he was. If she was in there, what kind of weapon might she have? How frightened was she?

"Elizabeth. Can you—can you come out?"

A shadow moved somewhere inside the darkness. His heart rose into his throat.

More movement, as if she'd taken a step forward.

Sunlight trickled into the space at the mouth of the cave. A dirty bare foot came into view. The tattered and torn hem of what must be a nightdress.

This was no ghost.

Chapter Seventeen

IT WASN'T ELIZABETH.

Jason's entire body shook with emotion as he took in Sally's disheveled appearance.

A bolt of mixed emotions hit him. Relief. Disappointment. Love. Guilt.

"Sally?" he asked, voice rough.

She stared at him, unmoving. Halfway inside the cave, as if she were afraid to come any farther.

"It's Jason."

Still she didn't speak. He left her to her silence as he took in her appearance.

Her nightdress was ripped in several places, the hem completely tattered. It looked to be stained with blood in several places. Her arms bore scratches. There was a scar at her jaw. Her eyes were sunken, skin reddened by the sun, stretched tightly over the bones of her face. Her wrists looked fragile.

"Are you—?" he took a step toward her, but she shrank

back, and he froze. He held his hands up in front of him. "It's all right. I'm here—I'm here to help you."

"J-Jay-son?" The word was fractured, her voice rough from disuse. She coughed.

Tears filled his eyes. "Yes. Jason."

"Edith?" She edged forward slightly, still hesitating in the mouth of the cave.

If she'd been out here in the woods alone for an entire year, she couldn't know what had happened. Had she guessed? How had she become separated from the company? Questions pressed inside him, but he could only shake his head, unable to find words to tell her that the rest of their family was gone.

"I have some food—in my pack."

Her expression took on a feral look that frightened him for a moment. He backed away, moved to his horse while keeping an awareness of her in the mouth of the cave.

He grabbed some hardtack and the last of the biscuits Paul had brought him, Maddie had gifted him.

Shadows angled down, a late afternoon breeze kicked up. Sally watched him warily as he approached. He tried not to crowd her, stayed at arm's length as he handed her the food. She watched his hands with wide-eyed focused attention and then fell on the food, stuffing it into her mouth. Her hands were like claws as she grasped at it.

"It's getting chilly," he murmured.

He had so much to ask her, and of course, he wanted to help in whatever way he could—surely she didn't intend to stay out here. But he needed to attend to the most pressing matters first.

He'd stay here overnight. And a fire would be a must as night fell.

It took some time to gather the twigs and branches enough to keep a fire going. Sally stayed in her cave, licking her fingers and watching him sweep the ground clear of decayed leaves several yards away.

"What happened?" he asked quietly as he arranged the twigs into a small bundle that would light. "How did you come to be alone out here?"

"Trapped." Her raspy voice. From this distance away, he had to strain to hear her. "I woke up. Trapped in a hole. Buried. Dark."

She'd been buried alive.

But she'd survived.

It took a moment for the realization to sink in. She must've been inside an air pocket. A miracle her bones hadn't been crushed to dust beneath the tons of rock that had fallen.

"The company searched for nearly a week," he said. He couldn't look at her as he said the words. The grief was still too raw. "Mostly—" he had to clear his throat. "Mostly we found bodies."

He remembered when they'd found a young girl, dehydrated and with two broken legs. He'd been angry and envious at the same time. As he'd treated her, his hand shook for the first time, he now realized.

"I heard sounds. I screamed."

Jason could've sworn they'd covered every inch of the mountainside in the six days that they'd searched. But there'd been areas where rocks slipped and slid beneath a body's boots, where another rockslide seemed imminent, and the wagon master had ordered them to stop.

Had Sally been trapped in one of those areas?

The fire crackled beneath his hands. He fed in more twigs, aware when she crept out of the cave. She was limping. He watched closely. The way she moved seemed to indicate something broken, perhaps a bone in her foot that hadn't healed correctly.

Oh, how she must've suffered.

"No one came," she whispered. She held her hands out to the flickering flames, and he saw more scars across her palms.

"Did you—dig out?"

She nodded. "Everyone gone."

She must've nearly died of starvation and dehydration if it had taken her that long to escape her prison of rocks and gravel.

"And... after? I heard tell of soldiers traveling this way. There must've been other wagon trains..."

She stared at the fire. Shrugged. "I hid."

Why? Hadn't she wanted to be found? Starving and alone in the wilderness? A snowy winter, where food would be scarce? She had no weapons, at least nothing that he could see...

"May I?" he gestured toward the cave.

She shrugged again, and he took that as permission. It didn't make sense that she would stay in the wild, avoid humans who could've helped her. Had something happened to her mind when she'd been trapped and left behind?

Inside the cave, the last vestiges of afternoon sunlight illuminated a small, blackened fire ring. She'd had heat at some point. A very primitive bow drill lay near one wall. There was a very dirty part of a blanket, a dented pot. Odds and ends. Had she scrounged through the wreckage to find these things? It must've taken weeks. Or months.

Outside the cave again, he watched his horse's tail twitch. The animal blew.

Guilt weighed on him. He should've searched longer.

Convinced the wagon master to stay. Stayed himself. He'd been mired in his own grief and anger at the Almighty. He couldn't have saved Elizabeth or the children, but he might've helped Sally.

"I'm sorry," his voice rough with tears.

She stared into the distance. Coughed. The wet sound of her cough worried him.

"Where is Edith?" she grunted the words.

"Gone," he said quietly. "She's gone. Died in the rockslide."

She stood and stalked off, waving her arms in an agitated manner. "No!" she wailed. "No!"

He watched helplessly, not knowing whether or not she would attack him if he approached and tried to offer comfort.

Edith. That's what the soldiers had heard her say.

"She was—right there." Sally paced back in his direction, eyes wild, expression distraught. "I heard—the loud."

The roar of the rockslide. That's what she meant.

"I tried—to reach for her." She was shaking and wailing now.

And he understood. Sally must've woken in those frantic seconds before anyone had understood what was happening. The children loved her and often fought for the chance to sleep next to her. He hadn't remembered.

And that night, it must've been Edith.

The force of the earth spilling around them must've torn his daughter from Sally's arms.

"I'm sorry," he said. A new wave of grief swept him, an echo of what Sally experienced in this moment. Had she held out hope all this time?

Her cries quieted. She must've known. Surely she must've guessed.

Grief was a strange affliction.

A long time passed, the two of them staring at the fire, her coughing occasionally. Night fell around them, but he didn't get his bedroll. He'd offer it to her anyway.

He cleared his throat when the fire burned low. "There's a caravan traveling a few days ahead. To Oregon."

For the first time, thoughts of Maddie intruded. The beat of relief he'd felt earlier echoed inside him again.

Sally was alive. Elizabeth was gone.

He wasn't married. Hadn't betrayed his vows.

He could go back. Try to win Maddie's heart.

"We can leave in the morning," he said. "Join the company."

"No!" A bout of coughing that rattled her entire body followed her sudden outburst. She backed away from the fire. "No, no no! Won't leave Edith."

"She's not here." He stared at Sally, who was breathing hard and looked wild eyed in the near-dark, the flickering fire illuminating her skinny frame. Half-starved.

And she wanted to stay.

"Edith. I should've saved Edith."

Will you ever forgive yourself? The question Maddie had asked him all those days ago echoed inside him.

He'd done the same as Sally was now, hadn't he? Believed that if he'd only been stronger, if he'd woken sooner, if he'd pushed to camp somewhere else...

Believed that if he'd been in control, everything would've been different.

Believed he'd failed his family.

Sally wanted to stay isolated. Dying slowly.

Jason had thrown himself into his work. Going without

sleep, without adequate food, punished himself. Dying on the inside.

Look at all you've done.

He had worked. But he hadn't lived.

He would never know why God allowed the rockslide to take so many lives. Would never be free of the grief of loving and losing his family. But what had happened wasn't about Jason's strength. Or lack thereof.

My strength is made perfect in weakness. Words from a Scripture Jason had read long ago and tried to forget slipped from his heart into his mind.

Jason hadn't wanted to love Maddie. Had done everything he could to avoid her. And it hadn't mattered. God put her in Jason's path anyway. Had used her to bring his heart back to life.

Elizabeth was gone. There would be moments when Jason found himself drowning in that grief. But he'd been given a second chance at love.

He'd broken Maddie's heart when he'd left. He knew it. Felt the same brokenness in his own. But now that he'd found the truth, found Sally, God was showing him the freedom waiting for him.

His heart was free to love again.

But first he had to help Sally.

* * *

Dawn was breaking as Maddie and Belle picked their way through the woods. Helplessness swamped her. She'd acted impulsively, following Belle into the woods at dark. She'd hoped to find the boys within ten minutes and then everything would magically go back to normal in camp.

Maddie stumbled over a protruding tree root, barely catching her balance before she fell to her hands and knees. She stood for a moment in the near-darkness, listening to her own ragged breaths. Belle was a silent shadow several feet away.

"All right?" Belle murmured.

Maddie didn't answer, only trudged forward.

Instead of a triumphant return to camp, Maddie and Belle had searched in the woods for most of the night. At first, there'd been far-off lanterns, distant shouts that let her know that others from the company were searching, too. She'd been so quick to leave camp, to prove herself, that she hadn't thought to bring a lantern. Or a compass.

By the darkest hours of night, she and Belle were hopelessly lost. Far out of range of lanterns and shouts.

And they hadn't found the boys.

When yesterday morning had dawned, she'd still held onto a kernel of hope. But they'd hiked a dozen miles yesterday, hollering for the boys. Hollering for help. Up and down this side of the mountain. She'd kept her bearings, at least.

Or thought she had.

Hunger pangs hit late yesterday afternoon, and then night fell and her legs refused to go another step... and they had no fire, no bedroll.

And no tracker working in the company anymore. August was blind. He couldn't find her and Belle. Or the boys.

Something rustled nearby. Belle startled, causing Maddie's heart to pound in her chest. But she kept walking.

"This is all my fault," she muttered to herself. This time she was careful to step over a big tree root poking up out of the ground, more and more clear as the sun came up over the quiet woods.

"What'd you say?" Belle asked.

If there was one good thing about this ordeal, it was this young woman. They'd become friends over the past thirty-six hours of searching and suffering together.

"I said, this is my fault." Maddie waved one hand as she spoke. "All of it."

Belle was bright, though she'd admitted she had no schooling to speak of. She noticed things like the path of broken branches along a creek bed they'd followed for a good while yesterday. To Maddie's untrained eye, it looked like a boy with a stick had whacked off branch after branch.

But then that trail had stopped.

Belle loved to talk, but there was a shyness about her, too. She was one of the most curious people Maddie had ever met. Examining a leaf in wonder at its shape. Watching a flock of sparrows take flight or the high, small clouds scuttle across the sky.

Like she was experiencing these things for the first time.

Maddie hadn't scrounged up the courage to ask why she seemed so enthralled with the outdoors or how she'd come to work at the saloon. And now she'd managed to get her new friend—possibly her only friend in the world, including her sisters—hopelessly lost.

If they couldn't find the company today, their lives would be in terrible danger.

"I shouldn't have made that promise to Mrs. Miller," she said now. Shame coated her words. "Why did I think I could become an instant mother?" She thought of all the things she'd done wrong, culminating in this terrifying ordeal. "I'm not fit for it."

"That ain't true." The fierceness in Belle's voice threw Maddie off balance, and she had to steady her steps.

"I been watching and listening for weeks. Longer'n that, if you count when I was sneakin' around camp. I seen you with those kids every day. Sitting with your arm around Alex. Singing to Jenny with a smile on your face. Praising Paul for his hard work."

Belle's words created a burst of warmth inside Maddie, though she was surprised that Belle hadn't mentioned the hours of actual caretaking for the children.

These were the moments that Belle noticed?

They splashed through a small creek, the shock of cold water a reminder of the night they'd passed huddled together on the cold ground, trying to sleep.

Had Alex and Paul done the same out in the darkness somewhere? Two boys alone couldn't survive in this wilderness. What if she couldn't find them?

A sob took Maddie by surprise, emotion overwhelming her at last. She stopped walking, aware of Belle hovering nearby. She covered her face with her hands, unable to stem the flow of tears.

"I thought I could be what the boys needed. Jenny, too." Her words emerged muffled through her hands. "I thought I could be there when my sisters expected it, too, keep up with all those tasks—"

But everything had fallen apart.

"That's dumb."

Belle's firm statement surprised Maddie into a beat of silence. She wiped away the tears on her cheeks, brows crinkling as she looked at her friend.

Belle stood with hands on her hips, looking somehow both fierce and uncertain. "I seen a lot of men."

Seen. Oh.

"All of them—every one—thought my worth was in my body. In my actions." She glanced away, as if afraid of finding judgment in Maddie's expression.

"But I don't believe it," Belle said fiercely. A single tear slipped down her cheek. She whisked it away with her sleeve.

"The Bible says that God 'knit you together in your mother's womb.'" The Scripture burst from Maddie's lips before she'd consciously thought of it. "God created you. He loves you."

She'd meant the words for Belle, who looked shocked and then ducked her head, frowning.

But the words sank into Maddie's heart anew.

You knit me together in my mother's womb.

She'd let Seán tell her she wasn't worthy of his love. Believed him. Before that, she'd found her worth in the praise from her father, from Stella, when Maddie worked at chores or kept their home peaceful and quiet.

She'd lost herself somewhere. Forgotten that God always found her worthy. Worthy enough to send his Son to earth to die.

It didn't matter that Seán didn't love her. That Stella was unhappy with her. Lily, too. Maddie might be imperfect, but she was a child of God. A beloved daughter.

The knowledge filled her with a steady light. A peace she had never known.

She couldn't know what would happen with the boys, whether they'd be found. Whether they'd be taken away from her. Whether she'd lose Jenny.

She did know now that no one could take away her identity. And there was peace in that knowing.

She wanted to shout it to the treetops and the mountain

towering over them, needed to share it with Belle—but when she glanced at her friend, Belle was staring into the distance with her head cocked.

"Do ya hear that?" Belle whispered.

Suddenly alert, Maddie strained her ears, held her breath. Only heard the whisper of the wind in the leaves overhead.

But Belle's brows came together. "Voices," she murmured when Maddie sent her a questioning glance. "I think it's the boys."

Fierce hope lit in Maddie's chest. She glanced around at the vast woods. "Which way?"

Belle was still listening. When her feet carried her to the south—at least Maddie thought it was south—Maddie followed.

A hundred yards on, she heard a dog barking.

Tommy!

The faintest sounds of boys shouting.

Her heart picked up speed. They'd found them!

But then the tenor of the boys' voices registered. They sounded terrified.

Something was wrong.

Chapter Eighteen

JASON RODE through the early-morning stillness. He knew they were hours away from Hollis's company, maybe even another day behind, if he pushed his mount for a fast clip. But he remained alert for the first signs of camp life. A horse blowing. The scent of woodsmoke on the breeze.

Sally stirred where she barely leaned against his back. She was so light that he could almost forget she was there. She certainly hadn't added any weight to bother his horse. He'd pushed on through the night, only stopping for a short rest. Sally had dozed off and on. Sometimes when she woke, she startled. But the longer they'd been together, the more cognizant of her surroundings she became, though she remained quiet and alert.

His heart filled with the anticipation of seeing Maddie and the kids again. He didn't know if he could wait for a moment alone with Maddie to tell her all he'd realized. But there was also a heaviness in his spirit. He hadn't been able to find words to explain to Sally his relationship with Maddie.

Sally seemed so fragile. It had been everything he could do

to get her to agree to come with him. He'd begged, cajoled, explained that she wouldn't survive another winter alone in the wilds. It was a miracle she'd survived once.

He'd plied her with medicine for the cough, and it already seemed better after only eighteen hours.

He had to find a way to show Maddie how much she meant to him and yet be sensitive to Sally's needs. She had been Elizabeth's family. She was his responsibility now, until she was back on her feet. Or forever, if need be.

His horse sidestepped, shying away from—

Bear scat.

It took only a glance to recognize the lumpy, berry-filled mess for what it was.

Sally grunted as Jason readjusted in the saddle. If he'd been alert to his surroundings before, he was doubly so now.

Then he heard shouts in the distance.

It couldn't be Hollis's company. They were still too far from the trail Hollis had been following.

A sense of foreboding crept down his spine as he wheeled his horse toward the noise. They'd only gone a few paces when he made out a far-off roar.

For one second, he was pushed back into the memory of that night with Maddie, before he'd even known her for the woman she was. A noise in the dark, a handful of terrified moments. Feeling the protective urge he'd tried to deny but somehow couldn't.

Bear.

"I'm going to let you down."

Sally didn't protest, but her eyes were wide and fearful as he linked his arm through hers and gently lowered her from the horse's back.

"Take this." He pressed his revolver into her hand. "There are six shots. I'm going to see if I can help. I'll come back."

His words seemed to reassure her even as she shrank back against a wide pine trunk. He couldn't wait. Not if someone was in trouble.

He kicked his horse into a gallop with only one look over his shoulder to ensure Sally was all right. She hadn't moved an inch.

Racing through the woods, he heard barking. It sounded like Tommy's distinctive bark, but it couldn't be. Hollis wouldn't have come this far south.

Yet the shout that followed the barks sounded an awfully lot like Alex.

Another unhappy roar blasted through the woods. Jason barely breathed as his horse crested a ridge and a little valley unfolded before him. He reined in, taking everything in at a glance as time seemed to stop.

Tommy, barking and growling, dancing and backing away in front of two bear cubs easily three times his size.

And Alex. And Paul.

What were they doing so far from camp?

The thought froze and disappeared as he registered Alex's screams for Tommy, who was blatantly ignoring his calls, while Paul was trying to pull his brother away.

Because a big black bear was barreling down the opposite hillside toward them.

He hadn't formed a thought before he realized the blur of motion coming from another angle was Maddie. And Belle at her side, both of them wearing identical terrified and determined expressions.

His thoughts crystallized.

If only he'd pushed his horse at a faster pace.

If only he'd never left the company.

If he'd—

The old voices disappeared in a quick, steady beat of warmth that pulsed through him.

He couldn't control this. He might lose all of them.

But he would choose to trust God. And to fight.

He kicked his horse once more and flew down the hillside. Saw everything unfold all at once.

Maddie pushed Belle so that she wheeled off toward the boys.

Alex had gotten close enough to grab Tommy, but now the boy was frozen in fear.

Maddie ran at a breakneck speed toward a line between the bear and boys. She was holding something—a stick?

He was too far away.

Leaning low over his horse's neck, he reached for his rifle in its scabbard attached to the saddle. He didn't dare aim it toward the bear—it was already too close to Maddie and a wild shot could kill her. He pointed the barrel into the sky and fired.

His horse flinched, skin flicking, but the animal kept going.

So did the bear. It was as if the sow hadn't even heard the shot.

It was bearing down on Maddie.

"No!" The cry was ripped from his lips.

He was still a dozen yards away when Maddie drew up, directly in the bear's path, and swung the massive branch like a club.

It hit the bear in the snout even as the animal reached out a paw with claws spread wide, swiping right at her. The sow turned her face away after Maddie's hit connected.

But as Maddie spun away, he saw a flash of red. Blood. She went to the ground.

A shout from one of the boys, who'd run with Belle a good distance away.

The bear reared up on its back legs, Maddie tried to scrabble away on her backside.

Then Jason was close enough to ride between Maddie and the bear. He fired a shot even as his horse reared in fear, whinnying loudly.

Fired again.

The bear roared.

* * *

Everything happened too fast.

Maddie threw herself between the bear and the boys, swung her club with all her might.

She heard a man's shout as the branch connected. For one moment, even though it was impossible, her heart heard Jason's voice.

She thought she'd gotten lucky when the bear's momentum was stalled—but a slicing paw came at her. She turned, trying to evade it, but the glancing blow sent a knifing pain through her shoulder and spun her willy-nilly.

She couldn't find her feet, ended up on the ground, scrambled for purchase—

A horse thundered in. Two gunshots.

The horse reared and whinnied, but all she could see was its rider.

Jason.

The sow made a different sound than the roaring Maddie had heard before. This was more like a call. She quickly ran around Jason's still-dancing horse. Her cubs joined her and they disappeared into the deeper woods.

It was over.

Maddie was trembling all over and could barely find her feet. Her upper back and shoulder pained with every movement. Where were the boys? Belle?

She registered their shouts from nearby, but she couldn't tear her eyes from Jason as he edged his horse nearer, reaching out for her from the saddle.

He swept her off her feet, the strength of his arms pulling her off the ground and across his lap in the saddle. His warmth and scent enveloped her as his hands briefly cupped her jaw, then dropped so his fingers touched both sides of her neck, so, so gently.

"Are you—?" He was cupping her shoulders, and she must've winced when he touched her right one. His fingers came away sticky with blood.

"It's not bad," she mumbled as he leaned awkwardly in the saddle, gently twisting her so he could look at it.

"It'll need stitches for sure. Look how the claw sliced you—"

"Not into the muscle."

He settled her again so he could see into her face, his mouth pulling at her soft argument.

Oh.

She could let herself fall into the intensity of his stare, the emotion swimming in his eyes. But she came to herself and tried to stifle the pounding heartbeats. Cast her eyes away from his face to search the woods around them.

Was Elizabeth nearby? Had he found her?

"Here come the boys," Jason murmured as rushed footsteps approached.

"Aunt Maddie!" Her heart pulled at the nickname from Alex's lips, spoken without forethought.

"Is she okay?" Paul asked. "She's bleedin'!"

The boys finally came into sight, Belle right behind them.

Maddie did her best to find a reassuring smile. "I'm all right."

The words sank in. She'd survived. Belle and the boys were all right.

Jason's hand flexed at her waist. Had he had a similar moment of realization? Things could've been so much worse. Would've been if he hadn't arrived just in time.

"She needs stitches," Jason repeated. "A bandage will do until we can make it back to camp, but let's move away from here quickly."

The boys agreed in murmurs. Jason started his horse at a walk and indicated they should follow. The horse's movement jostled Maddie's shoulder against Jason's chest, his arm still around her waist. It was too much for her aching heart.

"I can walk," Maddie said, voice choked slightly.

The boys were chattering from behind, their voices high and animated after their narrow escape.

"I can't bear to let you go." Jason's voice rumbled low. It took a moment for his words to register even as his arm tightened around her.

Tears filled her eyes. It wasn't right, not with Elizabeth somewhere out there...

"Jason, I can't—" She gasped the words, trying to lean away from his embrace. Knowing that he still cared about her broke her heart all over again.

She couldn't help seeing the awareness dawn on his face before she averted her gaze.

"Maddie, look at me."

She couldn't. But neither could she deny her base nature, because her eyes wanted to take him in from up close. Just once more.

He looked so serious.

"I was coming back to the company to tell you—It wasn't Elizabeth I found out there."

Not...Elizabeth?

He glanced over his shoulder. The boys' voices had grown quieter as Jason's horse outpaced them slightly, but Maddie could still hear them.

"I did find the ghost—the woman who'd been left behind. Elizabeth's sister Sally." He shook his head slightly. "She's severely malnourished. I don't even know how she survived. I barely convinced her to return with me. She's in the woods, just over that rise. I don't want to leave her for long."

He hadn't found Elizabeth alive.

He wasn't married.

He watched her face closely. Didn't seem to try to hide the sorrow in his eyes or his voice when he said, "She's gone."

He reined in, a muscle ticking in his jaw.

Oh, Jason.

Her eyes filled with tears. She knew how deep his grief ran. Had hoped, for his sake, that he would find a miracle.

"Maddie, I—"

The sound of running feet interrupted him. He let out a long breath through his nose, but a half-smile pulled at his lips. "They'll want to see for themselves that you're all right."

He let her down from the horse as gently as possible, but she still couldn't hold back a wince as her feet hit the ground. He was throwing his leg over the saddle to dismount when Alex flung himself at Maddie.

She caught him in a hug, unable to hide the indrawn breath that had Jason cautioning, "Easy."

But Alex had his face buried in her shoulder.

Tommy danced around their feet, barking.

"Hush," Jason ordered the dog. "Lie down." By some miracle, Tommy laid down in the leaves, panting.

Belle hung back a few feet, eyes watching the entire interaction. Jason approached her, and Maddie heard him explaining about Sally, asking Belle if she would go and fetch his sister-in-law while he bandaged Maddie. Belle left moments later.

"I thought you was a goner," Alex mumbled into her shoulder.

Paul hung back a step, looking half-afraid and half-shamed. "Why'd you do that?" he asked hesitantly. "Run toward the bear?"

Ever since his mother's death, Paul had rebuffed Maddie's comforting touches, but something in his expression or the set of his shoulders gave her the courage to lift her good arm from around Alex and extend it toward him.

Paul's face crumpled as he stepped forward, allowing her to tug him into the embrace, her arms full of two boys. She didn't even care about the pain in her shoulder. Barely felt it.

"I'll always come for you," she said, dipping her head to press her face briefly into Paul's hair.

When she raised her head, her gaze connected with Jason's. He hadn't made any declarations, but there was a new steadiness in the depth of his eyes, a warmth as he took in her and the boys.

After a few moments of reassurance, allowing the boys to catch their breath and all of them to realize they were alive and—mostly—unharmed, Jason said, "Let me bandage that wound."

The boys stepped back. Maddie didn't miss the quick swipe of Paul's sleeve beneath his eyes.

"Sit down," Jason said.

And since her legs still hadn't stopped shaking, she complied.

He knelt on the ground behind her. "I'm sorry about this."

There was a quick tearing sound before her sleeve came away from the bodice of her dress. Cool air slid across her skin and made her shiver.

"What are you lot doing so far from camp?" Jason asked. "And why hasn't Hollis pushed on farther?"

She flinched at the first cold bite of antiseptic. And was glad that, for this moment, she couldn't see Jason's face where he worked behind her.

Alex scuffed the toe of one boot across the ground. "They was gonna kill Tommy," he mumbled without looking up.

Jason's hands went still, his grip resting on her shoulder. "What?"

Paul looked extremely guilty as he spilled all of it. The blow up in camp. Threats that Jenny and the boys be separated. Their decision to take Tommy and run away.

Jason went back to tending Maddie's wound, quickly fashioning a bandage that wrapped beneath her armpit and around her neck. Each brush of his fingertips sent goosebumps scattering down her neck. But when he helped her up with a hand beneath her arm, she saw his thunderous frown.

"We shouldn'a run off," Alex said when Paul's words ran out.

But Paul was still tearful. He wouldn't quite meet Maddie's gaze. There was something else.

His chin jutted out. "Ma made me promise to take care o' Jenny. Cuz she's so little. But I—I wanted to run away. I cain't do it. Not without you."

She left Jason's side to embrace the boy again. He cried almost silently, as if shamed to have said the words.

"That's a big promise for a boy," she said as his cries died out. Jason had put a hand on Alex's shoulder. "Watching out for her doesn't mean you have to care for her every hour of the day. That's a mother's job. Not a brother's."

Her gaze met Jason's again. Echoes of what he'd said to her as she'd explained away the duties of her childhood passed between them.

"God brought us together to be a family," Maddie said firmly. "I know it. In my heart." Including Jason. Whether he was ready for that, she didn't know. But she would wait, if needed. "And I'm not going to let Hollis, or Mr. Larson, or Mrs. MacGuire or anybody separate us."

Paul lifted his head, eyes shining with hope. "Really?"

"Really."

Alex let out a whoop. Tommy jumped to his feet.

"Here comes Belle. And someone else," Alex said.

Belle and what must be Sally were still a hundred yards away, traversing carefully down the incline. Maddie gave Paul one more squeeze and then let both boys run off to meet them.

Jason tucked a glass bottle into his bag and straightened to his full height.

She was opening her mouth to tell him everything she'd realized, everything she felt, when he strode to her and took her waist in his hands.

"When I left," he began gravely, "my heart broke because it belongs to you."

Her own heart leaped in response to the beautiful words.

"Once, I thought I would never be able to love again. You've taught me otherwise. I love you."

Tears quickly filled her eyes and overflowed. "Jason, I love you, too."

He chuckled as he thumbed away her tears. This man who'd been unable to crack a smile when she'd met him was laughing. Maybe this day was meant for miracles.

And then he dipped his head to kiss her, and she met him with a fervor that the moment deserved—until the motion of throwing her arms around his neck pulled at her wound. She winced.

"Easy," he whispered against her lips, his own forming a smile. "We'll have the rest of our lives together. If you'll have me."

She let her kiss be her answer.

Far off whoops of joy cut their embrace short. And when Jason explained that he'd need some time to sort things out with Sally, she took the memory of his kiss into her heart where she'd keep it until things could be settled.

Jason had come back.

He loved her.

He wanted a life together.

Chapter Nineteen

"HEY! DON'T SPLASH!"

Jason glanced up from the creek bank where he was cleaning a mess of fish that he and Paul and Alex had caught over the past hour. The two boys had begged to keep fishing with lines tied on long, straight sticks while Jason had started to do what was needed for their supper tonight.

But Paul was retaliating when Alex didn't stop splashing, shoveling water with his hands toward his brother, pole forgotten on the bank. Which would get them even more wet.

Downstream several yards, where the water hit a wider place and was only two or three inches deep, Maddie stood barefoot, her skirt tucked up, holding both of Jenny's hands in hers as the tot stomped in the water and giggled.

Maddie glanced up. Their gazes connected. A wave of love and warmth washed over him. He didn't shy away from the pulse of grief, of missing Elizabeth, Hildy, JJ, Edith. It was all part of him. The good and the bad. The loving and the sorrow.

She cut her eyes down and back up, a silent order from

afar for him to pay attention to what he was doing. Smart thinking. He didn't want to nick a finger with this sharp knife.

He let his mind wander to the events of the past weeks as he finished cleaning the last two fish. When they'd rejoined the wagon train, Hollis and everyone else had been worried sick about Maddie and the boys. No one knew about Belle, so they hadn't known to worry about her, too.

Jason and Maddie had asked for a private audience with the wagon master and had a long talk about the children. About the promise Maddie made to their mother. About Jason's intention to marry her as soon as he spoke to Stella and Lily.

Hollis had seemed relieved that Jason was back, and that he would be part of the new family. He hinted that he'd wanted the children with Maddie, but Jason's return would make it easier for the other pioneers to accept.

Maddie had bristled but kept quiet. She'd gotten what she wanted—and he'd told her frequently how much he loved her for standing up for the children. She'd cried when she'd reunited with Jenny, and the girl had clearly called her "Mamie." Jason figured it was a mix of "Mam" and "Maddie."

There'd been a discussion a few nights later, after the wedding celebration with the entire company, about what Maddie and Jason should be called. Paul and Alex couldn't quite come to call them Ma and Pa. And that was all right. The boys settled on Uncle and Aunt. And if Jenny's "Mamie" changed to "Mama" as she grew older, there'd be more discussion to reassure Paul and Alex that their parents wouldn't be forgotten. In fact, Maddie brought them up in conversation almost every day.

Sally had settled uneasily into their family unit. She rode

in the front seat of the wagon most days—Belle remained inside—staring at the horizon. She didn't speak often, seemed to have trouble with the noise and busyness of camp when the wagons had circled up. She'd gained a little weight, but Jason didn't know how to reach inside her, to speak to the part of her that seemed broken.

But Maddie had simply accepted her as part of them. She spoke to her gently and didn't seem to care if Sally didn't respond. Last night, Sally had even reached out and gripped Maddie's hand as she'd been serving supper. A quick squeeze, the first sign of life from Sally. Of course it had been Maddie who'd brought it forth.

Jason still woke up from nightmarish memories. He had just last night, holding back a scream trapped in his throat. There'd been a fractured moment where he hadn't remembered where he was—and then Maddie, somehow sensing his distress, though she hadn't woken completely, rolled toward him in the darkness inside their tent and buried her face in his chest. His arms came around her of their own accord, and when he'd matched his breathing to hers, he'd been able to drowse until he finally fell back asleep.

When he'd been quiet over breakfast, she'd simply clasped his hand. Knowing he was deep in grief, willing to be there with him.

His love for her had grown by leaps and bounds in the week they'd been married.

The one dark cloud was Lily. She'd withdrawn from both of her sisters. Her distance hurt Maddie, and he wished there was a way he could help.

"You almost got a hook in my eye!" Paul complained.

"Boys!" Maddie's quick admonition settled them down in a pinch. He shared a smile with her.

After he finished up and they collected all their belongings and started back to camp. The boys ran ahead, Tommy hanging back with Jason. The dog—and the boys—had received a stern warning. One more mishap, one more dead chicken, and the dog would be put down. Jason had started liking the little dog and had worked for several days to keep him close.

Keeping one eye on the boys, Jason let his free hand—the one not holding the fishing rods and tackle—touch Maddie's back. She was carrying Jenny.

"Shoulder all right?"

She sent him a sideways crooked smile. "It's healed up, remember?"

The wound had been shallow and, thankfully, there had been no sign of infection. But he could still worry over her if he liked.

He was leaning in to steal a kiss, a quick brush of his lips against hers before they arrived back in camp and he would be forced to wait hours and hours until everyone was abed to kiss her again, when Jenny piped "Mamie!"

In a fraction of a second, Maddie's eyes filled with tears. She laughed as she wiped them away. "Sorry. So childish."

Not for the first time, he wanted to kick the fiancé who had made her feel that way. And then also thank the man for breaking her heart and sending her away.

He held her stare until she could read how very serious he was. "I was a dunce to make you feel unworthy—even for a second. I love every part of you. Even the sentimental ones."

New tears filled her eyes, and he offered her his hanky, overflowing with love of his own.

Like Job in the Bible, Jason had lost everything. He would

never forget his first family, never stop grieving. But his house and his heart had been filled with joy again.

Maddie was joy. As were the boys. Jenny. Even the dog.

He'd never stop giving thanks.

* * *

Maddie woke to the sound of Jason's low voice outside the tent. It was late. Not many in camp were stirring.

She was drowsing, about to slip back into sleep when a thought struck that wouldn't allow for more rest. Though every muscle in her body protested, she forced herself up and out of the warm bedroll, pushed past the canvas flap and out into the chilly night.

Jason was there by the dying fire, but she was surprised to find Paul at his side, both of them tucked together with a quilt over their shoulders.

A beat of concern had her pushing away the nagging thoughts that had sent her out of the tent. "Everything all right?"

"Couldn't sleep," Jason said. She couldn't be sure whether he meant himself or Paul, though she remembered her husband's soft snores as she'd fallen asleep not long ago.

Husband.

The newness of that title hadn't dissipated one bit. Mrs. Goodwin. She belonged to Jason. And he belonged to her.

Jason lifted his arm on the side opposite where Paul sat, a silent beckon for her to join the pair.

"I forgot to hang the washing," she admitted softly, aware of Alex and Jenny just inside the tent's canvas.

There'd been a bit of chaos when she'd been putting the children to bed. Tommy had burrowed into the tent—where he most assuredly did not belong—and Alex had tripped over the tent line when he'd chased the dog out, giving himself a bloody nose. Jenny had needed extra consoling, and by the time Maddie had crawled from the tent, she'd forgotten about the basket of wet clothing she'd left on the wagon tailgate.

Jason used his chin to gesture to a place behind her. Maddie glanced over her shoulder to see all the clean laundry flapping gently in the breeze on the line strung between two wagons.

Jason motioned to her again, the blanket hanging from his arm like some kind of cape. "Come here."

She desperately wanted to join him, so she did, murmuring, "I'm sorry about the laundry."

He wrapped his arm around her shoulders, bringing the blanket along so that she was cocooned with warmth, tucked against his side.

"Nothing to be sorry for. I should've let you know I'd hung it while you were tending to the children."

It wasn't fair to him. Wasn't she supposed to be a better wife than that? He'd been run ragged this afternoon helping a young boy who'd gotten too close to a rolling wagon wheel and had his toe crushed.

"I should've plucked that grouse for our breakfast," she said, eyes mesmerized by the last tiny flames flickering over the red-hot coals.

"It'll keep," he said. "You work too hard."

She wrinkled her nose at that.

"Jenny's diapers are gettin' worn," Paul offered quietly from Jason's other side.

Diapers. Cloth to sew them would be a pricey commodity —if it even existed—at the next fort.

Jason shook her gently, chasing away the tension that had come to tighten her shoulders. "We'll make do."

His voice was steady and warm. Unworried.

The uncertainty that wanted to plague her dropped away in the remembrance of what she'd learned in those early-morning moments with Belle while searching for the boys.

God didn't need her to work herself to the bone, worry over diapers or breakfast or laundry. He'd given her a family. He would provide what they needed.

She leaned her head against Jason's shoulder, soaking up his warmth. He set his jaw against the top of her head. "It'll be all right."

The three of them sat in the quiet night, watching the last of the sparks dance up into the sky until Paul stretched and rose. "I'm goin' back to bed."

"Goodnight." Her voice echoed Jason's.

"He all right?" she whispered after the boy had gone into the tent.

"Mmhmm. Missing his ma and pa. Just needed someone to sit with him."

"Are you all right?"

Jason leaned into her, dipping his chin to drop a kiss on her head. "Yes."

There was a slight movement inside the wagon. Was Belle awake? The young woman had been extra jumpy over the past few days. Maddie had frightened her without meaning to when she'd needed to fetch supplies from the wagon. She'd thought Belle had been more settled when they'd returned from the woods. Had something happened that Maddie hadn't noticed? Had someone in camp discovered Belle?

"I can hear your thoughts whirling," Jason murmured.

"Like you heard Paul get out of bed?"

Her husband had to be the lightest sleeper on the planet. Or perhaps that was a necessary part of his job, being woken at all hours to treat an emergency.

"When I heard him wake—" Jason broke off. When he spoke again, she could barely hear him. "For a few moments I was trapped in my memories."

Her breath caught. For a second, thoughts swirled. How she might never live up to his memories of Elizabeth. That perhaps she was only second best.

But a deep breath steadied her, and she remembered Whose daughter she was.

She clasped his hand loosely in hers. "Did your children like to snuggle in bed with you?"

Jenny was an earlier riser, but on the mornings when Maddie couldn't face daylight for another few minutes, she'd found that tucking the girl beneath the quilt with her and Jason calmed the girl enough to allow her to lie and babble and coo until it was time to get up.

"JJ," he said without having to think about it. "He liked it when I laid in bed to read to him before he fell asleep. The older he got, the longer and longer he wanted me to read."

She listened to him talk until the fine tension she hadn't realized he was carrying slipped away into the night.

He flexed his hand beneath her gentle hold.

"No shakes?" she asked.

"Not anymore. I feel... hopeful. Content. In love with my wife."

Warmth enfolded her like sunlight on a hot afternoon. Since his return, Jason had often told her how he felt. She never tired of the thrill of hearing it.

"Is it possible all of our dear children are abed?"

She heard the smile in his voice and turned her head

toward him. He angled his body so they were facing each other and brought his hand up to cup her jaw.

There was adoration in the glittering way he looked at her. "I will never..."

She had to close her eyes as he dipped his head and brushed a featherlight kiss over one eye.

"ever..."

A kiss to her other eye.

"...stop giving thanks..."

A kiss at the corner of her lips.

"...to God for bringing..."

A silly brush of his lips over her nose.

"...you into my life."

A single tear slipped down her cheek as he gently tilted her head up, his lips gently claiming hers. She returned his kiss, her fingers slipping into the soft, fine hair at the base of his neck.

His kiss felt like everything she'd thought she'd left back in Dublin. Like a new beginning. Like coming home.

Maddie had never expected to become a mother overnight, to have three children in her care. With every challenge they'd faced over these past weeks, she'd grown a fierce love for the children, a love that would never fade.

And being with Jason... she'd never expected someone like him. Strong. Intelligent. Courageous. With a tender heart hidden beneath his gruff exterior.

God had poured out bountiful blessings on her. He'd provided a healing path for both of them.

Epilogue

A SHADOW MOVED behind the Fairfax wagon.

For a moment, Coop thought his eyes were playing a trick on him, the flickering flames from the fire casting dancing light and darting shadows. But he stared long enough into that spot to see the dark figure move again. A person's shape, lingering behind the wagon, outside of the circle of safety, where he didn't belong.

He might not care about Leo's approval anymore, but Maddie Fairfax had patched him up more than once, and he didn't want anyone stealing from her. If there was a thief near that wagon, Coop would catch him.

He pulled the knife from his boot—he'd learned to keep it with him for protection. He was better with a knife than with his revolver—and he was a crack shot.

Years of sneaking out of the house through the kitchen window meant his steps were near silent, even in the dry summer grasses.

The crinkle of paper being folded. The soft, deep scrape of a barrel being pushed in the wagon bed.

He was only steps away from the corner of the wagon now, though the canvas still hid whoever was back there. No hint of illumination from a lantern or candle. Whoever it was in there was barely moving, barely breathing.

His stomach twisted slightly when he thought of the punishment this man or boy would receive. Hollis was a tough wagon master and didn't tolerate stealing.

He closed in on the edge of the canvas, hovered by the side of the conveyance so he was out of sight of whoever was inside there.

Now he heard the soft sound of someone chewing. Gulping down whatever food they'd found, more like. Then a near-silent footfall—he was coming out!

Coop sprang at the very moment the man started to crawl out of the back of that wagon. He had the element of surprise. He closed his arm around the culprit's waist and his other hand around a slender forearm.

The body was slight and rangy. Must be a boy—maybe a preteen.

The moment Coop had ahold of him, the boy struggled. One sharp elbow hit Coop's ribs with enough force to cut off his breath. He barely missed the head thrown back, meant to catch his chin or nose.

The boy twisted in his grasp, writhing and squirming for all he was worth.

But Coop was bigger. Stronger.

Somehow the kid didn't make a sound as he struggled, as Coop dragged him around the edge of the wagon and into the faint light thrown by the fire a good ten yards away.

"Stop fighting," Coop said. This kid—

He finally looked down, got a glimpse of—

Not a boy after all.

A young woman.

The realization swept over him as he got a whiff of scent from her hair. Rosewater.

He released her waist but kept hold of her wrist. She scrambled as far away from him as she could get while they were still connected by his grasp.

Coop finally got a good look at her.

She was slight, with brown hair that had come loose, or maybe never been put up in the first place. It hung in stringy waves over her face, as if she was trying to hide herself from him any way she could. The worn shawl around her had gone askew in the struggle, hung off one shoulder.

She was breathing hard as his eyes swept over her dress. It wasn't anything like the simple homespun clothes worn by the other travelers. It was some kind of shiny material, something that would have caught notice if she'd been out in the daylight. Purple maybe. Black lace at the neckline—far too low a neckline to be decent. And she was barefoot.

She was skin and bones, and he was sure he'd never seen her before.

She shook like a leaf as she pulled the shawl up to cover herself.

"Hey," he whispered. He didn't know what he meant to say. Something comforting maybe, because she was nothing like what he'd expected to find inside that wagon.

Her eyes cut to him, wild and terrified, and he felt a kick of recognition so strongly that everything around him seemed to freeze. The bugs went quiet, breeze stopped blowing.

There was only her. And him.

"You saved me." Because she had. That night when he'd been far too deep in his cups and nearly drowned. "I never got a chance to thank you."

He'd looked for her in every face in camp. Started to think maybe he'd hallucinated the whole thing. Now his angel's eyes locked on him, dark and fathomless.

More words lodged in his throat, but he was suddenly afraid of saying the wrong thing. She struck him like a newborn foal, a wild horse, untamed. Frightened of him and everything around her.

"Do you—do you need help?" he asked quietly. "My brother is a captain—"

"Let go!"

He was so surprised by her hissed words that he didn't hold on when she yanked her hand away.

"Wait!"

She didn't wait. She disappeared into the darkness outside the circle of wagons.

He was only a step behind her, hand out to trap her wrist again, but she slipped through a small space between a stack of crates and a barrel while his foot caught on a saddle someone had left lying on the ground. He stumbled. Regained his balance, rounded the wagon.

But when he ducked to look into the shadows beneath it, she was gone.

He wheeled on his heel. It'd only been a matter of seconds. She couldn't have gone far. He scanned for any movement, but the fire was on the other side of that wagon and here it was all darkness and even darker shadows.

Where—?

He thought he caught fleeting movement from the corner of his eye and ran several steps out into the prairie.

Nothing.

His breaths sawed in and out of his chest.

She was gone. That much was certain.

Who was she? His angel. A thief? Why sneak around?

He'd never seen her in their wagon train. Dressed like she was, he suspected she was a woman of the night, but... how had she snuck into their company?

She'd been frightened. Terrified of him. It had been there in the urgency of her struggle against him, the silent fury of her movements.

Every woman of his acquaintance, Alice included, would have shrieked, shouted, cried out. Why had *this* woman stayed silent?

Where had she gone?

What if she needed help?

What if he'd scared her off for good?

* * *

"Can I talk to you?"

Lily was buzzing with energy, even though she should be sleeping. Harry's words from earlier in the evening chased around her mind.

She was curled up beside Harry atop his bedroll in the cowboy camp. The fire was dying, only a few feet away. It was late. Two other cowboys sat in the shadows across the fire while they shared a bottle, their voices a murmur in the darkness.

Lily turned her head slightly and her ear brushed Harry's broad chest. One of his muscular arms banded her waist, and he snored softly, his breath warm in her hair.

She couldn't stop thinking about how he sought her out tonight after supper.

Lily toted a heavy pot full of dirty dishes toward the creek. Washing up in the cold water was her least favorite chore. She'd only just passed the wagon and gone out into the starry night when a shadow moved nearby. She startled and almost dropped the pot. Heart pounding in her ears, she recognized Harry's strong features in the moonlight as he swept his hat off his head and ran one hand through his hair—a sure sign of agitation.

She didn't miss his wince when the movement must've pulled at the still-healing muscles in his stomach.

Her heart pulsed with compassion before she quashed the soft feeling. He'd told her to leave him alone.

And she was still reeling, trying to come to terms with being an unmarried mother. It simply wasn't done. Every God-fearing family on this wagon train and in Oregon would shun her.

She didn't know whether she could stand face to face with him without the hot emotion inside crushing her.

She started to brush past him when he spoke. "Can we speak for a moment? Can I—?"

Without waiting for an answer, he reached to take the heavy pot out of her hands. But he gasped under its weight and the entire thing fell to the ground, scattering utensils across the dirty ground.

Lily stared at the mess, thinking that the spill represented her life at this moment. Everything out of order. A mess too big to contain. Maybe even too big to be fixed.

Harry wasn't looking at the utensils. He was staring at her, one hand pressed to his side, while his expression was a mix of chagrin and frustration.

"I'm sorry," he blurted.

"For dropping my pot?"

He frowned, the fierceness of his expression giving her pause. "For pushing you away. I—I didn't want you to see me at my weakest."

Fury swept through Lily with an intensity she didn't recognize. "What about before?" she demanded. "You said things that made me believe... I gave you my—my body in a way that a woman should only do with her husband. And you ignored me for weeks."

Shame swept over her as she said the words aloud. A mess, that's what her actions had created.

Harry watched her with that same shame in his expression. But his jaw firmed with determination. "I saw you talking to Ed Halverson—I was jealous and I got all mixed up in my head. Lotta folks look down on me 'n the other cowboys. And—" For a second, he gave her his profile. She saw the muscle ticking in his cheek. And then his gaze was back on her, lit with a fire from within. "I done some bad things. In my past. I sure enough don't deserve someone as beautiful—as pure-hearted as you."

Her heart softened at the confession. She'd heard some of the other women gossiping about the hired hands. How cruel was it to look down on someone because they needed work and took what was available?

If what Harry said was true, if he'd really questioned whether he deserved her, could she give him another chance?

"I—I love you, Lily. When this journey is over, I want to prove I can be the man for you. Build you a house—"

She buried her smile in the crook of her elbow, a smile she couldn't hold back when she thought of how she'd thrown herself at him. Thought of the kisses they'd shared, the promises he'd given her.

Harry loved her. She loved him.

He'd spoken the words she'd been too afraid to utter when they'd been together weeks ago.

After they'd cleared the air, he'd helped her gather the dirty utensils and plates, apologized when he couldn't carry the pot to the creek for her. He stuck by her side when she washed up, watching for danger.

He'd asked in a low voice whether she thought her sisters would approve of him. And had she told them about him?

She'd taken a turn to apologize, admitted to her own failings.

After they'd lugged the clean dishes back to camp, he'd threaded their fingers together and led her back to the cowboy camp, where they'd had coffee and curled together under his blanket, talking under the starry sky until he'd drifted off.

Lily was so happy. Surely if Harry meant for them to be together, meant to build her a home in Oregon, surely he was thinking of marriage. She would broach it in the morning.

And... she had to tell him about the baby. He would be happy. She knew he would.

He shifted at her back. A change in his breathing told her he'd come awake.

Someone else was moving nearby, rustling in their bedroll.

"I gotta get up. My turn for watchin' the cattle." His voice was a rumble in her ear.

She needed to go back to camp as well. Stella likely wouldn't notice her absence. And with Maddie distracted by the handsome doctor and her adopted brood, she might not realize Lily wasn't tucked in her tent where she was supposed to be.

But her sisters weren't the only people in camp. Some of the other pioneers, like Mrs. Smythe were nosy busybodies and might notice if Lily wasn't where she was supposed to be.

Harry didn't seem in a hurry to get up. He nuzzled his nose into the place where her neck met her shoulder, while one of his hands came to rest on her belly, over her dress and shawl.

Lily could feel her heart beating through her skin at that point where his hand hovered over where the baby must be.

She opened her mouth to tell him. "Harry, I—"

A strident rattling noise interrupted what she would've said. Harry froze.

What was that?

She started to lift her head, unease heightening her senses.

And Harry's hand suddenly gripped her hip in a painfully tight hold.

"Don't move." He barely breathed the words.

And it was only then that she registered the narrow-bodied animal coiled and posed to strike only a mere foot from her face.

A snake.

Everything happened too quickly.

Harry threw out his hand. There was a blur of movement. She thought the snake struck, but Harry rolled his entire body away with a violent motion and she was thrown over his body to the grass beyond.

He cried out once. She shrieked at the pained sound.

She pushed to her hands and knees and blinked against the flickering firelight in time to see Harry grab at his neck—and then fling the four-foot-long critter into the darkness beyond the cowboys' circle of bedrolls.

Harry sat up, face flushed and eyes glassy. A trickle of blood seeped down his neck to his shirt.

He put one hand to his neck.

"Someone help!" she cried out.

Another cowboy, one whose name she didn't know, moved in their direction even as she crawled across the ground toward Harry.

Whose face had gone alarmingly pale. His breath rattled shallowly in his chest.

"Harry, darling—"

"What happened?" the man asked as he came beside the two of them and squatted down.

"There was a snake—a rattling noise. It struck."

Harry was now struggling for breath, eyes glassy.

"Maddie!" Lily screamed her sister's name, but every muscle felt frozen and locked in place—she couldn't make herself stand up to fetch her sister.

A shadow approached out of the darkness. Another cowboy.

"Fetch the doc," the cowboy at Lily's side ordered. "He's in a bad way."

The shadowed man in the darkness immediately started jogging toward the circled wagons.

"Tell him it's a rattlesnake bite!" The cowboy called after his friend.

A rattlesnake. No. No, this couldn't be happening. She'd seen a dog bitten by a rattlesnake in the early days on the trail. The poor animal had suffered for hours before the man who owned it had put it out of its misery.

"He-he'll be all right, won't he? Can the doctor take the poison out?"

She clutched Harry's free hand as the other man pulled her beloved's hand away from the wound on his neck. Two round marks marred the skin where the snake's fangs had pierced into Harry's neck.

"I dunno," the man muttered from behind her shoulder. "Never seen a wound in the neck like this—I don't like it."

Harry slumped and his hand jerked free of Lily's as he fell onto his back on the grassy ground.

"Harry!"

Lily didn't realize she was shaking his shoulders until she was pulled bodily away.

"Let me go!" she shrieked. Why wasn't the cowboy helping Harry? He was pale and still on the ground as she tried to yank away from the man clutching her shoulders in an iron grip.

"You ain't gonna help him like that—"

There was Dr. Goodwin, running toward them with his coat flapping open over his nightshirt and his black bag in hand.

It was only when Lily saw Maddie slightly behind, a shawl wrapped about her shoulders and her hair loose, that she collapsed to the ground in tears.

She was aware of the cowboy standing behind her like a silent sentinel. Through a gaze blurred by tears, she watched Doc kneel over the man she loved, the man she'd planned to spend her life with.

Her new brother-in-law exchanged a serious frown with Maddie and Lily's sister stood to her full height and moved toward her. The man at Lily's back seemed to fade away into the night.

Maddie's brows were pulled together in concern and she glanced back at the circle of wagons before reaching out for Lily.

"What are you doing out here—?"

Lily shook off her hand. "Help him!" she cried out. "The doc needs your help. You have to—to save Harry."

Lily's voice shook on the words as sobs broke free.

When Maddie reached for her again, Lily didn't protest as her sister's arm came around her shoulders.

And then the doctor was there, too. "He's gone. The poison entered his body too close to his brain and heart—"

"No!" Lily wailed. "No!"

"Lily."

Maddie's firm tone might've been the only thing that could break through the crushing grief sweeping over Lily.

"Calm down," Maddie said slowly.

Lily couldn't.

But when Maddie's head turned and Lily realized that there were torches being lit, that others from the wagon train were stirring, she was overcome with a realization that she was alone in a compromising situation with a bunch of rowdy cowboys. One of whom was...

She couldn't even think it.

"Are you injured?" Doc asked. "Did the snake strike you?"

She shook her head as silent tears slipped down her cheeks.

Maddie came close and shielded Lily from view of the others who approached from camp.

Harry had saved her. He'd thrown her completely out of the way and taken the snake's strike—a strike aimed directly at Lily's face.

He was dead. Had died rescuing her.

Maddie led her away from the awful tableau as more men approached, more torches lit the night.

Lily couldn't help staring over her shoulder as she allowed her sister to lead her numbly away.

The man she'd loved was gone. And with him, the future she'd only begun to dream of.

* * *

Thank you for reading LOVE'S HEALING PATH. I hope you loved Jason and Maddie's romance. You'll see them again in FREEDOM'S DISTANT FRONTIER...

Lily is drowning in grief, mourning the man she once loved, when she finds herself in a compromising position and wrangled into an arranged marriage with a hired hand she barely knows.

Matt has been traveling with the Oregon-bound wagon train on a secret mission to recover a valuable family heirloom. He knows Lily's family is involved, but the closer he gets to Lily, the more he wants their pretend marriage to be real. How can he be falling for the woman he's investigating?

As danger looms, Matt must protect Lily at all costs, soon finding himself torn between his duty to protect her and the secrets he's keeping...

ONE CLICK FREEDOM'S DISTANT FRONTIER NOW >

For my Family.

Acknowledgments

With special thanks to my beta readers Benita and Benecia who gave such thought-provoking insights on this book before any one else got to see it. You'll never know how much I appreciate your generosity with sharing your time and thoughts.

I'm endlessly grateful to my proofreaders Lillian, Mary-Ellen, Benecia, and Shelley for helping me clean up all the little errors (there were many!)—and to my early/advanced readers who caught even more that snuck through. Hugs!

A special thank you for my readers

I want to extend a heartfelt thanks to my readers. Your inspiring reviews, heartfelt emails, and each and every interaction online make every step in my writing journey worth it. This book is dedicated to you.

Thank you for picking up not just this book, but the ones that came before it. Whether you've been with me from the start or just joined, your support is truly appreciated.

I hope you can escape into these books, find love, recognize parts of yourself in the courage and tenaciousness of my characters.

With sincere thanks to (listed in alphabetical order by first name):

Agnes P, Alesha, Alfred Tong, Alma, Alyson Widen, Alyssa Tillett, Amber Kraker, Amy Gaebel Lewis, Amy Shippy, Anastasia Corbin, Andi P, Andrea Maddox, Angeline Farrow-Douglas, Angi, Anita Blackwell, Anita Leonore Homberger Schaer, Anita Rohn, Ann La Bianco, Ann Sharp, Anna Arvidson, Anna Gonzalez, Anne Lewis, Annette, Annie Shelton, Antonette Roestoff, April M. Linz, April Renn, Ariel Ornellas, Barb Raymond, Barbara G. White, Barbara R., Barbara Van Norman, Becky Boyce, Becky Larson, Belinda Maloy Chasarik, Bessie Shepherd, Beth C Smith, Beth Caballero, Beth Pirtle, Beth Riggen, Betty Ann Sharpe, Betty Jo,

Beverly, Beverly Crowley, Beverly Hurst, Billie Corbin, Bonnie Joyce Johnson, Bonnie Kampmann, Bonnie Purnell, BookWorm, Brandi Mincey, Bridgette K. Shippy., Bud Bivens, bunny, C P McIntyre, Callie Marshall, Cara Lee Ward, Carla Illikainen, Carlee Ashcroft, Carol A. Helm, Carol Abbey, Carol H. Sell, CAROL HULSEY, Carol Jarrett, Carol Lang, Carol Ray, Carol Sell, Carolee Doeden, Carolyn Bryant, Cassandra Garcia, Cassie Garcia, Cathy Whittington, Cecily, Charlene Herring, Charlene Weber, Charlotte Jolly, Chasity McPeek, Cheryl Smith, Christa Oliver, Christie Murrow, Christina L Smith, Cindy Burrell, Cindy Kidwell, Cindy Lou, Cindy Slawson, Clara Perkins, Colleen Crigler, Colleen Marie Lynch, Cortney M Engman, Crystal Stewart, Cynthia Coleman, Cynthia Whitman, Dali Castillo, Dawn Ard, Dawne Itnyre, De Vullo, Deann Montgomery, Deanna de Moulin, Deanna Newman, Deanna Wheeler, Deb Graham, Debbie Meers, Debbie Rines, Debbie Waring, Debi, Deborah Clark, Deborah Cooney, Deborah Crawshaw, Deborah Kinchen, Debra Birmingham, Debra Rylander, Dee Manning, Denise Glisson, Desiree Luhnow, Diane C. Johnson, Diane Shannon, Dianna Garland, Dianne M. Cole, Dianne Smith, Dixie, Donella, Donna Christian, Donna M. Rickey, Donna R parcel, DonnaR, Earl Broome, Ed Rappe, Elaine Kiefer, Elizabeth H., ELLADEE Chauvin, Ellen Siler, Emily Criddle, Esther Searcy, Eunice Koster, Eva, Flora Gatzemeier, Frances Scruggs, Gail E Hollingsworth, Galyn LaMaster, Ginny McCoy, Gloria Williams, Grace E. Kerr, Grammy Cece, Greg Posey, Gretchen Fike, Hannah Hoover, Heather Byrd, Heather Louise Bentley, HeidiLorin Callies, Helen Adams, Holly Bleggi, Hosanna, Indie, Indie Swinford, J H Kercheval, Jan Tomalis, Jane Shull, Janet "Lime" Leimenstoll, Janet Demaree, Janet Russell, Janice Tomlinson, Jannette LaRose, Jasmine M.,

Jeanne M. Ondo, Jeannie Ellis, Jeannie Weiser, Jen S, Jennifer Gordon, Jennifer Huppert, Jennifer R Woody, Jennifer Riddle, Jessica Ramos, Jessie L Bell, Jo Evans, Joan Smaldone, Jodi Shadden, John Sperling, Jolie Zeller, Joy Wolfe, Judith Lasseigne, Judy, Judy Kelly, Judy Lipcsak, Judy Schexnayder, Julie E. Finlinson, June Nelson, Kaitlyn Raney, Karen de Castro, Karen Grattan, Karen Waymire Zimmerman, Karla M, Kathe Everson, Kathleen Snyder, Kathy McCauley, Kathy Oliver, Kathy Rice, Kathy Salyer, Kathy Trim, Kay Garrett, Kay R, Kellie McBeath, Kelly Conrad, Kelsey Scanlon, Keri Baker, Kim Wells, Kotie Oosthuyzen, Kunita R Gear, Kunita R. Gear, Lady of the Lodge, Lana Hicks Burton, Laura Harris, Laura Skelton Garcia, Laurie Smith, Laurie Thames, Lilia Aguilar, Lilian A. Moore, Linda Berres, Linda Bicha, Linda Farabaugh, Linda Faye Deneau, Linda Flugrad, Linda Foster, Linda Fowler, Linda Henderson, Linda Kushnir, Linda M, Linda Marion Hill, Linda McFarland, Linda S., Lindy Miller, Lisa, Lisa A. Lagnese, Lori M Fulk, Lori Raines, Lorraine Austin, Luann, Lucy Lowden, Lucy Melugin, Lynda O., Lynette Hall, Lynne, Malgorzata B., Mandy Bentley, Marcia Patton, Margaret Fraleigh, Margaret N, Maria Blodgett, Maria Mast, Marianne Josefsen, Marion Prisca, Marlene Moore, Mary Ann Speel, Mary E Knuth, Mary Jane Wood, Mary K., Mary K. Burkett, Mary Z, Mattie Miller, Maxine Ohlson, Mdhudson, Megann Zeigler, Melanie Anderson, Melissa Ann Whited, Melissa Butcher, Melissa Hartwell, Melissa Pettersen, Merrill, Michelle Malcom, Michelle Rhden, Misty G, MJ Hagler, MollyE, Monica, Monica Schultz, Mrs. John Wayne Brown, Jr., Nancy C. Vance, Naomi J. Kenney, Natasha P., Nicole House, Nida, Nina Banks, Norma Burks, Pamela Hagen Duarte, Pamela Hammock, Pat Brown, Pat Damon, Patricia A Goplen,

Patricia B. Hawes, Patricia Dempsey, Patti Long, Patti Meister, Patty Fontenot Duplechin, Patty Szoke, Paulie, Pearl E Bird, Peggy Ann Mantzey, Peggy Charlene, Phyllis Bullock, Phyllis Willett, Rachel Blanthorn, Rebecca L. LeDoux, Regina G Turner, Renata Hornshaw, Renay Parker, Renee, Renee McDonald, Rhonda Myers, Ridaa, Rita M, Robbie Pink, Robin Lee Pierce, Robin Sweitzer, Robyn Bujdos, Ronica Fody, Ronnie H Davis, Rosalie Brooks, Roslind Haynes-Stewart, Roylene Shaw, Ruth Ann Campbell, Sally Garnaat, Sandra Owens, Sandra Phillips, Sandy glunz, Sara Elisabeth, Sara White, Serina H., Shanda Perkins, Shannon McFerren, Sharene Devitt, Shari Roberts, Sharon & John Marks, Sharon Bollinger, Sharon D Riggs, Sharon Hampton, Sharon Landers, Sharon Marks, Sharon McCluskey, Sharon Meier, Sharon Miles, Sharon S., Sharon Sands, Sharon Stites, Sharon Timmer, Sharon W. Steward, Shawn Moultrie, Shawna Moore, Sheila Elmore, Sherri Merrill, Sherry Antrim, Sherry Brown, Sherry J. Miller, Sherry Jane Miller, shirley hargrove, Sigrid Torgersen, Silvana DeCicco, Sonya Riddle, Stacey C. Head, Starr M, Sue Ashlock, Susan Berresheim, Susan F. Fletcher, Susanna Klein, Susi Moffitt, Sylvia Echave Stock, Sylvie Rayne Malcom, Tami Burritt, Tamira Scarberry, Tammy Rafeld, Tammy Shotts, Tanya Taylor, Tauni Paul, Taylor Coffey, Tedgena K Stoops, Teri Ware, Terri Camp, Terri McNabb, Terrie Beckett, Theresa Cassell, Tiija, Tina L Tanner, Tina Rice, Toni, Tori, Tracey Fisher, Tracey Hockman, Tracie Smith, Tracy Rose, Tricia Lee, Vena Hill, Vernona Graham Hale, Vicki Peek, Vicki West, Vida V Arrington, Virginia Campbell, Vivian Pearson, Vonda Eggleston.

Want to connect online? Here's where you can find me:

GET NEW RELEASE ALERTS

Follow me on Amazon
Follow me on Bookbub
Follow me on Goodreads

CONNECT ON THE WEB

www.lacywilliams.net
lacy@lacywilliams.net

SOCIAL MEDIA

Also by Lacy Williams

WAGON TRAIN MATCHES

A Trail So Lonesome

Trail of Secrets

A Trail Untamed

Wild Heart's Haven

A Rugged Beauty

Love's Healing Path

Freedom's Distant Frontier

WIND RIVER HEARTS SERIES (HISTORICAL ROMANCE)

Marrying Miss Marshal

Counterfeit Cowboy

Cowboy Pride

WIND RIVER LEGACY SERIES (HISTORICAL ROMANCE)

The Homesteader's Sweetheart

Roping the Wrangler

Return of the Cowboy Doctor

The Wrangler's Inconvenient Wife

A Cowboy for Christmas

Her Convenient Cowboy

Her Cowboy Deputy

Catching the Cowgirl

The Cowboy's Honor

Winning the Schoolmarm

The Wrangler's Ready-Made Family

Christmas Homecoming

Heart of Gold

Courted by a Cowboy

SUTTER'S HOLLOW SERIES (CONTEMPORARY ROMANCE)

His Small-Town Girl

Secondhand Cowboy

The Cowgirl Next Door

COWBOY FAIRYTALES SERIES (CONTEMPORARY FAIRYTALE ROMANCE)

Once Upon a Cowboy

Cowboy Charming

The Toad Prince

The Beastly Princess

The Lost Princess

Kissing Kelsey

Courting Carrie

Stealing Sarah

Keeping Kayla

Melting Megan

The Other Princess

The Prince's Matchmaker

HOMETOWN SWEETHEARTS SERIES (CONTEMPORARY ROMANCE)

Kissed by a Cowboy

Love Letters from Cowboy

Mistletoe Cowboy

The Bull Rider

The Brother

The Prodigal

Cowgirl for Keeps

Jingle Bell Cowgirl

Heart of a Cowgirl

3 Days with a Cowboy

Prodigal Cowgirl

Soldier Under the Mistletoe

The Nanny's Christmas Wish

The Rancher's Unexpected Gift

Someone Old

Someone New

Someone Borrowed

Someone Blue (newsletter subscribers only)

Ten Dates

Next Door Santa

Always a Bridesmaid

Love Lessons

NOT IN A SERIES

Wagon Train Sweetheart (historical romance)

Copyright © 2025 by Lacy Williams

All rights reserved.

No part of this book may be reproduced in any form or by any electronic or mechanical means, including information storage and retrieval systems, without written permission from the author, except for the use of brief quotations in a book review.

www.ingramcontent.com/pod-product-compliance
Lightning Source LLC
LaVergne TN
LVHW051341310125
802553LV00011B/367